ROOTS REDEEMED

OTHER CROSSRIVER BOOKS
BY TRACY MICHELLE SELLARS

ROOTS RUN DEEP SERIES

Roots Reawakened
Roots Revealed
Roots Redeemed

ROOTS REDEEMED

ROOTS RUN DEEP SERIES BOOK 3

TRACY MICHELLE SELLARS

ST JOSEPH, MISSOURI USA

To my Lord and Savior, Jesus Christ.
You reached down with Your loving hand and rescued
me from myself when I didn't even know I needed saving.
You have my life, my heart, my all. I am Yours.

"Now unto him that is able to keep you from falling, and to present
you faultless before the presence of his glory with exceeding joy,
To the only wise God our Saviour, be glory and majesty, domin-
ion and power, both now and ever. Amen." Jude 24–25 KJV

ONE

Waterford Cove, Virginia
February 14, 1899

This is what I've been missing out on all these years." Amber Graham whispered the words that were more of a realization than a question as the carriage rounded a corner in the Wright's long driveway, revealing what she'd always known lay just across town.

But it wasn't the palatial home or the expansive acreage that made an ache nine years deep twist in her stomach. The three Wright sisters stood on the front porch, waving their hellos. If only it was the four Wright sisters, Amber thought.

The painful reality that she had missed her chance intensified as Amber ascended the steps and was enveloped in welcoming arms. Sheila Wright appeared behind her daughters on the full-length porch and the four of them urged Amber indoors. She didn't need to be prodded. For the last two weeks when she wasn't in the lab testing new battery designs for Professor Henning, she'd been at the university's weather station, studying the plummeting temperatures. Getting in near the fire sounded just about right.

"Mother, you remember Miss Graham? When I saw her at the King's Castle last weekend, I said to myself, Yvette, that girl works too hard. Get her on over to the house and show her a good time."

Millicent Wright beamed an electric smile at her sister. "The best idea I'd heard in a while, if I do say so myself. Even I know when it's time to call it quits."

"Of course I remember you," Mrs. Wright said as she drew Amber into a warm embrace. She let go with a squeeze. "Welcome, my dear. I can tell already you're going to fit in nicely with this lively family."

As Amber's coat was taken and the talk whirled around like her like snowflakes in a blizzard, she realized the Wright home was quickly becoming a study in contradictions. Women who had numerous staff at their disposal chose to greet their guests in the freezing cold. Opulent rooms that at first held her at a distance with their ornate bric-a-brac suddenly seemed to change their mind about her as the girls invited Amber to take any seat she pleased.

A camelback sofa beckoned and Amber's fingers immediately felt over the brushed velvet upholstery. Rumor had it that Millicent, Yvette, and Winifred had been adopted into grandeur, though Amber had never imagined such extravagance. But she'd lived under enough temporary roofs to realize that the countless comforts money afforded weren't what she craved. Things that could be destroyed by fire or water didn't last. She wanted the deep, abiding love of a family, no matter the address. Amber would take dusty carpets and frayed furniture any day if it meant she could be a Wright.

"You're just in time," Yvette was saying. "The others will be here shortly."

"Others?"

"Oh, yes. There will be at least one more girl. Edith. And then Trey, of course. He's upstairs most likely trying to make himself so handsome that neither you nor Edith will be able to resist his charms." Yvette giggled. "We needed some men for us, too, so I invited Ryan, and he's bringing three school chums that also know Trey. This is going to be a hoot."

Amber swallowed and looked to Mrs. Wright for some sort of an explanation. When Amber accepted the invitation, she'd had no inkling this was to be a party. Maybe she should have stayed inside her little cabin. She could have spent the better part of the evening making weather charts from the data she'd collected or journaling her findings on how to get the most lead in a glass cylinder to make an efficient but durable battery.

Mrs. Wright didn't seem to notice Amber's dismay and instead was bent over stroking the head of a golden retriever who had taken refuge by the fire. Amber was intrigued. Unlike a party that very clearly had an equal number of boys and girls and an agenda to match, animals were something she was completely comfortable with.

Amber got up from her seat and stooped to catch the dog's eye. "What's your name, little mama?" It was obvious the family pet wasn't long in bringing a litter into the world.

"This is Emma. As you can see, she's going to bless this house with puppies any day now." Millicent joined Amber at the hearth, daintily dipping at the waist in her darling yellow dress to pet Emma. As the dog's ears were stroked, she cast a grateful look at her owner. "Don't worry, dear," Millie murmured. "You're going to do just fine."

"Why don't we go up to our room?" suggested Yvette. "It'll give us a chance to make ourselves even more enchanting for the boys."

Mrs. Wright waved them off. "You girls go on ahead. Mr. Wright will keep me company while I watch out the window for the others."

Amber found herself trooping up one side of the double staircase, a mirror of itself that was lined with photographs of various shapes and sizes. One family picture caught Amber's attention. She paused in her ascent to have a closer look. An orphanage stood as a backdrop for a younger Mack and Sheila Wright who knelt and encircled three young girls in their arms. April 1, 1890 had been written in the bottom right-hand corner. Amber knew the date well. The photo had been taken twenty-four hours before she had wearily knocked on the door of the orphanage known as the King's Castle. The ache that had settled in her stomach upon arriving at the Wrights twisted even tighter.

The other girls were already well ahead of her, the musical colors of their skirts rounding the corner at the top of the steps. Amber hoped she wasn't being rude taking her time, pausing to look at more photographs as she went. It would have been better if she hadn't. Candid pictures of the sisters with their new family were interspersed with the ancestral heritage the girls had become heir to. She caught a blurry image of her brown skirt reflected in a glass-framed photograph and scurried up the rest of the flight.

Despite the fact that none of the photographs included Amber, these were the sisters of her heart. They were the visitors at the orphanage whom she most looked forward to seeing. The ones who came early and stayed late.

Mr. and Mrs. Cole had even let their daughters stay the night on occasion, although it had been ages since they'd had one of their famous slumber parties. All the girls at the orphanage would push their beds into a great circle, leaving the center open for a pretend campfire. The tall ceilings with the addition of the gardener's ladder lent the perfect opportunity to construct the grandest tent any of the girls at the King's Castle could dream up. The hooks from which they had strung extra sheets tied together were still there. Amber had seen them hanging from the rafter beams yesterday when she had gone upstairs to read a story to one of the littles who had come down with a bad cold.

As she came to the doorway of the sisters' grand bedroom and saw the fuss they were making in front of the mirror, Amber stood stock still for a moment. Of course. It was Valentine's Day. February 14. The most romantic day of the year. Amber should have known there was some special occasion that had caused Yvette to extend this unusual invite. But for as often as the girls had come visiting at the orphanage, this was the first time Amber had ever been asked to step foot inside the Wright home. This could turn out to be quite the night.

"I think I'll change," Millie was saying. She never could keep still for a moment. "What about the emerald one?"

"Do be serious," replied Winnie. "Green? You'll look as mournful as St. Patrick's Day. No, I do believe a deep rose would suit you better."

"I like Amber's brown, to be perfectly honest," came a deep voice from the doorway.

"Trey! Be off with you," Yvette said. "We're just about to change.

Honestly. I'll tell Mother."

The handsome, overgrown boy tossed a slow wink at a mortified Amber. "Go on ahead and tell her. She'll be thrilled that I'm hoping to draw your guest's name from the jar."

Amber didn't know what he was talking about, but she knew the look he threw her wasn't one that brothers used to tease and torment their sisters with. She had been the recipient of that sort of innocent ribbing on too many occasions to count. No, Trey's wink meant he was setting the evening up for the wolf to chase the rabbit.

As Amber turned and watched Trey saunter down the hallway, a new possibility dawned in her mind, illuminating the horizon of the future, compensating for the past. It was a completely unique approach to make up for all she had lost. Lord willing and if she played her cards right, she could become a Wright after all.

♦ ♦ ♦

"They're here!" came the call from Mrs. Wright.

Many sets of footsteps could be heard stomping snow from boots in the foyer below. The sisters gave little squeals, then straightened their skirts and donned placid looks just in time to descend ladylike down the twin staircase to receive their guests. Amber wasn't fooled. For the last half hour, speculation had abounded as the girls argued over who they thought would be paired with whom.

Shy and sly grins came from the four gentlemen who were allowing their coats to be taken by the butler and another of the family's staff. They straightened their collars and Amber noticed one young man had a small striped sack in his hand. Another knock at the door brought in Edith, a girl with golden hair whom Amber didn't know.

"You wouldn't believe the snow coming down. We'll be getting another inch or two while we're here, I shouldn't wonder."

Amber recognized the speaker as an upperclassman from Waterford Cove University, Ryan. She couldn't remember his last name. He smiled at Amber as Mrs. Wright ushered them all into the drawing room.

"What's he doing here?"

Amber turned to see who had hissed the words and found Trey bending down to Yvette's ear.

"I invited him, dear brother. Now, play nice."

"Yeah, yeah."

Mrs. Wright clapped her hands. "Settle in, everyone. And welcome. Please, whatever you do tonight, make yourselves at home. Mr. Wright will also be popping into the room from time to time throughout the evening, I am sure. It was at a gathering much like this that he and I met, you know." Edith and the Wright sisters exchanged coy and knowing looks. Sheila Wright looked pleased as she recounted the tale. "My Mack here was a last-minute addition to the Valentine's party that year held right here in this room. I had my eye on another beau at first, but the good Lord intervened. I'll let you guess who drew my name." Everyone chuckled politely.

"And we're glad of it, Mother." Trey was the epitome of a perfect host as he stood and went to his mother, kissing her hand. "We shall all have tales to tell when the night is concluded." He turned to the crowd. "But before we pair off for games, let us adjourn to the dining room."

Amber kept her eye on Trey as the group moved to take their seats for dinner. Both his straight hair and his eyes were inky-black, a most becoming color with his fair skin.

And to her surprise, he was pulling out her chair. "Do sit down, Miss Graham." He sat ceremoniously and leaned a little too close. "Or may I call you Amber?" He didn't wait for a response. "I was hoping to sit with you at dinner tonight." He offered her a smile, one she was sure he used often for getting what he wanted. "That way I can convince you to help me tamper with the jar so I'm sure to be paired with you."

Amber nodded and unfolded her napkin, placing it in her lap. Anything to give her a moment to collect herself. Trey Wright was being downright flirtatious with her. It felt all wrong and all right at the same time. This was what she had wanted. Hadn't even dared hope for.

"Wright, old man. Thought you'd have spent the night taking your father's runabout for a spin. Didn't figure you for party games." Ryan had taken the chair on Amber's right and was leaning forward with his elbows on the table. Something in the tone of his voice told Amber this would be an interesting exchange. Trey's lips were pressed into a tight line as he ignored Ryan completely. Maybe she could help smooth the rough waters these two seemed to have between them. She always had been interested in bridges. Time to build her first one.

"So, are you two in some of the same classes at school?" Neither responded as the first course was served, a lobster bisque with a side of bacon wrapped scallops.

"Thank you," Amber said to the maid. The girl blushed and hurried away. Maybe it wasn't proper for guests to speak to those who were serving them. But whenever she waited on others at the King's Castle, she felt honored when someone took the time to look her in the eye and acknowledge the hard work she had put in.

"You'll be hoarse if you thank the hired help every time they come in. The Wright family plans on treating their guests well tonight," Trey said.

"That's right," Millie spoke up from across the table. "After a five-course dinner, we're going to play Heart Lottery. Afterwards, we'll retreat to the ballroom on the third floor and have ourselves a little dance before coming back down to play more games."

"I hope it doesn't snow too much," put in Yvette who was sitting on Ryan's other side. "I'm hoping to stay up late tonight, and I don't want the weather to send anyone home early." She put on a sweet little pout and smiled at Ryan.

"I agree," said Trey. "I don't want anyone to miss the game I've got up my sleeve to bring the evening to a close."

At this, the others began to speculate what Trey meant, especially when he said it with that glint in his eye. But no matter how hard they tried, he wouldn't spill the beans; only told them they would have to wait and see.

"I hear you're interested in the sciences," Ryan commented to Amber.

"My reputation precedes me." Amber responded calmly but her curiosity was piqued. "How did you know who I was?"

"You're all the talk around the engineering department. Isn't she, Wright?"

Trey looked like he would like to stab the chicken that had just been placed in front of him. "Yes," he said, giving Amber his complete attention. "I hear you've got your hands in just about every lab and workshop there is on campus. Not that I'm surprised. Ever since they began admitting women, the female population has been showing its face more and more in our little world."

The way Trey spoke the words made it sound like he felt infringed upon. But Amber knew the hours she spent helping the professors were valuable. "I like puzzles, mysteries. Unsolved problems. It's just the way I see things in my head."

"Ah, yes, the feminine mind. Always working overtime," said Trey.

"Do you have any interest in automobiles?" Ryan asked.

Amber felt like she was at the football match she'd watched last fall between Waterford Cove University's team and a nearby rival school, each man working to steal the ball back. One so bold yet proper, the other quiet yet confident.

"Figuring out the best way to do anything is always something I'm interested in. What are you studying?" Amber had seen Ryan many times in the hallways at WCU but they'd never spoken. He was regarded as brilliant by other students yet she knew he kept his head down.

"My major is engineering. Lately, I've been pretty focused on my senior project." When she prompted him to go on, his pale blue eyes took on a new light. "My design pairs an electric motor with a gasoline engine. You get a quick start with the help of a battery and the longevity of distance with a standard gasoline engine. And if you want an amazing burst of speed, you can run them together at the same time." Ryan shrugged. "It's all managed by a simple lever clutch system."

"That sounds amazing. I would love to take a look sometime. Professor Henning ordered some supplies last month to have me start mocking up a few different battery models." Amber put down her silverware and felt her eyes grow wide. "I wonder—"

"You want to know what Ryan is studying, do you? Oh, let's see,"

Trey cut in. "Well, he's inventing new ways of interrupting conversations I'm having with nice young ladies like yourself. He's getting his masters in relentlessly pestering me to share with him the secrets of my trade. Gasoline motors, mind you." Trey sat back and cocked his arms above his head. "And he's trying to cogitate a pitiful design to get himself recognized in the automobile industry." Trey looked smug and boldly put his arm around Amber's shoulders. "You just stick with me, honey, and leave the likes of him alone. He'll flunk out of everything good life ever throws his way."

◆◆◆

That's the kind of gal who could do anything she put her mind to.

Ryan Pierce had been watching the Scottish beauty all night. It wasn't simply Amber's shimmering red hair that caused him to keep his eye on her. She'd handled the tense conversation between him and Trey with poise, even managing to tease them about being enemies and somehow easing the tension at the table. And she'd done it all with a heady mixture of innocence and charm. He'd never spoken to her directly at university, only seen her sailing in and out of classrooms, doing the professors' bidding. But the way her face lit up like fireworks when she spoke transformed her from someone he had never known by name to a woman he couldn't wait to learn every single thing about.

"Your turn, Ryan." Yvette was in charge of managing the silly parlor game he was being forced to play. Next time he would double check the details of the activities before accepting a last-minute invitation to some party. He should be working on his design.

Ryan glanced at Amber, who could be found at any given time next to the dog. He could see her mind wasn't on the gathering any more than his was. He put his hand into the large jar and said the first prayer he could remember sending heavenward in a long time. Maybe, just maybe, God above would see fit to let him draw the name he knew he'd have on his mind for days to come: Amber Graham.

He took his time, feeling the smooth papers contained within. He was certain now that one of the Wright sisters had filled all of them out, so he couldn't go by the sense of touch if he was hunting for a particular one. And he was.

No, he'd have to rely on good old-fashioned luck and maybe God's favor. He opened the folded, rose-colored note and released the breath he'd been holding. Edith was certainly a nice-looking young woman. The Wright sisters were enchanting, if not a bit immature. But when he looked at the paper in his hand, it was Amber whose name was written in scrawling penmanship.

"Well? Don't leave us in want, friend." Another of the men was clearly as anxious as the others.

"If it's Yvette, we'll all be happy, won't we?" said Winifred, looking at Millie with a nod.

Ryan didn't care if any one of them had cast their vote for him. He walked over to where Amber sat near the fireplace petting the family dog. "If you'll have me?" he said so only she could hear. Too late to realize his mistake, he looked back at the group. Someone new had already pulled out another name, ready to see what fate had in store for them. But it was the lethal look Ryan caught in Trey's eye that caught him off guard.

Placing his hand on the dog's stomach, he chose to take no notice. This gem of a woman was so close he could hear her breathing, yet he couldn't quite bring himself to look her in the eye. He'd done too much. He hadn't yet done enough.

He looked up when she said, "It would be a pleasure," and was powerless to look away. "But first you have to tell me your last name," she added.

Ryan stood and pulled her up with him. This was completely out of his realm of comfort. He was the best liar he knew. Could fool anyone into believing whatever he wanted them to. He was a master at taking from people what they didn't know they wanted to give. He could do this. He could hide the truth and pretend he was someone else, just for one night. One little Valentine's party.

"Looks like everyone has found their match." Mr. Wright came into the room with his wife on his arm, saving Ryan from having to answer. The hosts had dressed for the event and were the mirror of wealth and hospitality as they preceded everyone to the ballroom. Electric chandeliers sent their beams to grace the gleaming dance floor as the couples took their places. Ryan tried valiantly to put aside his misgivings about his heritage. He even succeeded in ignoring Trey, choosing to forget their rivalry for the time being. They could pick up where they left off tomorrow.

For now, for this moment, Amber was in his arms. Maybe there was a God after all.

◆◆◆

"Please say you'll stay just a bit longer."

Amber considered Millicent's entreaty while watching occasional pieces of snow stick to the parlor window. Out of all three Wright sisters, Amber felt Millie was the one who understood her best.

"It's too early to leave just yet, and I want to tell you all about Isaac Jennings. Isn't he just a doll? He asked me to go riding with him next Sunday, you know," said Millie.

"And I have been invited to attend tea at the home of Mark Holt," said Yvette. Thankfully her friend hadn't been too upset that Amber and Ryan had shared the dance and were partners for the game portion of the evening. Yvette had told Amber as soon as Edith and the boys took their leave, "Ryan's really more like the big-brother-type, anyway." Amber had been more than relieved. She didn't want to cause any waves.

"What about you, Winnie?" Yvette continued the current train of thought.

Winifred rolled her eyes. "Nothing to report here. I got stuck with Bartlett. No thank you. But I'm glad we held this little soiree just the same."

"Amber, you've been awfully quiet," Millicent observed, and Amber felt all eyes turn in her direction.

She sat on the edge of one of the sofas, observing the Wright's golden retriever scratch up her blanket again and again, never appearing satisfied with the results. The dog hadn't greeted anyone or barked when there was commotion in the room. In fact, Emma was panting heavily, even though the wind coming in through every little crevice around the window frame seemed to be making the room colder than ever.

"I think your dog might be going to whelp tonight."

The other girls dropped the topic of courting and instantly picked up the exciting matter at hand.

"This will be our first time delivering puppies. I'd better go get Mother." Millie was already rounding the corner into the foyer as she finished speaking.

A howling wail could be heard outside the well-built home. Then came a loud snap and a jarring crash.

Trey and Mr. Wright seemed to instantly appear from wherever they had been hiding out after the party. Mr. Wright opened the front door, and Trey looked out the large picture window, even though the lights from inside made it nearly impossible to see out.

"It's a tree, Sheila. Came down because of the ice, I suppose. With a little help from the wind," Mack Wright said in answer to his wife's unasked questions as she joined her husband in the foyer.

"Goodness, me." She peeked out the front door quickly then slammed it shut. "That cold goes right through the bones. No one is going to be going anywhere in this weather."

"It's not a problem," Amber spoke up. "I can still make it home. But first, I'd like to ensure you have everything you need to help Emma here. I believe you are in for a long night." Amber chuckled. "One of many, after these pups are born."

"I won't hear of you going anywhere," said Mr. Wright. "And if I'd have known the others would be traveling on streets that might be blocked by downed trees, I never would have sent them out." Mr. Wright checked his watch. "After midnight already anyway."

"Yes, dear, you're in the right. Amber, you must stay. We'll have our driver return you to your home tomorrow when it's safe to travel."

Yvette came to Amber's side and squeezed her arm. "We'll set you up in our room. We'll pretend there are four Wright sisters." Winifred and Millicent looked at her pleadingly.

"Looks like I'm more than outnumbered," Amber said ruefully.

She risked a glance at Trey. He had his hands in his pockets as he leaned against the parlor's cased opening. And he was looking at her. He grinned, saying, "The university's called off classes for the week because of the cold. So, if you're up for it and there's enough snow, maybe we could build a snowman tomorrow before you go back to the orphanage. Good night."

She cringed at his mention of the fact that she still lived on the King's Castle property at the ripe old age of almost twenty. But she knew Trey didn't mean it as a dig. The orphanage had been the home of his own sisters at one time in their lives. They each had their own story, as did she.

As everyone scattered to either gather supplies for Emma or to get ready for bed, Amber thought about the turnabout the night had taken. When Yvette conned her into coming over for a quiet afternoon of taking tea and catching up with old friends, she had never expected this. Thrust into uncomfortable conversations, coerced into playing ridiculous party games, turned round and round on the dance floor, not by Trey but by some stranger, and now kept overnight when she had work to attend to.

No, this wasn't what she had foreseen. But maybe by spending an entire day with the Wright family, she had been offered the perfect opportunity to make herself a permanent fixture in this home. Unlike that fateful day nine years ago, this time she wouldn't be too little, too late.

TWO

I really ought to go to bed," Amber said quietly to the new mother and her pups as she noted the time on the grandfather clock.

"I hope you're not telling poor Emma that. Looks like she needs you."

Amber got up from her position on the floor in the dimly lit room. Emma lifted her head to look at the intruder.

"It's just Mr. Wright," Amber cooed. "You're fine." She looked at Trey standing there so casually, as if it were completely natural for both of them to be in pajamas and robes. "Looks like she's going to make a pretty good mother. Guess my work here is done."

"Don't go on my account." Trey held up a hand. "And please. It's Trey." He walked over to the fire. "I thought I might find you here. I knew my sisters wouldn't be able to stick it out. I imagine growing up at the orphanage has put you at a disadvantage, but not in matters like this."

Amber bristled at his insinuation. "I believe the people who cared for me gave me the best upbringing I could have had, given the circumstances. And, yes, we used to have plenty of dogs around. Not so much anymore. I wish that was the case." Amber felt a sudden jealousy when she glanced at the puppies. Six of them, all nuzzled up to their mother. Cozy. Safe. Cared for. So close to another beating heart that they could most likely hear it inside their own heads. Not feelings she was at all familiar with.

She pulled her borrowed robe tighter. "I think I'll go make good use of the bed the girls made up for me. Been a long night."

"Good night, then."

"Night." Amber passed Trey as she made her way to the foyer. A single light at the top of the staircase made it easy for her to make her way safely to the top, just as the possibility of a relationship with Trey beckoned her further into the refuge of the Wright family.

At the dinner table, he had seemed genuinely interested in conversing with her. When Ryan had drawn her name, she had caught a look of distaste on Trey's face. And had he just sought her out in the wee hours of the morning or was it simply wishful thinking?

One thing was for certain: it was too late to piece it all together tonight. She crawled into a bed that had been pushed up next to Millie's and melded into the plush mattress. In a matter of minutes she'd fallen into a dream where a gardener was harrowing the soil on his hands and knees. Into the waiting earth he planted one lone seed. Tiny. Insignificant. Lifeless.

But the master of that garden never stopped watering that little seed, never stopped protecting it. He sang over it. Stayed up all night just to make sure it was safe. Guarded it during the day against infiltrating enemies. By the time she awoke, it had become an enormous tree, lush and bursting with life.

♦ ♦ ♦

Through slitted eyes, Amber could see morning light softly coming through the three tall windows that stood like loving, watchful eyes over this room the Wright sisters had shared for many happy years.

Yvette was already talking about how it was the perfect morning to go outside now that wind had died down. Winnie was brushing her brown hair with meticulous strokes while Millie was bustling around the room, informing her sisters in a loud whisper they would need to loan their guest something fresh to wear for the day.

But Amber had something more important to do than join in the conversation. Math. It had been nine years since the day the seed of a word had taken root: home.

In the cold basement of a church where she and five others took refuge, rumors had spread from cot to cot. They were tall tales, Amber was certain, for who could believe that a large factory had been shut down and was now an orphanage that never turned a child away?

Amber would lie on her back and watch the water trickle down the sides of the stone walls and picture in her mind's eye this magical place. It sounded heavenly. It may not be anyone else's dream come true, but it was hers.

Food at the ready. A warm bed. People who would care for her. No more moving from place to place. No more hiding in the shadows to keep safe in bad neighborhoods. No more being thrown out on her ear when she couldn't work fast enough in the factories.

Home was waiting for her if she could only find a way to get there. To an underweight eleven-year-old with nothing over her head but a leaky old church, the dream took root and wouldn't let go.

She had been nine years now under the care of Garrett and Justine Cole and their close friends, Christian and Summer Titus. Good years. Ones she was grateful for.

Even so, every day she faced familiar, haunting questions that wouldn't let her heart rest. It was one thing to go about her day, either with her volunteer work at the King's Castle or for the professors at WCU. The busyness helped to build a wall that kept out the hound dogs whose names were "If Only" and "What If?"

Here at the Wright's, experiencing first-hand what she'd missed out on, their howling had become a din so loud she could hardly think. If only she'd had enough gumption to climb aboard that wagon and hitch a ride to Waterford Cove a day sooner. What if she had set her fear aside and stopped doubting she could make it to the orphanage by herself?

Multiply nine by three hundred and sixty-five. Amber did the math to perfection, could see her slate from the King's Castle schoolroom with clarity. Carry the four. Nine times three plus five. She curled up into a ball with her back to the light. More than three thousand days. It was a sickening sum. She wished she hadn't done the calculation.

But there it was, and now she'd never be able to forget it. If only she'd been able to escape her doubts just a little sooner, she would have woken up in the brilliant light of this very room every morning for the last three thousand two hundred and eighty five days.

"Should we go without her? Mother is calling us for breakfast."

Amber caught the single drop of wetness that had rolled across her cheek, sat up and threw the covers off. Even though a fire was blazing in the room, she could feel the chill coming in through the thick walls. "Good morning."

She put on her bravest face to greet the sisters, the one she'd used when visitors came to the King's Castle and left with a child in their arms, a child that wasn't her. She was well-versed at donning an expression that said it didn't matter. A smile that showed happiness for everyone else's luck.

No, that wasn't quite right. It wasn't luck that Mack and Sheila Wright had come to the King's Castle before Amber had arrived bone weary. Starving. Bruised. It had been the Lord's will that Millie and Winnie and Yvette had been there and she hadn't. It had been God's doing that she missed being a part of a family by one day. A mere twenty-four hours.

"Millie laid out a dress for you. Quick, put it on. Breakfast is ready," Winifred said.

"I'm afraid I can't get myself presentable in time." Amber yawned and took in the girls' appearance. She knew they'd already been at it for at least half an hour.

"Winnie, dash downstairs and tell Mother we need five minutes," Yvette said then turned back to Amber. "We'll all help you. Run to the commode and come back as quickly as you can. If my sisters could help sneak me out the other night and make my bed look like I was sound asleep, we can pull this off in nothing flat."

There was no time to ask what Yvette had been up to that required evading Mr. and Mrs. Wright. Amber hustled to do her bidding, and with Winnie back from passing on the message, four pairs of hands made quick work of Amber's appearance. For nearly two years, Amber had been getting ready in her small cabin by herself. It felt strange to be a part of a cluster of giggling girls again.

Even though she no longer slept in the big house, she knew at any given time she was welcome there. In truth, she was a bit lonely in her little cabin that sat near the front of the property. Coming in early to start breakfast or helping the big girls learn a new skill always brought back those first stirrings of home she had experienced upon setting foot in Waterford Cove.

"Thank you for waiting," Amber greeted her hosts when she and the other girls entered the dining room. "I'm afraid I overslept a bit." Too late she realized it would have been more appropriate to let Mr. Wright speak first. That was the kind of thing she never gave a thought to in the home where she'd spent almost the last decade. The King's Castle teemed with life and movement and was too happy a place to observe formalities and proper decorum. Even the strict schedule the Coles adhered to didn't deter the children from boundless camaraderie as they learned and played and grew.

"You're not to worry, my dear. We would have gladly waited a good while longer," Mrs. Wright said as she indicated where Amber should sit. Everyone was in attendance this morning. She was surrounded by good-natured joking and smiles on every side. Amber felt like a sea sponge that couldn't get enough of the heavenly liquid of family soaked into her pores.

"The sun looks like it might come out," Trey commented, turning his head to look at Amber as he placed a big bite of eggs florentine in his mouth. He chewed while he watched her.

Amber knew better than most girls the opportunity she was being handed with Trey Wright. She would not fudge this. All of her time with the older boys at the orphanage taught her that a young man only looked at a girl like that if he was interested in more. Teasing, she knew, usually began the dance of courtship.

She glanced out the window nonchalantly. "Yes, it looks like it actually might turn out to be nicer than last night." Start small, she told herself. Don't appear too eager.

"Then after breakfast, we can go out and romp in the snow for a bit, eh?" Trey didn't look his sisters' way as he spoke the question.

"A winter wonderland awaits," Yvette put in, attacking her oatmeal with renewed vigor. She was always up for some sort of adventure. "And then after supper, we can play that new game Trey taught us last night."

It was more than tempting to set her other responsibilities aside and pretend she was already part of this household. But it was time to face reality. This wasn't her home; she didn't truly belong here. "I can only stay for a little bit. The Coles and Tituses will be worried about me."

"We could send a message to them if it's troubling you," Sheila said in her friendly way. "Why don't you stay a few days? After all, any guest who comes into the kitchen offering to help like you did last night is officially part of the family."

Amber hesitated. "Really, I mustn't."

"At least promise you'll come Saturday and stay the day," Millie prompted as she clasped her hands under her chin.

"Saturday then." Amber felt filled to the brim with their affection.

"Do you need someone to come and get you?" asked Sheila.

"Sure she does," Trey said, leaning to the side and bumping shoulders with Amber. "I'll pick her up and bring her over." He twinkled his inky-black eyes at her. "And I'll take her home this afternoon."

"Please pardon the interruption," the butler intoned from the dining room entryway. "Allow me to present Mr. and Mrs. Wright along with your nephews Abel, Henry, and Thomas." With that, he stepped to the side as a short, older couple came in. Behind them, three youngsters with red cheeks and noses crowded into the room.

"Grandmother! Grandfather!"

Amber stayed seated while all three Wright girls pushed back their chairs and came to hug the newcomers. Even from where she sat, Amber could feel the cold coming off of the guests' coats and scarves and catch the unique smell of freshly fallen snow.

Mr. Wright stood and posed the question that was surely on everyone's mind. "Pops, what in the world are you doing out in this weather?" Anyone could see that even though Mack Wright was scolding his father, he was pleased to have the visitors join them.

The three youngsters who had also come in, the oldest not more than eleven or twelve, shouldered their way past the affectionate group and loudly seated themselves at the breakfast table while Mack and Sheila Wright welcomed everyone in voices loud enough to be heard over the ruckus. Yvette and Winifred were going on about the puppies, and Millie was filling any conversational gap with details of last night's party. Amber had never seen anything like it. Come to think of it, she had never been in the presence of this many people who were related to one another.

Now the table boasted eleven family members. If she were included in that count, that would make an even dozen. And if the boys' mother and father were in attendance, not to mention Sheila Wright's own parents and any other extended family members such as aunts and uncles and other cousins, why the number would be astonishing. It was already almost an embarrassment of riches.

She remembered a Christmas long, long ago when she'd had the traces of what might be called a home for a time. Some friends had joined her and her caretaker's little holiday for two, and the extra beating hearts had made that room feel full and merry.

The strangers, though, had come and gone quickly. They patted her small head and told her that surely Saint Nicolas would put something in her stocking come morning.

She hadn't understood what they meant until many years later when she had her first Christmas at the King's Castle. Christian and Summer Titus had taken her under their wing and made sure she felt included in decorating the large four-story house and baking holiday treats. When the other children gleefully hung their stockings on Christmas Eve, Amber stood back, wondering what it was all about. Those had been happy days, learning what it felt like to be loved and to love in return. But being in this room with these people felt different somehow. This soothed her soul. This felt permanent.

Watching the Wright family give each other cheery kisses and good-natured ribbing brought to mind the tree she had dreamed of the night before. She could see it now as a family tree, branching out with a hundred arms, bursting with hope for the future, supported by healthy roots underneath. Like a parable Jesus told His disciples, even though the mustard seed seemed to be the most insignificant because of its size, it grew to become the largest of all, providing protection and provision. That's how she wanted her life to be. Future generations of Wright's nestled in her and Trey's branches.

She glanced at Trey to silently communicate her joy, hoping to share the moment, but he was looking at nothing in particular and his lips were turned up in an aloof, if not polite, smile. Come to think of it, he hadn't said a word since the butler interrupted him. Amber wondered why he seemed to be the only one who wasn't thrilled at this turn of events.

♦♦♦

Beyond a shadow of a doubt, Ryan Pierce was about to go mad. Absolutely overboard. He sighed in vexation and pulled a hand down his clean-shaven face. If he could change his last name, steer his future toward a safe and prosperous harbor and get far away from the ill repute of his father, he was fairly certain he would come into his right mind again.

The next step to sanity was going to have to be a smaller one, though. For the moment, Ryan would settle for getting out of the house. "Father!" he bellowed. "I'm going up to the school." He slammed the door behind him, not truly caring if the man had heard him or not.

Unfortunately it was too icy this morning to hop on his electric bicycle. Its double electric motor would have gotten him to Waterford Cove University with enough speed to appease his agitation. Making the mile walk was usually an option as well, but the air was biting cold this morning. Better to ask the family driver to take him in the carriage. While he rode in the somewhat warmer cab, he could get in the right frame of mind and further formulate his plan.

His leather-bound notebook sat unopened in his lap as he watched the passing scenery. His mind worked better when his eyes weren't on the columns, the calculations, the drawings, when he could see life happening around him. And this particular drive was proving more interesting than others. More than once, Gerrard had to steer the horses around trees that had given in to the violent trio of wind, ice, and freezing temperatures that had been assailing a good portion of the eastern part of the nation for the last couple of weeks.

Not many Waterford Cove residents were out and about today, even though it looked like this never-ending storm system might be giving them some reprieve from the unprecedented cold and precipitation. The elaborate homes of his and his father's neighborhood looked as though they were still nestling each family safe and secure inside their well-constructed walls.

The atmosphere felt almost like a white Christmas, everyone home with those they loved. Everyone but him. Christmas, holidays, family dinners were niceties others enjoyed. The Pierce drawing room, devoid of jolly gatherings and cut spruce with beautifully wrapped gifts beneath, was a place he avoided at all costs. Being in the house for more than a quick sleep and a meal here and there made his stomach feel like it was turning inside out.

Ryan was glad he would be able to avoid Christmas for another ten months as he took in the empty streets and carriage houses filled with horses and conveyances with no one in any hurry to leave.

If his ideas took flight, the scene before him wouldn't last much longer. One day, when he went past these same homes, something would be different. The horses would be put out to pasture. The buggies relegated to family members who had extra room on nearby farms. In his inventive mind, he could easily see the outbuildings housing a new type of transportation: the automobile. Most of them were wide enough to have two parked side by side.

His father scoffed at Ryan's ambition for his unique engine modifications, said he wouldn't amount to anything without the Pierce family name behind him. School chums told Ryan to put his mental energy to better use. But he was positive that soon Waterford Cove's streets, not to mention roads across the country, would no longer belong to four hooves and crudely fashioned wheels. Pneumatic tires, robust batteries, and cars that could go the distance would rule the future. So would he. And it would happen faster than anyone could blink.

"I'll jump out here." Ryan disembarked and made his way up the icy marble stairs that led to the Engineering and Modern Sciences building. Professor Henning was bound to be there and when he tried the door, sure enough, it opened easily.

The air was chilly inside the cavernous building, but he ignored the sensation while his long legs ate their way down the hall.

He had spent the last three and a half years in WCU's laboratories and classrooms. This was the place where his mind could leave behind the trappings of the past and move forward into the future. It was in these rooms where his dreams of becoming a self-made man had first taken root. In these walls he would make his great escape from the Pierce family legacy.

A perfectly executed flyer caught his eye as he reached to open the door to the mechanical engineering workshop.

First Annual Waterford Cove University
Automobile Endurance Race
Display Your Senior Project
Green Flag 1:00 Easter Day, March 19th
Register to Enter by Feb 22nd
First Place Champion to Receive Cash Prize &
Once-in-a-Lifetime Interview with Two
Automobile Industry Leaders,
Benz and Daimler
Good Luck to All Participants

That Professor Henning. This was his doing. Ryan was sure of it. No one else on campus had the kind of connections Paul Henning did with automobile manufacturers around the world. Yet, Ryan was curious to find out how Henning got Benz to agree to come to a small, albeit notable, university like WCU.

Ryan copied the flyer's details in his notebook and smiled to himself. This was it. Beyond perfect. More than he could have hoped for. He didn't know where he would get a vehicle but that seemed insignificant when compared to sitting down with the best of the best and sharing his invention.

"Mr. Henning," Ryan said, swinging the door wide and striding in to the room, "consider me officially signed up."

THREE

"Ma y I take you driving next week after this weather lifts?" Those had been the last words Trey had spoken to Amber yesterday as he looked down at her pleadingly from his cozy spot inside the carriage while she stood in the falling snow. She may have won the fight to go home, but she had readily waved the white flag when she'd looked into Trey's eyes and heard him ask permission to see her again.

The snow was still coming down this morning as Amber took the familiar path from her cabin to Christian and Summer Titus's cottage. As she kept her skirt above the dampness, she thought of how her face might have appeared when she'd answered Trey's question, sincerely hoping she hadn't seemed too enthusiastic. Amber had been out with other young men, but when compared to the possibilities that awaited her with Trey, those other experiences were merely trifles.

"Amber!" Mirabel and Fiona's round blue eyes danced with hers as the Titus's door flung open. "You're here!" said Mirabel. "Mommy, she's here! She's not lost in the snowstorm like you said." Both of Amber's hands were taken captive by the children as they led her into the kitchen where Summer was kneading dough on the counter.

"I'm so glad you're all right. Come here, you!" Summer set her work aside and grabbed Amber by the shoulders. Her friend of almost ten years gave her a tight squeeze, then set Amber back away from her again. "Oh, bother. I got flour on your sleeves."

Amber glanced down and turned her upper arms just so. Sure enough, a set of handprints was left behind. But Amber didn't brush them off. They were evidence someone other than the Wrights appreciated her company.

"Where in the world have you been?" Christian Titus came in through the back door, carrying a big armful of wood. The man who had been a father figure to her since she was eleven years old set down his load and looked at her expectantly.

"Sorry to have worried you all in vain." Her conscience chastised her thoughtlessness. "I was with the Wright family. I didn't tell you, Summer, that they had invited me over for the afternoon. That was the day before yesterday. Valentine's Day."

"We made heart-shaped cookies for Val-um-time's," Mirabel piped up. She was sitting on a stool in the middle of the homey kitchen, swinging her stockinged feet so they banged in rhythm against the center worktop. "Mommy said you could be lost in the snow."

"Or frozen to deff," Fiona put in. She was sitting on top of the island itself, nibbling on one of the famed Valentine's cookies.

"Fiona," said Summer reproachfully. "I said nothing of the sort." She looked at Amber. "We were just concerned, that's all. I didn't see any smoke coming from your chimney when it cleared up yesterday and I could finally get a good look out the window."

Christian straightened from where he had been stoking the fire in the wide hearth. "Little did we know you were in such good hands, Little Bumble Bee."

Amber felt a warm, homey feeling whenever Summer or Christian called her by their own special nickname. It brought back memories of the first night they'd tucked her into bed at the King's Castle. Christian had seen her fiddling with her special bee necklace and had dubbed her their Little Bumble Bee.

"Praise the Lord. We can always trust our heavenly Father to take care of us," Christian said in his deep voice. Amber knew from the bits and pieces of his own story he sometimes shared that statements like that didn't come easily.

"Have a cookie, Amber." Mirabel stopped her swinging momentarily and grabbed a cookie from a plate on the counter. "This one's the prettiest."

"Did you make this one all by yourself? It's beautiful." Amber admired the creation and took an obligatory bite. She was glad she did when Mirabel rewarded her with a smile revealing two missing front teeth. These were her people, even if there were no familial ties. She had been like a big sister to Mirabel and Fiona, had held them as infants, pushed them in their carriages for hours, wrapped Christmas presents for them each year.

"This weather has given all of us a chance to do some of the things we've been wanting to do." Summer lifted Fiona from the counter and held her on her hip. Mother and daughter with their fair Norwegian features rubbed noses. "Like make cookies, right?"

Fiona nodded contentedly.

"Yes, and Amber, you'll be proud of me." Christian grabbed a box from the corner near the table. "I brought out these old Pinkerton files I've been meaning to go through. Defunct, most of them, I'd think by now. But my itchin' fingers have been wanting to take a peek. See if any of these unsolved cases need to be brought back to life again." He rummaged about in the box and pulled out a white folder. "This one here in particular."

"Anything special about that one?" Amber caught the look Christian and Summer exchanged as she asked the question. It seemed as though there was a story to be told.

"It was Christian's first case. Almost twenty years ago, wasn't it, honey?"

"Twenty-one this summer. Twenty regarding the other matter." Christian's face took on a faraway look. Amber guessed that whatever this was all about, it was personal to the Tituses.

Summer sent the children to play in their bedroom while Christian and Amber took a seat at the kitchen table near the fire. Summer pulled out a chair as Christian opened the file and began to lay out each piece of paper, one by one.

"It's his system. He likes to have all the papers in a certain order."

"Helps my mind to make sense of all the pieces if I think of it like a puzzle."

"Remember all those nights in the great room of the King's Castle when we used to stay up late and put puzzles together?" Amber had such fond memories of every moment the Tituses spent with her during those formative years. She felt certain Christian's problem-solving mind had rubbed off on her, for she often found their train of thought quite similar.

"You asked if there was anything special about this case." Summer drew Amber's attention away from her attempt to read Christian's handwritten notes upside down. Nothing about what she could see looked especially official.

"I could ask the same question of you, Amber. Did anything out of the ordinary happen at the Wright's?" Summer looked across the table with a knowing expression. Had her friend already deduced the possibility of Trey and Amber striking up an attachment?

"As a matter of fact, something sort of did happen." She fingered her necklace as she considered how much to share. "Trey Wright asked me to go driving with him next week if the weather is good enough. He saw me home yesterday, too. And I'm invited to spend the day with the Wright family on Saturday." Saying the facts out loud sounded even more ridiculous than when she repeated them in her own head. To hold out any kind of aspiration that she would be enveloped into a large, loving family bordered on absurdity. But hold out, she did. Amber only hoped she wasn't entering a fool's paradise.

Summer beamed. "That is the most exciting news I've heard this year." Her friend's reaction deflated Amber's surging anxiety. Summer always knew the right thing to say. She stretched out her hand to take Amber's. "I know you haven't found the one God has for you yet."

Amber looked down.

"That's not to your discredit." Summer glanced at Christian. "This wonderful man came into my life not only after many failed attempts, but also only after I was willing to give God my hopes and dreams. All of them."

"That's easier said than done, I'm sure." Around Thanksgiving, a boy who had stayed at the orphanage in years past stopped by to visit with the owners. When Amber had laid eyes on him again, she recalled the many nights he had taken center stage in her dreams. She had prompted him to stay longer than he'd intended, and they had sat under the red maple, talking for a spell. But like her other attempts at beginning a lasting legacy, nothing came of it.

Last summer, Amber had tried to catch the eye of the pastor's son before and after church services, but he never once glanced her way. At WCU, she was always aware of who came in the room and if they were married or not. When it came to courting, she felt like it was her first week helping in the chemistry lab, mixing and matching elements, seeing what combination she could come up with. A little of this, a pinch of that. Shake and stir. Then nothing. All her aspirations hadn't produced even the smallest reaction.

Since the party, however, she felt for the first time she might be blending together the right mix of ingredients. Mr. and Mrs. Trey Wright. It had a nice ring to it.

"Don't forget," Summer was saying, "God knows what's ahead and He's in control. Remember the words of Jeremiah. 'For I know the thoughts that I think toward you, saith the LORD, thoughts of peace, and not of evil, to give you an expected end.'"

Summer was right. God must have a plan, and as Amber looked back on her time at the Wright's, she could see it clearly. God had given her one shot at securing a promising future: someone to love her who also had the ability to give her a deeply rooted family tree all in one fell swoop. She'd better get her slingshot polished up and in working order, for she had two birds to kill with one stone.

◆ ◆ ◆

A five-day head start. It could be just the edge Ryan needed to win the race. Trey Wright and the other seniors whom Ryan predicted would try and jockey for first place had no idea what would greet them Monday morning when classes resumed. He chuckled. They were all cozied up in their houses, playing chess by the fire and squandering the day away. Not him. Ryan would be miles ahead by the time they were scrambling to get ready.

"What are you laughing about?" William Pierce strode into the study where Ryan was hunkered down at his desk, papers spread out before him.

Like I would tell you. Ryan took his time looking up, pretending to finish marking something with a pencil.

"I need you to go down to the bank today, son. Payment was due yesterday." His father's voice turned to a whine. "And of course, we couldn't get down there with this weather."

Ryan kept a passive look on his face, but his heart rate picked up a few notches. He could read between the lines. If William was asking him to run this errand, there was more to it than his father having a busy day ahead. He needed Ryan to do what he didn't have the skills to do himself—dodge payment on the house. Maybe his dad was living more on borrowed time and money than Ryan was aware of.

When Ryan didn't respond right away, William said, "Don't tell me you're too busy with your doodads and contraptions to help out your old man."

Ryan drew fresh air into his lungs and bent again over his work. "I've got a lot to accomplish here, so, no, I don't think I'll be—"

In one smooth motion, William's arm shot out like a drawn sword, sending Ryan's papers flying in every direction. He placed his hands on the now-empty desk and towered over Ryan. "You will do as I say, boy."

Then as quickly as the storm had come, William seemed to regain control. He straightened his collar and sat down in an empty chair, leaning back and crossing his ankle over his knee, as if it were completely normal to explode like gasoline poured over fire. It was the same mask of innocence William put on for neighbors and clients. "You know it's as much for your benefit as it is mine," William said coolly.

Ryan didn't have much exposure to know how other families were run, but if he ever had one of his own, William Pierce wouldn't be a part of it. Calmly and methodically, Ryan bent to begin picking up the physical evidence of William's fury. He'd learned from a young age to hide his reaction to his father's outbursts under an exterior of nonchalance. "I'll head down there in a bit," he said evenly.

"See that you do. And when you return, come to my office. We have to work out our strategy for getting this company prospering again. Remember, we have a meeting with that new investor Saturday afternoon."

Ryan put his copy of the Endurance Race flyer on the bottom of the stack of papers as he stood up, but its words were imprinted in his mind. It wouldn't be long now and he could sever ties to this joke of a family for good.

♦♦♦

Amber's nerves felt like they were paralleling the swing of what the papers were referring to as The Great Blizzard of 1899. Up a little, down a little. A small burst of warmth, then back to freezing cold. Icy layers on top of snow. The resulting outcome was becoming a bit slippery.

After she'd visited with the Tituses the other day, she'd come home and wrapped up the weather logs she was compiling for the meteorologic professor at WCU. Amber ran her hand down the columns, pleased with her work, but her mind was on something else.

Trey had said he liked the brown dress she'd worn to the Valentine's party, but Amber wasn't so certain. His mother and sisters wore the most up-to-date styles. Surely Trey compared Amber to the women in his family and the girls who ran in his circle.

Amber stepped to her small looking glass and admired how her new shirtwaist set off her eyes and hair. This particular shade of blue had always been her color. The Coles and Tituses had provided the cabin for the most modest rent Amber could imagine in exchange for the time she put in at the King's Castle. Her paycheck at the university covered the rest of the rent and gave her enough to live on. Still, she wondered if the new outfit she'd purchased this morning had been worth the expense.

She came to a quick conclusion as she went to answer the heavy knock at the door. If the deficit in her small savings and the extra half an hour spent on her hair would secure her a place next to Trey Wright, then it was worth the sacrifice. She swung the door open wide and looked her future in the face.

"Wow. Didn't expect you to clean up so nice." Trey stood on Amber's small doorstep, a box bearing the name of a well-known Waterford Cove chocolatier in his hand. "I like my girls with a little meat on their bones. Here." He held the sweets out to her.

Amber hoped Trey wouldn't find anything else about her that was lacking. He didn't even have to be giving her the time of day. She would do everything within her power to not be found wanting.

"Thank you. Should I leave these here or bring them along?" Amber said, leaving him on the step and grabbing her coat and gloves. She picked up a knitted hat, too, but after a moment's hesitation set it back down. To save her hair, she would forgo the warmth.

"Whatever you decide, do it quick. This wind is biting."

"Sorry about that." Amber left the chocolates on her dual-purpose dining room table and work space. She would open the small box later tonight and savor each nibble as she reflected on the little moments this day would hold.

The same driver who had provided transportation for the party waited patiently as she and Trey climbed inside. Trey tapped the side of the door and they were off.

"Tell me all about Amber Graham," Trey prompted, leaning back against the seat with one arm stretched out beside him.

Amber fingered her necklace. "Goodness. All about me, hmm? From your sisters' accounts of their visits to the King's Castle, you probably know more about me than I do." She chuckled softly to hide her discomfiture.

"You know, you're probably right. Why waste time with idle words when I already know what I need to?" He held up his hand with his fingers splayed out while the carriage rolled along the slushy street. He grabbed his index finger. "First of all, you're beyond beautiful. I could look at you all day."

Amber blushed at the flirtatious comment. He thought she was beautiful?

Trey touched his middle finger. "My sisters love you. Mother approves, and so does Grandmother. When I reminded them I was picking you up today, they were practically planning our engagement party."

Amber knew her cheeks had grown a shade darker. Was this really happening? In past experiences, it was Amber who was always two steps ahead of the other person. This time, Trey seemed to have bounded alongside her. Maybe they really were two peas in a pod.

"Third," Trey said, ticking off his ring finger, "you need me. You stick with me and you won't have to scrounge around for a measly paycheck at WCU. Women shouldn't work." Trey stopped his visual aid to grab her hand and run his thumb along hers. "These fingers should be smooth. Perfect. Just like you."

He seemed to have this all figured out. Flattery. Gifts. Altruism. Trey had gone quiet and she wondered if he'd finish his counting. "And numbers four and five?" she asked hesitantly. Maybe he couldn't come up with five reasons to be interested in her.

Trey let go of her hand and gave her a smile that reminded her of Lewis Carroll's Cheshire Cat. "For those two, you'll just have to wait and see."

♦♦♦

Ryan pulled out his Carmouche pocket watch. Almost four o'clock. Time to get going. It would make a good first impression if he showed up early to his next appointment.

"Son, you've been awfully quiet." William had put on his most charismatic smile. "I'm sure Mr. Blake would love to hear a young, creative mind like yours speak of the inevitable transition from the old-fashioned wagon to horseless carriages."

"Fast, reliable, sustainable, and independent transportation is what every American needs," Ryan looked Mr. Blake square in the eye, "even if they don't yet know it's what they want." He'd sold the same line a dozen times over to rich, gullible men who came in from all over the country.

Mr. Blake walked around William Pierce's pride and joy, a car that ran on gasoline. An eclectic automobile his dad had dubbed the Chariot. It was for this worthless contraption that Ryan had coerced the bank manager at Waterford Cove Holdings to extend William Pierce's mortgage. When Ryan had learned the truth about the Pierce family's financial situation, he determined that buying William four additional days was more than he deserved. His father had made a fateful error sending Ryan to do his dishonest deeds. Again.

"How much in the account?" Ryan had asked the teller.

The young man wrote down the amount of twenty-five dollars. Ryan glanced at the paper and held his back ramrod straight, putting on the persona of a businessman who was simply doing a cursory check of his finances. Nothing to be concerned about. Nothing save the fact that what was left wouldn't begin to cover their expenses.

Ryan turned his attention back to Mr. Blake, making sure he appeared relaxed yet confident, convincing this man he believed in his own words 100 percent. "Yes, Mr. Blake, if you want to find a horse and buggy ten years from now, you'll have to look one up in a history book." Ryan took a deep breath. "If you get in on the ground level now, your returns in the future will be unprecedented." He could do this. He could make this one final sale before breaking off on his own.

The man rubbed his short beard. "I don't know. I never got an education myself, and I've been saving so my son can go to Waterford Cove University. Took my father's floundering business and made it the success it is today. It's been hard work, I tell you, but I've got almost enough in the bank that my boy could begin attending this fall."

"You'll be able to send him all four years if you invest now, Mr. Blake," William said.

Ryan had always known he was selling a bunch of rubbish, telling people what their ears were itching to hear while knowing full well the Pierces couldn't deliver. The Chariot was simply a cobbled together machine made from various parts and pieces William had taken from other hardworking inventors. It couldn't travel more than two or three miles without breaking down, and if it surpassed that test, a few more would reveal the Chariot's other inadequacies. No profit had been turned and every dollar investors gave went to pay Pierce household expenses.

Yet never before had Ryan considered the implications of his deceit.

How many families had lost hard-earned money because of him? How many little ones had to go without because their fathers succumbed to the fiction he fed them? And it wasn't just the niceties of life that were on the line. If he finished this transaction, he knew in full disclosure he'd be robbing Mr. Blake's son of an education. That he couldn't do.

"That's right," William put in with an eye on their guest as Mr. Blake bent to inspect the axle. "With a mere three hundred dollars, you could see a rate of return of twelve percent within the year."

Ryan flipped open his watch. Four ten, now. He glanced anxiously at the door.

Mr. Blake was putting his gloves back on. "I think I'll need to talk with my wife before I make any decisions."

A bad sign, Ryan knew from experience. If an investor wasn't convinced in the first few minutes, it made Ryan's job ten times harder. *Good for you, Mr. Blake. Get out of here while you still can.*

"And of course, I'll require a ride in your little contraption before I sign anything. Want to make sure it's everything you say. Good day," the man said and began walking toward the door.

William stepped into the man's path. "Have you heard the news? Come middle of March, everyone in town is going to be lining the streets to watch the First Annual WCU Endurance Race. You can rest assured this vehicle will not only be a competitor, but with Ryan driving and the new innovations that the Chariot uniquely possesses, we're sure of the win. Sales will skyrocket. That can only mean more money in your pocket. You can finally secure that education you want for your son."

Their guest shot raised eyebrows Ryan's direction. Ryan schooled his face so his shock didn't show. As far as he was aware, he was the only one besides Professor Henning who knew about the race. *Father must have looked through the papers on my desk.*

For some time now, Ryan had been building the muscles to emerge from the confines of the cocoon he lived within. With a sense purpose and one final push, he broke through the wall, severing the cords that bound him to his father's treachery. Looking at William across the open interior of the Chariot, he said in a wooden voice, "I will be behind the tiller, and I will win. But it won't be with the Chariot."

Mr. Blake looked intrigued. "No?" he asked.

William's face turned bright red.

Get used to it, Father. I'm just getting started.

FOUR

William Pierce held his tongue and watched his son casually amble out of the carriage house behind Mr. Blake. It wouldn't do to have the investor see William explode, a fury lit by the match of Ryan's insolence.

William stood out by the street next to his sorry excuse for a son and waved as Mr. Blake's two-horse carriage pulled away. "How dare you?" he said under his breath. "Get in the house. Now." He said the last word with what he hoped was enough menace to execute his authority.

His tone must not have been adequate for instead of obeying, Ryan was speaking with Gerrard.

"Don't you worry, Mr. Pierce," the family driver was saying. "I'll have you on the road in a jiffy."

William grabbed Ryan's arm and swung him around. "Just where do you think you're going?"

Ryan shrugged him off and didn't look him in the eye. "Nowhere that would interest you."

William would not be put off so easily. "Try me."

Ryan turned and walked away. Fine. They could just have it out, right there in the drive for all the neighbors to see. "I'll not let you leave until you tell me what you were trying to prove back there. Mr. Blake gave me the 'I'll have to ask my wife' speech. You know what that means." William stood between Ryan and the carriage. "I had him in

45

the bag with that race comment." He curled his lip. "You broke this; you're going to fix it."

Instead of his son giving in to his demands like usual, Ryan shot around him quicker than William could react. In a matter of seconds, the carriage was heading west.

Ryan didn't know the half of it. This was way more than making payment by Monday so the bank didn't take the house. William spun slowly in a full circle, hands in his pockets, taking in the grandeur of his home, his neighborhood. He would not lose this life he had built. Couldn't lose it. Would dig in his nails and hang on for all he was worth.

Without Mr. Blake's money in hand, William would be forced to extreme measures. That stunt Ryan pulled back there was the final push to the other side of the line. A line that William had promised himself he wouldn't need to cross over, ever again. Yet there he stood, staring at the inevitable.

Tonight after dusk, he'd knock on a door he hoped he'd never have to darken. Looked like old Hippocrates was right when he said, "For extreme diseases, extreme methods of cure."

♦ ♦ ♦

Only two more days and the dash to win the extraordinary honor of garnering an interview with Benz and Daimler would begin. The starter's pistol had already gone off in Ryan's head, every muscle spring-loaded for the challenge.

If everything went as planned this afternoon, he'd be that much closer to ensuring not only the win, but the latitude of achieving his own success. Someone whom others would honor and esteem rather than toss to the side when they'd used him up or had enough.

"Come on in, Ryan," Mack Wright shook hands with him across the desk. The mid-February sun was slanting in low through the leaded windows flanking the bookcases in Mr. Wright's bright study. "How can I be of assistance?"

Time to put on the charm. But he didn't need a reminder to do what was already second nature. A long list of dos and don'ts when it came to currying someone's favor wasn't necessary to review. Fabrication of the truth was a skill he'd been perfecting as his father's front man since he was no more than a youngster.

"Mr. Wright, thank you for agreeing to meet with me. Or may I call you Mack?" Ryan perched on the edge of the chair and spoke to the older gentleman as a humble colleague.

"Absolutely." When asked indirectly if they would be willing to drop the formalities, most people answered positively. It put them at ease to know they could relax and be themselves. Elbows on the desk, Mack steepled his fingers while tapping the tallest ones on his chin. Sure signs of a great thinker and someone who had something on his mind.

Very interesting. Ryan guessed he would have been the one to break the ice. The end result would be better if Ryan got Mack talking first.

"You look deep in thought." A statement Ryan knew was difficult to leave untouched.

"How could you tell?" Mack laughed softly and leaned back in his chair. "Sheila's forever telling me I'm easier to read than *The Adventures of Pinocchio*. Guess she's right." He got up and walked to the window.

This man didn't seem content to stay in one position for long. Ryan knew from Mack Wright's reputation around Waterford Cove that in all things, he was considered a mover and a shaker. "Spring'll be coming on soon."

"Yes, sir. Before we know it." From experience, Ryan knew small talk was full of hidden layers left unsaid.

"Change is good, wouldn't you agree?" Mack turned, hands behind his back and regarded Ryan with a look that was hard to interpret. "You've known my son for how long now?"

This was not a question Ryan had anticipated. But he could roll with it. "Almost four years. Started together as freshmen at WCU," Ryan said pleasantly. No need for Mack to know the bad blood that existed between them. "Met him in algebra class that first year."

"I thought as much. He mentions your name from time to time at the dinner table. If you want my opinion, I think he's a little jealous of you."

Mack came to stand in front of Ryan and leaned against the desk with his arms folded on his chest.

"You don't say? I always thought he was simply antagonistic." This visit wasn't going at all how Ryan had hoped. Maybe it hadn't been such a good idea to let Mack steer the conversation.

"No, that's not it. It's as simple as this: he knows you're better than him. And he'd hate it if he knew, but all of his hostile statements against your scruples and aspirations have allowed me to form a very high opinion of you."

Looking down for a split second, Ryan chuckled. "Not too high, I hope."

"High enough that when you asked for this meeting—the reason which, I promise we'll come to in a moment—I thought it would be the perfect chance to ask you for a favor."

How ironic. "What can I do for you?" Ryan asked sincerely and looked at Mack with an open gaze. Something new stirred within him at the thought of working for a man of integrity.

Mack sighed and moved to sit in the chair next to Ryan's. "Trey's a little scattered right now. His mother is worried. He's set his sights on local politics with an eye on getting to the state level someday. But his grades are dropping, and he's shown time and again that even with all his aristocratic dreams, he lacks gumption. Follow through. I'd like to help him get his head out of the clouds and on to what God's gifted him with. After graduation, he's welcome to come work for me, of course, but he's always been better with hands-on projects than financial ones."

Ryan tried not to shift in his seat. Why was Trey's father sharing this with him? Ryan had never been particularly fond of his schoolmate, but ignoring him was better than seeing him as a person, someone with faults that could be named. Someone whom others cared enough about to help with those failings. Someone with a future. It was easier to toss a taunt or two in Trey's direction every now and again than to think about what he needed and how Ryan could help.

"I can see I've made you uncomfortable. Never fear. I think you'll appreciate where I'm going with this. Come Monday when school resumes, you're going to find out what Professor Henning and I have been planning for months. There's to be an Endurance Race mid-semester. I assure you," Mack paused with a twinkle in his eye, "the winner will be well rewarded."

Ryan smiled. Now the prize money and the interview made more sense. Mack Wright would know the right people to ask to get Benz and Daimler involved. Professor Henning was just the person steering the ship; Mr. Wright had built the boat. "I've already been hard at work to get ready for it, sir."

Mack's eyebrows raised. "Is that a fact? Well, son, good for you. And good news for my purposes here. You see, I was going to offer to be your sponsor."

Ryan could not have been more surprised. "But that's what I came here to ask you." He knew the look on his face was incredulous.

Mack laughed out loud. "Well, I'll be. I hope you're a believer then. I think God Himself orchestrated this little meeting."

"It's getting harder to ignore that potential fact. But, Mr. Wright. Mack," Ryan caught himself. He must remain casual. Professional. "If I may, why would you pull the rug out from under Trey like that?"

"I don't see it that way at all. Just the opposite, in fact. Once Trey knows you're a force to be reckoned with for the win, it'll light a fire under him so hot he won't be able to do anything but jump." Mack chuckled softly. "Here's how I see this going. I've got the runabout out in the carriage house and a Packard that should be arriving any day. I'll give you the money you need to buy your parts, and you can pick up the runabout when my other car gets here. How does that sound?"

"Father?" Winifred, the most diminutive of the three Wright sisters in Ryan's opinion, popped her head into the room. When she saw Ryan, she nodded at him politely. "Dinner will be ready soon."

"Tell Mother I'll be there in a minute." Mack looked at Ryan expectantly. "And we'll need another plate added to the table tonight. That is, if Ryan here will accept our invitation?"

"Yes, sir. In both regards. May we talk about specifics after dinner?"

"Of course." Mack paused by the study's door and turned back to Ryan. "I love my son. Let there be no doubt about that."

"Don't worry, Mack. I can tell you're a good father. That's worth a lot these days."

Mack regarded him curiously, and Ryan wished he hadn't let that last statement slip. It showed vulnerability, something that didn't hold water in business dealings. Better to let Mack leave their discussion with assurance of Ryan's tenacity and confidence.

"And I'll make Trey work harder than he thought possible." Ryan grinned broadly. "But that doesn't mean I'm going to let him win," he said with a wink.

Mr. Wright slapped him on the back good-naturedly as they went out into the hall. It was then Ryan saw a most unexpected and pleasant sight: Amber Graham walking gracefully to the dining room. Was she here at Trey's request or as a guest of the Wright girls?

Either way, he'd be able to gaze at her angel face all evening. He buttoned his suit coat and stepped a little lighter. This was shaping up to be one of the most intriguing days he'd had in a long while. Most intriguing, indeed.

◆ ◆ ◆

This was the fullest Amber had seen the Wright family dining table yet. Grandmother and Grandfather Wright and their other grandsons had evidently stayed on through the rest of the week, for they were still in attendance. It made Amber wish she had decided to extend her visit as well. And another guest had also joined the dinner party. Ryan sat to her right, just as he had on Valentine's Day. She shyly glanced sideways at him.

He really had been a nice companion, patient with her on the dance floor and making her feel comfortable during the parlor games afterward. He seemed affable enough when he spoke to others, but a lonely quality also hung about him. She should offer something nice to say.

"Thank you for being my partner at the party. It was a lovely evening."

Ryan smiled. "It was my pleasure. I've had one of the tunes we danced to in my head ever since." He seemed more at ease now that she'd gotten him talking.

"And I can't get your hybrid design out of my head. I like to see how things work and how I can make them better. Like I was starting to say the other night, Professor Henning has me working in the lab with batteries. I've even been staying after school to experiment with his leftover supplies."

"Hybrid. I like that. Taken from the hybridization that's being done over in the Ag Department."

"Don't you know it's not proper to talk about work over a nice meal?" Trey interjected.

Not this again. Trey took his seat on her other side and Amber felt sandwiched between the two men.

"Forgive me. You're correct, of course. Where are my manners?" Ryan answered calmly, surprising Amber. From the interchange she had witnessed during the party, Amber thought he might bite back. There were always a few boys at the orphanage who worked hard to prove they were the king of the castle. This scenario seemed to be no exception.

"I'm taking Amber driving next week," Trey announced unexpectedly.

"Sounds nice. Maybe—"

A sudden wind slammed against the house, cutting Ryan off and causing the dining room window to rattle violently. The young Wright cousins along with Trey and Ryan jumped up and ran to peer out. Despite the deepening dusk it was easy to tell from the *ping ping* against the glass what they were up against. Another ice storm.

"Come, boys," beckoned Mr. Wright. "Sit back down and enjoy your supper." He turned to his wife. "Sounds like more of the same. Maybe worse this time."

Mr. and Mrs. Wright's nephews skipped back to their chairs, hooting. "No school Monday, that's for sure," the oldest of the three said as he heartily shoveled soup into his mouth.

Amber remembered days at the King's Castle when something would change the status quo. A new litter of puppies to take care of instead of studying zoology. An unexpected donation that allowed Garrett and Justine Cole to purchase new shoes for everyone with enough left over to buy an extra treat or two. A new girl to join the big girls' room or another baby to love on. Unanticipated blessings that came just when the present state of affairs was beginning to feeling humdrum.

Grandfather Wright spoke up. "I've never seen anything like it in all my born days. But I say let the wind howl. We're all snug inside this well-built house." The pleasant older gentleman winked at Sheila behind his spectacles. "Your father did a fine job building this place and we're still enjoying its benefits today. We'll just hunker down here until this passes." This time he looked at Mack. "That is if you don't mind our stay extending a bit longer?"

Mack smiled gently at his father and included his mother in his warm gaze. "I wouldn't hear of you trying to make it home in this treacherous weather. No, you stay right here." He looked around the table at his other guests. "That goes for the rest of you as well. Ryan. Amber." He made eye contact with each of them in turn. "Please, make yourselves at home. You are more than welcome."

Ryan and Amber glanced at each other and shared a small smile. She wasn't sure if Ryan was thinking the same thing as she, but judging the light behind his eyes, it was a distinct possibility. It felt good to be included as part of this family, even if only for the span of a few hours. She murmured her genuine thanks and resumed eating, glancing every now and then at the faces gathered around the table. It seemed the Lord was shining His favor upon her. With Trey at her side for the rest of her days, she would ensure the miracle she needed to be officially grafted into this wonderful family.

Millie interrupted her daydream state-of-mind when she squealed. "Amber, your bed's still all made up. Let's have dessert sent up to our room and stay up as late as we can."

"Oh, yes. Let's," Yvette said. "A real slumber party, like we used to have at the King's Castle."

"What's this?" asked Grandmother Wright. The small woman peered at Amber from the end of the table. "Did you used to live at the orphanage, too, dear?"

Amber blushed. "Yes, ma'am. Still do, as a matter of fact. Now I have my own little home on the property." How she hated to speak of anything that magnified the reality that she didn't really belong anywhere. Not truly here, as an interloper, even if it was a welcome one. Not in the big house anymore; she was too old to bunk down with the others every night. Not with a husband of her own; she'd never been able to make a good match. Not as a smaller piece to a bigger whole of anything that would last. No roots. No future.

She was still just going from one interim to another, living on charity, praying she could scrape by, always on the fringes of pre-existing people groups. A behind-the-scenes worker bee at WCU. An occasional guest at Christian and Summer Titus's dinner table. An extra hand at the orphanage.

Trey cleared his throat and pushed back his chair. "Yes, Amber grew up at the orphanage, but let's not speak of it. Excuse me. Mother, Father."

Trey's reaction clearly indicated he was either embarrassed or ashamed. If only she could change her past, or at very least, hide the remnants that still clung to her. Trey was striding from the room and didn't look back. Should she go after him? No, that wouldn't look right. They weren't a couple. They had no understanding to speak of. Amber's face was still hot as she wondered what to do next. Best to not mention the King's Castle again in front of this man she wanted to make an impression upon.

"What moods that boy has," said Sheila. "Pay him no mind." She was looking at Amber. "You just go off with the girls now and I'll have your desserts sent up shortly."

Millicent, Winifred, and Yvette each came in turn to give their grandfather a quick hug and their grandmother a kiss on the cheek. Amber stood awkwardly waiting for them to finish when unexpectedly, Grandmother Wright motioned her to come near.

She grabbed onto Amber's hand and while the older woman's skin felt paper-thin, her grip was strong, immovable. Amber did not know until that moment how much she had lost by not knowing her own grandparents. Who had they been? Were they still alive? If she looked, would she be able to find them? Swift tears filled her eyes. So much had been taken from her. And that meant she had so little to give.

"My dear, don't let your past dictate your future. Do you believe in Jesus Christ as God's only Son?"

Amber nodded, aware the others in the room were most likely watching the exchange. But when she glanced up, she saw the Wright sisters had left the room and everyone else seemed wrapped up in their own interactions. She gave her full attention to the family matriarch.

"Then all is settled. The Lord's admonition to His people, Israel, applies to us today. 'Remember ye not the former things, neither consider the things of old.'"

Amber leaned down to better hear the woman's soft voice. She didn't want to miss one syllable.

"'Behold, I will do a new thing; now it shall spring forth; shall ye not know it? I will even make a way in the wilderness, and rivers in the desert.'" She patted Amber's hand. "Keep your eyes on Him and watch and see what He will do."

Amber boldly bent to kiss Grandmother Wright's lined cheek, praying silently she would one day not simply have the invitation to call this woman Grandmother but instead that they would share a last name, giving Amber official and permanent rights.

◆◆◆

It had been a long evening. Ryan's talk over after-dinner coffee in Mack's office had gone well, but at this very moment, he was wishing for his own bed. The worst of it was the torturous witness of Trey's clamorous quest for Amber's attention. That combined with Mack's insistence of letting Trey find out on his own about the race when classes resumed had Ryan's emotions more heightened than usual. It had been a relief to say goodnight to the household and close his guest room door.

Unfortunately, the place where he'd be laying his head was wedged in between Trey's room and the girls'. That meant shared walls on either side, giving him unwelcome access to what was going on behind closed doors.

He turned down the covers and was beginning to unbutton his shirt when he heard Trey's door creak open and footsteps passing by in the hallway. A moment later, he heard a knock, but not on his door. Most likely Trey was requesting access to the girls' room. Ryan's suspicions were confirmed as giggles ensued shortly thereafter. He couldn't make out the exact words of Trey's low bass, but after the sound of a door closing on each side of him, he assumed Trey had gone back to bed. Ryan put his ear up to the girls' wall. That was one way to find out.

"Amber, you simply must marry Trey," one of them said.

"It's a foregone conclusion as far as I'm concerned," said another. Amber, perhaps? Ryan hoped not.

"Oh, girls. You're jumping to conclusions. He's not really interested. Is he?"

Amber for sure this time. At least he could take comfort in her doubt of Trey's feelings. To Ryan, it was obvious Trey was in pursuit. It seemed Trey's sisters agreed.

"I tell you, he is. That boy has set his cap for you. He's never escorted a young lady over to spend the whole day, has he, girls?" More giggles. "You know what that means, don't you?"

Ryan wished his heart wasn't beating so loudly in his ears. It was difficult to hear their sopranos over the pulsing. The voices became more muffled the harder he strained, although the general tone in the room next door was all too clear.

Ryan huffed. *Just my luck to be witness to the dawn of Amber's affections for another man.* Would have been better to hear through the grapevine. He needed to get out of there for a while. Maybe come back after they had quieted down for the night.

Stealing silently into the hall and closing his door with the knob turned so no *click* would be heard, Ryan made his way downstairs. A change of scenery would help him contemplate his next move. The twin staircase was dark, as was the foyer, but a soft glow came from the fireplace in the front room. Next to the hearth lay the Wright's golden retriever with her new litter. He stooped and noted a homey, pleasant smell. He had no idea something so small, so common really, would possess the ability to bring him into the right frame of mind. Ryan stroked their smooth little bodies while whispering meaningless words to the mother.

"Just the same idea I had." The words were spoken softly from the cased opening. Amber stood there with a huge smile on her face, but she wasn't looking at Ryan. "Aren't they just the best? I had no idea I'd be here again so soon to see how much they've grown." She bent next to him, the flames alighting on each strand of her hair, making her look more alive than the average girl.

She was so perfect. So right. So wholesome. Everything in Ryan yearned to be with her, but yet he hesitated. She was too perfect, right, and wholesome to want to be with him. She deserved the Wright family. They would treat her well and give her everything he never could.

She picked up one of the puppies and cuddled it close. "How in the world could anyone think there isn't a God when they hold a newborn in their arms?"

Ryan wasn't sure if she was asking the question rhetorically or to him specifically. He kept quiet and picked up one of the litter. Its eyes were still closed and it was hard to tell if it was a boy or a girl, but Ryan knew one day this dog would bring joy to someone, somewhere.

"To be honest, I've never thought about it that way," he heard himself saying. Amber Graham made him want to be open, honest, unbarred. "I've never held a newborn, or even a baby before." He looked up and gave her a half grin. "Of any species."

"Never? That's something. I've been holding babies since the day I came to the King's Castle." Amber picked up another of the velvety-soft creatures and sat cross-legged, giving the two puppies a nice little nest between her legs. "As soon as I got there, Mrs. Cole had me helping in the nursery. That is, when I wasn't doing my lessons."

"Did the orphanage have many babies? I would think it would be older children whose parents had died."

"You'd be surprised at the myriad circumstances that bring children to the place in their lives that they would need to be housed by strangers. Abuse. Neglect. Abandonment. Death. Ugly things that follow you around, no matter how much you try and escape them." Amber looked down, focusing her gaze on the puppies.

"If you don't mind my asking, which one of those brought you there?"

"All of them," she said matter-of-factly.

Ryan reeled back an inch or two. That was startling. Amber seemed like such a well-rounded girl. She obviously had an intellect that soared above her peers. She was a bright light with an even brighter future.

He knew he'd lose sleep over her confession. "All of them?" He hoped it was an accident that she'd used the word *abuse*. That shouldn't happen to any child. None of those things should, yet he'd experienced all of them himself.

"Yes." Then she straightened her shoulders and lifted her chin. "But that was a long time ago. No need to dredge up the past." She put the dogs back with their mother and her hand seemed to automatically go to the necklace she'd been wearing the last time he saw her.

"What do you have there?" Ryan hoped he wasn't overstepping invisible boundaries.

She looked down quickly, the necklace still in her hand. "Oh. I didn't realize I was fiddling with it. Summer's always trying to get me to break the habit. Says it's not ladylike."

"Who's Summer?"

"Sorry. Summer Titus. Christian Titus's wife. Besides the Coles, they're the first people I met when I came to the King's Castle. Now they live just one house over from mine on the King's Castle property. Their little girls, Fiona and Mirabel, are very special to me. I love them to pieces."

Ryan put the puppy he'd been holding back with its mother as well. He felt a hollow place open up inside at the mention of Amber's close relationship with these people. He didn't know why he should feel that way. He shouldn't begrudge her the chance to have what he never did.

"But the necklace?" he prompted. "What's that on the front?" Amber ran her finger over the raised image. A dragonfly perhaps?

"It's a bee with its wings spread out. See?" She turned toward the fire and Ryan repositioned himself to have a closer look.

"It's quite something," he said, his breath coming a little quicker. He was so close to her now that if he had the nerve to look up, their faces would be mere inches apart. Better to focus on something other than the girl in front of him. "I wonder how the bee is attached." He peered closer. "Or if the artist carved it all from one piece of gold." Not only was the multi-dimensional bee life-like, truly its own work of art, the engraved background of vines and flowers seemed to make it come to life. "It's exquisite." Reluctantly, he backed away, his fingers itching to stroke the raised surface of the necklace, to have in his hand something that must still hold Amber's warmth.

"I think so, too. Whoever made it had an eye for beauty and design. I'm too scientific to be so creative. The bee seems to be mid-flight, don't you think?" Amber dropped her hands to her lap. "It's all I have left of my mother."

"What about your father?"

Amber's eyes flashed. Ryan knew that look. He'd gone too far, forgotten himself during this personal exchange with a near stranger in the dark of someone else's home. Their meeting seemed fated, just like his discussion with Mack had been. It was strange how God felt closer now than He had in a long time, maybe ever, as Ryan let his guard down and was simply being himself, wasn't trying to con someone. "I'm sorry. It's none of my business."

Amber reached out her hand but stopped before she touched him. "No, no. You're fine. I'm sorry for my reaction. It's just that no one has asked me that in a long time. Goodness, I can't even remember when. Maybe when I first came to the orphanage. They always want to know things like that. But after I got settled, I realized none of the others wanted to speak of long-lost mothers and fathers, not the way you would think they would. I guess it's just easier to pretend they never existed. Like all of us had always been there, with no family ties to a future but also nothing confining us to a disagreeable past. When you don't speak of it, it's easier to forget you were destined to be alone."

"But you're not alone. You just said so. The Tituses. The Coles. Now the Wrights." Ryan swallowed. The next words would be some of the hardest he'd ever had to say. Probably because they were the truth, something he wasn't as comfortable speaking as its counterpart. "You seem to belong here. And I think they all agree. From Grandmother

Wright all the way down to Trey. You're wanted here."

The words brought with them a hideous finality, a gavel of judgement proclaiming nothing could ever come of a relationship between the two of them. Ryan realized in that moment that although he wanted to win the race, wanted to get out from under his father's oppression, he needed Amber. The truth tasted bitter, but gauging Amber's reaction, his words were just what she needed to hear.

◆◆◆

I'm too good for this. William Pierce picked his way through the dark, trash-strewn alley and held his breath against the mixture of sewer and onions, a combination he hoped to never again encounter. He swore under his breath as he stepped in something that squished underneath his shoes.

Number 6. William stood on the sagging stoop and knocked. He put his hands in his pockets, hoping to keep them there throughout the duration of this disagreeable visit.

William felt tall and powerful as he stood waiting for the door to open. Bringing his anger about the missing money to the forefront of his mind always gave him a bizarre, otherworldly feeling of unnatural strength. Over the years, he had used those emotions again and again to fuel the drive to let others take the fall so he would end up on top.

The plan to take that money was no exception. It had been the perfect set up, too. Everything planned down to the last detail. Then things had begun to go south. Their three-person crew had dwindled to two after Tabitha had up and married some guy and moved away. Traitor. That meant more work for him as he prepared to rob prosperous Waterford Cove Holdings. But in the end, all he had to show were months of his life wasted. Gone, just like the ten thousand dollars he'd held in his hand for so brief a time. But it was out there somewhere, taunting him with its possibilities. And it was his.

"What're you about, bangin' like that in the middle of the night?" A woman in a ratty nightgown opened the door a crack. "You drunk?

Get on out of here."

William shoved his toe into the space between the door and the jam, blocking the woman's attempt to shut him out in the cold. "Go wake up Joseph. Tell him Will is here."

The woman's eyes squinted for a moment, then recognition seemed to dawn. She obeyed, hollering over her shoulder, "Joe! Looks like your past is finally here to haunt you."

The creak of a floorboard, the rustle of clothing, and the scuffling of feet reached William's ears before Jelly Joe appeared. William stamped his icy feet, but by the looks of the squalor these people lived in, the inside of the house wasn't going to be much warmer.

His suspicions were correct as Joe regarded him without a word and motioned with his head for William to come inside. Joe led the way to a table near a wood stove that lent only the faintest hint of heat. The woman disappeared down a short hallway, leaving the living room-kitchen combination for the two men.

"Thought I was seeing a ghost," Joe said, turning his back on William to stoke the fire and put on some coffee.

"Nope. Just me. In the flesh." He regarded the man whom he once would have called a friend. Friends did things for each other. Got their comrades out of scrapes. Stole items or information for the good of the other. Stood by in hard times.

Joe didn't take a seat at the kitchen table like William expected. He leaned against the work counter and crossed his arms over his huge stomach. "Why are you here, Will?"

"Cut straight to the point, don't ya?" William cringed at how easy it was to slip back into old patterns. This was just a brief stop along the journey of his life. A temporary detour. He'd worked too hard to leave this life behind to begin acting like he was on the same level as these people. Ruffians. Criminals of the lowest order.

"You left me in the lurch," said Joe, a trace of fire lurking in his bloodshot eyes. "Tell me somethin' worthwhile. Cuz I don't take too kindly to the likes of you bargin' in on my sleep."

"I think you know why I came. I need the money. And you're the perfect person to help me find it."

Joe's gray-yellow beard shook with laughter. "What a joke." William didn't like the way Joe emphasized each word. "You serious, Will? You must be in quite a fix to come knockin'. But hey, I already knew that."

William narrowed his eyes. "What do you mean?"

"I mean," said Joe, coming to the table and looming over William, the bulge of his protruding belly still giving testament to his nickname, "that for the last twenty years, I've been keepin' tabs. Watching you. Following your failures and successes, knowing that sometime soon, all my hack-shaw work would come in mighty handy." He smiled, revealing several missing teeth. "Looks like that day of reckoning might finally be here." Joe started down the hall, calling back over his shoulder. "Follow me."

Joe stood in the doorway of small room and leaned against the jam, allowing William access. The six-by-eight foot space contained one lone desk and a wobbly-looking chair. It also held a sight that made William's stomach turn sickeningly.

His eyes darted to read the words on the newspaper clippings that haphazardly covered the walls. *Lone Thief Takes All—Fraudulent Scammer on the Loose—The Chariot, A Rival for Benz?—Pierce Purchases York Mansion on Fifth Street—Jewelry Missing from Mayor's Home, Reward Money Offered for Information—The Chariot, an Automobile to Watch*

William's eyes grew large at the precision with which Jelly Joe had followed him through the years. Only a handful of the articles contained William's actual name and those that did were of his semi-legitimate successes. The rest were speculative on Joe's part. But he was eerily correct on most.

"I can see I've got your attention," Joe said victoriously, obviously feeling he had the upper hand. "Your desperation is gonna work to my advantage." Joe gestured down the hall toward the main room of the house. "As you can see, I could use the money, too. And I know more than you think I do. You need me."

William tried not to squirm. Tabitha and William had worked well together many a time, planning their three-person heists. Tabitha was always good for distracting their marks while the caper was underway.

Jelly Joe only filled in the gaps—he was the driver, did the grunt work when staking out a heist, was the one who cleaned up any lose ends. But it was William who had been the mastermind behind every job. And Joe knew it. The gang would have been made up of two ne'er-do-wells who couldn't rub together two stolen coins if it weren't for William's cunning and expertise.

"I was at your beck and call for too many years, pulling jobs you thought you were too good for. Doing your dirty deeds while you kept your hands clean." Joe sneered, an ugly look that made his face resemble an angered dog. "It's my turn now. I'll go pour that coffee so you've got what it takes to jump when I say how high because you just got yourself a job, Will. Working for me."

FIVE

Mind if I take a look?" Amber's hand was already reaching for the file, but she looked across her kitchen table at Christian Titus before picking it up.

"By all means. That's why I brought it over. Thought you might enjoy picking it apart a bit. I've had all week to look at it but haven't gotten very far." Christian gave his wife a loving glance. "We've been too busy making memories."

Summer left her spot in front of Amber's fireplace and came to lean against her husband's shoulder. "I know most people probably don't enjoy being shut in for this long, but we've loved every moment. It's given us a chance to slow down and take account of what really matters." Summer looked content, like a young girl just finding her forever love for the first time.

Like I would know what that looks like.

"I can give you a brief overview of the case," Christian was saying, "but I honestly don't want to taint your thoughts with my own. I'd love a fresh set of eyes on these documents. So, if you have some spare moments this week, go on ahead and use that analytical mind of yours. But no rush. This one's been unsolved for two decades; I think it can wait a good bit more." He said the last with a chuckle.

"But you have a history with this one, right?" Amber glanced at Mirabel and Fiona who were settled in front of Amber's small hearth playing with a few wooden toys she kept around for just such an occasion. She wasn't sure if their little ears should overhear whatever their father might say next.

"Yes," Christian said, but he didn't lower his voice. "Before I left the organization, I handed over all my case files to the director, of course, but I made notes on certain ones that I knew wouldn't leave me alone." He shrugged. "It was sort of a hobby for a while after I got hired on with the PD in Waterford Cove. But I got so busy with the force and the orphanage that these all got put to the side."

"Other than the weather, what made you dig this one out of mothballs now?" Amber was sure there was more to this than met the eye.

Christian looked quickly at his wife. Summer gave a small nod, almost imperceptible. "I think it's the date. Coming up on the twenty-first anniversary of the Waterford Cove Holdings Robbery of 1878. A grand total of around ten thousand dollars was stolen. It's still out there somewhere. And what's worse, no one was ever caught and our leads were purely based on assumption. This time of year especially makes me think of what happened during that season in my life. You see, this one was not only my first case as a Pinkerton, I've always had a hunch it also involved my first wife."

Long after the Tituses had made their way back home across the slippery February grass, Amber sat by the fire, pouring over Christian's carefully detailed notes. It was not unlike some of the projects Professor Henning gave her at the university. An assignment to dig into an unsolved problem. A commissioning to find a solution by means of trial, analysis, and discovery.

Amber wondered about the woman whose name had been underlined periodically throughout the papers—Tabitha—Christian's first wife. Amber had no idea until today that he'd even been married before. Had she been a criminal? How did the marriage end? Amber shuddered to think what it would be like to fall in love with someone who wasn't what they first appeared.

Lord, protect me from such a fate.

That morning, after some quiet prayer and Scripture reading in the

Wright's parlor in leu of church, the weather had lifted enough so that both Amber and Ryan were able to bundle up and take their leave. The passage the family had read together had very much refreshed Amber, but she had missed her own time with the Lord.

She jumped up and grabbed her Bible, turning to Isaiah as she walked back to the hearth. After she had flipped through a few chapters, she found the verses Grandmother Wright had spoken over her. She mulled them over as she sat looking out her window at the bare trees shaking their limbs in the cold breeze. The poor dears had most likely never endured such frigid temperatures in all their days. Amber could sympathize. But if these verses were just as applicable today as they were when they were written, then she, as well as the trees, could hold out hope. *I will do a new thing. I will make a way in the wilderness. Rivers in the desert.*

A new thing. Was that what God was up to now? All the nights she could have spent bonding with new sisters, all the days of missed family time together, and now suddenly the prospect of becoming a Wright held very real possibility. A clear path in the wilderness of Amber's life. Leaves being pasted onto her barren tree. It was too good to be true. Maybe that last fact alone was a clear sign God was the One at work.

Setting the Bible to the side, she reached for the file again but was interrupted by a sound at the door.

"Summer—" Amber began, opening the door for her friend.

"Surprise?" It took Amber a moment for her mind to assimilate that it was Ryan who was standing there. He had removed his hat and was bowing slightly, a boyish grin gracing his face.

"Yes, it is. Won't you come in?" Amber's heart was trying to return to normal speed as she stepped aside to allow him access.

Ryan wiped his feet on the mat. "Thanks. It appears to be thawing out a bit but I can't seem to get warm enough, you know?"

Amber cleared her throat. "Yes, the temperatures are rising, that's for sure. But I've still got the fire going as hot as I can get it." She watched his every movement, wondering what this man was doing at her house. She didn't know who his family was or where he lived, but by the sheer fact that he attended university and was connected to the Wright family in some way, Amber was well aware they weren't equals on any level. "Did Professor Henning send you?"

Instead of answering her question, her unexpected guest stood in the middle of her one-room cabin, turning in a big circle, seeming to take in every detail. His eyes landed on the floor in front of the fireplace.

"Excuse the mess. The Tituses were here earlier and I was working on something for Christian." Amber sat again on the hearth rug so she could straighten the papers, but out of the corner of her eye, she tried to see her home through the eyes of this wealthy man.

"Let me help you." Before she could protest, Ryan was kneeling in front of the her. "Do you want these in any certain order? Looks like you were really in the middle of something."

"They all belong in the same folder, so I can just stack them and put them in here." Amber held out her hand, indicating she had the situation under control. How embarrassing. She glanced over at the bed. At least the covers were done up.

But Ryan's eyes weren't on the clutter. They were fixed to the paper that lay on top of the stack he held.

"What is it?" she asked.

He looked up, his eyes a bit wider than usual. "Nothing."

Ryan handed over the documents, providing Amber with a measure of relief. These were something Christian had entrusted to her. She hadn't realized that when she'd agreed to help that she was also signing up for the responsibility of keeping them confidential.

"Allow me to help you up." A big hand was extended her way and she could do nothing but accept his assistance.

"Thank you," she said, adjusting her skirt. "As you can see, I was cold, too. Felt good to work right in front of the fire."

"If you'd like, I can move your table over so you don't have to sit on the floor." He laughed and she felt ashamed that she would be caught in such a position. "Don't be embarrassed. If you'll recall, I was doing the same last night at the Wright's."

His laughter no longer made her feel like she was being judged.

Instead, it broke the tension she felt, making it easy to laugh along. "Let's leave the table but bring over the pillows." When he seemed perplexed at her suggestion, she said, "Well, what are we waiting for?" Amber marched across the room, grabbed two pillows from the bed and plopped them at Ryan's feet.

Not missing a beat, Ryan went and grabbed two more. "Another for you, my lady, and one for me. But I haven't yet answered your question as to why I'm here." He sat cross-legged, placing his elbows on his knees, steepling his fingers at his clean-shaven chin. "Professor Henning didn't send me, although I believe he'd sanction this meeting."

Meeting. That meant this wasn't a social call. Amber lowered her eyes and pulled at a loose string on the rug.

"I sent myself. I wanted to speak with you about the after-school project you mentioned. My interest is piqued."

Amber was surprised Ryan would come to her rather than a colleague or even a professor. "How can I help you?"

"I believe we share a commonality. Innovation. Invention. Progress. Tell me more about the batteries you've been working on for Professor Henning."

"Has he shown you the prototypes in the lab?" she asked.

Ryan shifted on his pillow, putting his hands up to the fire's warmth. "I've only heard rumors. Henning's been quite reclusive about the designs. If I had to guess, he's gearing up to teach on the concepts in the fall term. Of course, I'll be gone by then."

"I think he's pretty excited about the possibilities. I can only imagine what larger-capacity batteries that are more portable will do for inventions yet to come." Amber looked at Ryan shyly. "I've been wondering since I saw you yesterday if a high-capacity battery is exactly what you need for your senior invention."

"You're right. In order to make this hybrid engine, as you called it, work, I've got to solve that piece." Ryan leaned toward her slightly. "You'll probably hear about this tomorrow at school, but there's going to be a race. A place I can take all the ideas that are in my head and turn them into reality." He looked bemused. "So far, it's mostly been on paper. If I can bring it all together, I see this as a real chance to make the automobile manageable for anyone who wishes to drive one. Benz and Daimler are going to be at the race, too. They could take this concept and run with it. Before we know it, the horse and carriage are going to be completely replaced by the horseless carriage." He grinned lopsidedly.

"I'd love to help." The words were out of her mouth before she fully thought them through. Was it wise to partner with someone she barely knew? Yet the picture he created was captivating. "What exactly do you need?" Maybe it would be best if she knew what she was getting into before she so readily volunteered.

"I'm glad you asked. And thank you for offering your assistance." Ryan looked at her thoughtfully. "I'm always by myself. It would be nice to work side by side with someone who shares my interests. I'll also need the supplies. Do you think Henning would let me buy some of what he's got?"

Amber wondered if he meant he always worked alone on his projects or if he was truly without anyone in the world. She would answer his question instead. "I think it's worth asking. He's got a supplier just down the coast. I know he could get more if he needed to."

"Wonderful. And I already have a strong lead on a Westinghouse three-horse-power motor," he said. "Going to buy it from the Waterford Cove Knitting Mill on the north end of town. Once I have the battery and can spend a good chunk of time in the carriage house putting it all together, I'll be set."

He said the last with such an air of confidence, Amber could do nothing but believe he'd accomplish what he set out to do. She wondered if his family owned an automobile that he was modifying. Amber knew there were probably less than fifteen cars in the entire town of Waterford Cove. Ryan's family must be very rich indeed. "Well, I think you've come to the right place." Amber smiled. This was going to be fun. "If Henning says yes and we spend a couple hours in the lab, we could get your battery ready. Maybe next week?"

A sound at the door came just before it opened slightly. "Amber? You still here?"

"Come on in, Christian." Amber stood hastily and glanced over at Ryan, who was looking so casual and at home on her floor. "Christian Titus, let me introduce you to Ryan—" She faltered. "I'm afraid I don't know your last name."

"Pierce," said Ryan, getting up nonchalantly and shaking hands with Christian. He didn't look the least bit chagrined by the situation. He was pumping Christian's hand and smiling an engaging smile. "Ryan Pierce. Nice to meet you Mr. Titus."

"Pierce you say?" Christian looked sharply at Amber, then back at Ryan. "What brings you to the King's Castle and our dear Amber?"

"I haven't been over to the big house yet, but you know, that's not a bad idea. I wouldn't mind seeing the fruits of your hard labor."

"It's not really mine to claim. I just help out where I can. Nonetheless, come on over anytime. I could show you around the property. There's more to it than you'd expect."

Ryan was still smiling. "I'd like that. And in answer to your question, I'll admit my reasons were a bit selfish. I'm hoping Amber will help me with a project I'm working on."

"Seems to be the common theme around here lately," Christian said good-naturedly. "Say, why don't you come over tomorrow afternoon and I'll show you the ropes?" His sharp look had vanished and the tension she'd first sensed in him now seemed non-existent. Perhaps her friend was feeling fatherly and it eased his mind to know Ryan was here for academic reasons. Amber told her heart that was fine. Just fine indeed.

♦ ♦ ♦

Waterford Cove Holdings Robbery, 1878. Unconfirmed Suspect: William Pierce.

The words from the file Amber had in her possession followed Ryan home. He knew his father had a sordid past, but it was never brought up in conversation. Could he have pulled off a bank robbery? Ryan doubted it. On the other hand, his father had always gone after what he wanted. Perhaps back in his younger days he had been more Machiavellian and less headstrong.

The afternoon passed quietly as Ryan's mind bounced between wondering why Amber would have a file with his father's name on it and formulating his plan for the Endurance Race. Amber. She had blown into his life like a fresh spring breeze off the Atlantic. He wanted to see her again. Needed to be near her. If he could get close enough, maybe he could leech from her what he was lacking. Purity. Companionship. Love.

But if his suspicions were confirmed and his father was implicated in a crime, and if Amber ever connected the dots back to Ryan, she would never give him the time of day. If she caught wind of the true Pierce family legacy, she'd run in the other direction as fast as her legs could carry her.

Even if he couldn't see her now, he needed to get out of the house. As he stepped outside, Ryan noticed that even in the slight evening breeze, the air had almost taken on a springtime feeling. If it was still like this in the morning, there'd be classes for sure. And if the temperatures kept rising, the ice and snow would be gone within a few days and life could resume back to normal for everyone along the Eastern Seaboard. But Ryan didn't include himself in that count.

In the morning, he would begin his day just as he had for the last four years. Up before the sun, a couple hours bent over his designs, a bicycle ride to WCU, followed by a full day of study and experimentation. It would be the same, but it wouldn't feel the same. Too much had happened. This last week had brought a confusing and exciting turn of events he never saw coming. Some he despised, some he needed, some he was scared he couldn't live without.

A redheaded angel he could never have. A head start at a once-in-a-lifetime shot to pitch his design to people like Benz and Daimler. A father whose poor decisions looked to be catching up with him. A small miracle in the form of Mack Wright's offer. And after hearing Mack read this morning from the big family Bible, a bewildering sense that there was a God who cared about him.

Ryan went to the side entrance of the carriage house and left the door open behind him to let in enough twilight to illuminate the front of the

Chariot. He walked around the car, noting its strengths but mostly its weaknesses. Its chassis was too heavy, its body too costly to reproduce in mass quantity, its gasoline engine almost impossible to start quickly.

Despite its shiny exterior, Ryan knew that in the rear of the chassis resided a carburetor that originally belonged to Mors, a cooler that had morphed from Galli's original design, and a brake lever Ryan himself had dug out of the trash heap behind the Engineering Building. But William Pierce was a whiz at metal fabrication, adept at making something look good from the outside, camouflaging mismatched parts and pieces that somehow resembled a whole automobile.

Ryan scoffed. He was done trying to sell this pile of junk to the sad sacks who believed every word he told them. He hoped for Mr. Blake's sake that his wife had put her foot down.

A puff of wind suddenly banged the door against the building's exterior wall. The force propelled it back on its hinges and slammed the door shut. The darkness seemed to have cast its unanimous vote against the light because Ryan couldn't see even the hint of an outline. Reason told him if he could reach out and touch the Chariot that he would be able to feel his way closer to the door, but rational thought didn't win this argument. Ryan felt panic rise in his chest as he reached out to touch something tangible.

Without warning, a thought flashed through his mind. A snippet of something Mack had read aloud that morning from near the back of the family Bible. "…him who hath called you out of darkness into his marvellous light."

The Chariot seemed a mile long as he inched toward what he hoped was the door. The light. Marvelous light. Isn't that what he had been moving toward? Away from the groping hand of his father's darkness, and instead steering in the direction of honest gains. Light. God's light? Did its source matter as long as he broke away? As long as he didn't follow his father's footsteps? In the oppressive dark, Ryan renewed his vow to never become like his father. He was better than that. He could rise above. He *would* rise above. Ryan reached the front of the Chariot and bravely took a step away from what was solid. Known.

He put both hands out in front of him, hoping to feel the hardness of the wall any time now. Even though he hadn't noticed it, his eyes must have adjusted in the last thirty seconds or so, for he could faintly make out the corner of the door where the twilight was trying to push itself back inside. Ryan lunged for it and threw the door wide.

The familiar objects in the carriage house were gilded by soft starshine when he looked back. *Some big fool I am.*

As he walked to the house, his father pulled up in the family's carriage. Alone, Ryan noted. William never went anywhere in town without their driver. He always held to the notion that appearance counted for everything. "Let them know by the way you carry yourself that you're worth something." Ryan had never known his father to set reputation to the side in lieu of convenience. To be considered unimportant, even by a stranger, was unthinkable.

"Where's Gerrard?" Ryan asked. Now that he thought of it, he hadn't seen the man all afternoon.

William waved away the question. "Had to let him go. He was becoming insolent."

I highly doubt that.

"Pay no mind to things that aren't important. It's time you and I focus on the matter at hand." William's tone was civil but Ryan knew better.

Nothing I haven't dealt with before. His feet carried him to his father, a darkness no light could penetrate, no matter how marvelous.

◆◆◆

Tabitha Murray. Amber couldn't get the name out of her head. She didn't know what was so special about it or the entire Waterford Cove Holdings case, but both had captured her imagination. It had been midnight when she'd finally turned down the wick on her kerosene lamp and lain in the darkness, her thoughts still racing.

Her efforts to relax apparently hadn't worked too well, for she had been up before dawn with the kind of energy that always came with a new project. Taking apart the whole and looking at the function of each piece was just as exciting as putting it back together. And now, she was racing along the path toward the King's Castle to attend to her morning duties.

"Goodness. What has you tearing around here this morning?" Elizabeth Edwards, the resident grandma at the orphanage, was stirring the morning porridge at the enormous cookstove. She glanced over her shoulder and shook her head at a breathless Amber.

A pile of scrumptious-looking scones next to a saucer of clotted cream caught Amber's eye, Justine Cole's doing no doubt. The King's Castle's founder was always trying to bring some of her English homeland into the details of everyday life for the children. "Sorry to barge in like that." She took a calming breath and a big bite of scone before answering. "I need to get through my chores as fast as I can. I have a full day ahead of me."

"I know a woman on a mission when I see one." Elizabeth smiled. Grandma E, Summer's birth mother, had been a part of Amber's life for years now, although it was hard to refer to her by the nickname. Elizabeth had three children of her own, the oldest not quite eight and the youngest still toddling about. If Amber couldn't start growing her family tree soon, she could always hold out hope that love would find her later on in life, like it did with Dustin and Elizabeth Edwards. *I hope it doesn't take that long.*

"Here's a little friendly advice," Elizabeth said gently. "If you weren't working two jobs and always doing a favor for someone or another, you'd be able to walk in here like a lady."

Amber gave Grandma E a quick kiss on the cheek before taking her leave. "Thanks for the advice." She swallowed the last of her breakfast, saying with a smile, "I'll take it into serious consideration."

The older woman, who was a spitting image of Summer, shooed her out of the kitchen with a friendly laugh. Amber peeked into the dining room, saying hello to those who had already begun setting the table for the morning meal. "Hello, John. Theo. Angela." Amber walked through the room, greeting each one by name. As her reward, she received sleepy hugs around her waist while she smoothed her hand over each young head. It took only a minute to set out the rest of the plates and napkins. "I'll catch up with you all tomorrow," Amber said to the room at large. "Today, I need to get scootin', so here I go."

Running up the stairs like a gust of wind, she stripped down the beds in the big girls' room as fast as her hands would let her. If she got these linens started while she talked with the girls who were still getting dressed for the day then she could think about the battery design while she mopped the floor. When she was through with that, she'd hop down to the first-floor nursery and love on the littles for a few minutes before helping Grandma E start the vegetables for lunch.

She was pleased when only an hour later she opened the pantry door to pull out the potatoes.

"Did you hear the news?" an excited voice said at her side.

Amber jumped. She'd been so engrossed in challenging herself to get these potatoes ready in less than fifteen minutes that she hadn't heard young Mirabel come into the kitchen. "What news is that?" Amber asked, looking up to see if Summer and Fiona had come to the big house as well. Looked like Mirabel had walked over by herself.

"Spring is here." Mirabel's missing two front teeth made it sound like she said "sling is here." "Isn't that right, Grandma?"

Elizabeth pulled up a stool at the counter and grabbed another peeler. She looked lovingly at her granddaughter. "Oh, yes. I'd say it's officially arrived."

"Is that a fact?" Amber glanced out the window where the sun had just peeped its head above the tree line. This far south of the nation's capital rarely saw the kind of weather the Great Blizzard of 1899 had brought. Typically by this time in February, the crocuses were showing their pretty purple heads, and Amber was beginning to anxiously look for buds on trees. Maybe Mirabel was more right than Amber had given her credit for, although the extended cold snap made it feel like "sling" would never come.

"Mother told me so. She says we can leave winter and Christmas and Val-um-time's behind and start getting ready for Easter." Mirabel paused in her energetic talk. "When is Easter?"

Amber put down the potato she'd been peeling. Her heart lurched but she schooled her face to appear pleasant to her little friend. "It changes every year."

"It does?" Amber could see Mirabel's six-year-old mind struggling to understand. "Is it coming soon?"

"Yes, but it's not always on the same day. Sometimes, it's not even in the same month." Amber would know. She remembered a birthday cake with no frosting that she had been given on her sixth birthday. The woman Amber had lived with for the first few years of her life had woken her up and told her it was her birthday and it was Easter and they were going to church. They never went to church.

"My birthday is Easter?" she had innocently asked Mrs. MacDonald.

Her caretaker's face had taken on an odd look. "Yes. Easter. Don't ever forget that, Amber."

The circumstances that had taken place that peculiar week in her young life had become muddled in Amber's mind over the last thirteen years, but she could still pick out a few precious memories that held some clarity.

Knowing her birthday was on a special day like Easter gave Amber a sense of identity for the first time that she could remember, but what she discovered later on that morning during what was called "Sunday school" was even more profound. The teacher had read from a book she said was the Bible. The words from the leather-bound volume assured the class that each one of them had been born for a reason. The woman told Amber that a man named Jesus Christ, who was God's own Son, loved her so much that He gave His life for her so she could be a part of the family of God. Forever.

The message she had readily made her own that bright Sunday morning took on an even deeper meaning in less than a week's time when Mrs. MacDonald took sick.

It struck Amber that she had been the same age as Mirabel when her caretaker had lain on her deathbed and given Amber a gift. "From your mother," she had said, laying a golden necklace in Amber's hand. It was cool to the touch and Amber had stroked it with her small thumb.

"She asked me to give this to you when you were old enough. You're not yet—" Mrs. MacDonald's words were cut off by a wracking cough. After a long moment, she continued. "But I can't wait any longer." The woman who had cooked her meals and washed her clothes and had never forgotten to say "good night" closed her eyes and whispered, "Two things, girl. Do two things for me."

"Yes, ma'am," said Amber. She squeezed Mrs. MacDonald's hand more tightly.

"Go to the woods out back and find the bee tree. Look really closely at it. There's something there your mother wanted you to have. I don't know what it is, but if you find it, hide it, and take it with you." The woman's voice faltered and Amber leaned in close. "Then go to the church I took you to. They'll know what to do. Take good care of yourself, Amber Graham."

Graham. A birthday, a last name, and a Savior who wanted her as His very own. But all those glorious gifts hadn't been enough when Amber slung an old bag of Mrs. MacDonald's across her shoulder and looked back at the little shack in the woods. Before she left, she searched those woods for what seemed like hours, looking for a bee tree, but Amber had no honey to take with her as she walked to the church.

Mirabel was plucking at her sleeve. "When is it this year?"

"When is what?"

"Easter, silly. Haven't you been listening?" Mirabel giggled and poked Amber in the ribs.

"Come here, you," Amber drew Mirabel into a side hug and kissed the top of her golden head. "I always listen when you talk. Easter is March 19 this year. About four weeks away. And you know what? I bet by then the tulips will be up. Tulips are my favorite flower. What's yours?"

While Mirabel chatted away about flowers and bunnies and the Titus's Easter traditions, Amber made quick work of finishing the vegetables. The other Titus girls came in as she was leaving. Summer greeted her mother with a hug and Fiona wrapped her arms around her grandma's leg. One day, Amber said to herself. One day I'll have a family to call my own. The Wright family.

"Good to see you, Mother. Amber," Summer said. "What are you girls up to this morning?"

"I've got an appointment, so I'll try to catch up with you this evening if I can," Amber said. "And I have a hunch that Professor Henning's going to have plenty of work waiting for me today since everything's been shut down for so long." She ruffled Fiona's hair and included them all in her smile. "See you later, then."

Amber wished she had a faster way to get to her next stop but her own legs would have to do. It was just as well. Walking would give her more time to go over the facts she already knew.

Tabitha Murray. Joe Schneider. Both names that were presumed acquaintances in William Pierce's previous crimes. Amber held her skirt up a bit higher and jumped over a puddle that was in her way. Pierce. Christian's notes indicated the man was the key suspect but that the robbery hadn't fit Pierce's known *modus operandi*; the location had been different from any the criminal had targeted in the past, not to mention he always used a three-man crew.

Amber mentally corrected herself. Three-*person* crew; not all of them male. That's where this Tabitha person came in. Or at least, that's what Christian had assumed.

Amber kept her mind working overtime as she made tracks to Waterford Cove's Main Street. Two more stops and she could catch the nine o'clock train.

"Excuse me," she said to a man who was stuffing papers into a tall filing cabinet behind a counter at City Hall. "Is this where I would find records? Marriage licenses, perhaps?"

He jerked his head to the far corner of the large room. "Ask Miss Childs. She'll give you what you need."

"Thank you."

"Can I help you?" A young woman with a sharp chin and high bun greeted her. Amber wasn't certain this stop would give her any leads, but it wouldn't take long to find out.

Amber checked her notes again, just to make certain she was asking the right questions. "Yes, I'm looking for information you might be able to provide on three different people. Marriage licenses. Deeds.

Birth records. Here are their names." Amber produced a scrap of paper.

"Marriages and births are public, of course, but I'm afraid I can't give you property data without consent of the owner." The young lady pointed to the name Tabitha Murray on the list. "I'm not certain if this would be beneficial to your search, but I can tell you right now that surname is Scottish. Seen plenty of those come through. Is she a family member of yours?"

Amber shook her head. "No, she's not family. But I'd still like to find out any information I can about her."

Miss Childs's face took on a conspiratorial look. "Naturalization records are public. Would you like me to try and find out if that woman immigrated to Waterford Cove County?"

"I honestly don't know if that would help, but, why not?" Amber shrugged. "If you wouldn't mind. How long do you think it'll take? I need to catch the nine o'clock train."

Miss Child glanced at the clock on the wall. "Why don't you stop back tomorrow morning?" she suggested. "I should have more information for you by then."

Amber placed her notes into her bag while expressing her thanks to the clerk. As she opened the door and stepped outside, the strength of the morning sun made the long weeks of hard winter feel long ago and far away. Piles of snow still remained but the air felt fresh and clean. Amber breathed deeply, letting the sense of adventure wash over her. If she could never know who her own family had been, maybe she could help a close friend like Christian fill in the missing links to his.

◆◆◆

A fresh, briny smell swept in from the sea and came with a cheerful welcome to greet residents on Waterford Cove's bustling downtown street of First Avenue. The breeze followed Ryan as he walked to Bijoux d'Artisan. Mr. Dandurand was certain to be busier than normal on this particular Monday in February. It seemed everyone in town had been kept within their four walls long enough. He guessed that was why he'd had no trouble pawning his electric bicycle this morning. People were looking for excuses to be out-of-doors.

Ryan's reasons for skipping his morning routine hadn't originated from cabin fever however. He needed to complete his next two errands and arrive at the Engineering and Modern Sciences Building before his first class started.

His father would think Ryan was doing this as a favor to him, but as he pushed open the heavy door of the shop, Ryan repeated the mantra that had been running like a locomotive in his head for the last twelve hours. *This is for me. This is for my future, not Father's.*

"Morning." Ryan took off his hat and placed it on the glass display counter. "What'll you give me for this?" Ryan's heart sank for a split second as he set the Carmouche pocket watch in front of Mr. Dandurand, a man who was a legend in Waterford Cove. It seemed to Ryan the Frenchman had been around since before the city was founded.

Ryan remembered his mother taking him to Bijoux d'Artisan as a little tyke, not tall enough to see over the counter. But that hadn't mattered. The treasures to be found under the glass were enough to keep even a five-year-old's attention. That was the first time he was ever in the shop, the day he had received the watch as a birthday present from Mother. The last time he would ever go on such an outing with her. She would leave before the summer was half over. She would die before his sixth birthday.

The store owner put on a pair of spectacles and flipped open the piece. "Not many of these made. Maybe fifty. I brought one just like this when I came over from France with my wife, more than twenty-five years ago."

"I think you brought that exact watch over with you, Mr. Dandurand. My mother bought it for me for my fifth birthday."

The man nodded, pushing his glasses back up onto the bridge of his nose and working the gears of the piece. "Sat here in the case for quite a while. Whenever someone would hear the price, they would always walk away."

That made Ryan smile. "Mother told me to pick out whatever I wanted and hang the cost." His smile faltered as he wondered if he could get as much out of the heirloom as he needed.

I'm sorry, Mother. But I'll be creating a better legacy with it. Just you wait and see.

"I remember engraving the back." Mr. Dandurand turned the watch over and read, "*To Ryan, from Mother with love. July 4, 1883.* Don't know why you'd want to part with it now," Mr. Dandurand clicked the face closed, "but I'll give you fifty for it."

The feeling Ryan would have when he walked out of the bursar's office with a zero-balance due on his college education compelled him to set negotiations aside and unquestioningly accept the man's offer. It was a fair price for such a valuable piece and he didn't have time to dicker this morning. "Done."

The absence of the watch's weight stayed heavy on his mind as he walked the two blocks to Main Street. The teller he had spoken with last Thursday was raising the shades of Waterford Cove Holdings' front windows. The man saw Ryan and after checking his pocket watch, held up four fingers, indicating the bank would open in a few minutes. Ryan instinctively reached into his pocket to check the time and came up empty-handed. He'd only been without his Carmouche for mere moments and already he could see this was going to be more of an inconvenience than he realized.

A young woman stepped out of the City Hall building across the street. Her red hair captured the glow of the morning sun as she stopped for a moment at the top of the steps and closed her eyes. Then she quickly turned her head both directions before crossing over to the bank. Ryan would know Amber Graham's purposeful stride anywhere, and he absorbed her every move as she came closer. From the way she walked right past him without looking his way, he could tell she had yet to notice his presence.

She tried the door to the bank and when it didn't give, went to peer in the window, her hand blocking the sun's glare.

"They should be open in a few."

Amber jumped when he spoke the words near her ear. "Ryan. You certainly know how to get a girl's heart pumping." She laughed softly and readjusted the bag on her shoulder. "What brings you down here? I thought classes would have started by now."

"Sorry, Miss Graham." He bowed low but kept his eyes on hers, capturing her in what he hoped was a charming twinkle. "I could ask the same of you. I thought you kept busy at the King's Castle before heading to the university to lend your proficient skills."

The bank doors opened from the inside and Ryan held out his hand, indicating Amber enter first. The two-story embossed ceilings and wood-paneled walls shone against the polished floor. Amber slowed her step as though she were inviting him to walk beside her.

"I don't know about proficient," she said as she looked up at him in a friendly way. "Maybe just efficient. There is a difference."

How he loved her banter. "Most likely that's true, but I also have no doubt you possess both in exceeding quantities. That, along with many other admirable qualities, I'm certain."

"Sir, I don't think you know me well enough to make such assertions." Amber winked at him as they came to the teller booths. "Excuse me, please." She stepped to the counter and asked to make a withdrawal.

It took a moment for Ryan to realize the teller was speaking to him. His eyes were too full of the Scottish beauty next to him. *The more assertions I make about you, Amber Graham, the more convinced I am that I need to know you better yet.*

SIX

R ound trip to Oakwood Hills, please," Amber said, opening her little clutch. Hard-earned money she didn't mind parting with. It was escapades like this that made her feel useful. Alive. As though her inquiring nature was of value, even if it was being used simply to satisfy Christian's curiosity. But it would be fun to surprise the Tituses with some new bit of information she might find.

"Train leaves in a few minutes, young lady. Better get on board before you miss it." The ticket master handed her some change.

"Thank you. I will." Without paying mind to the other passengers, Amber seated herself with Christian's notes from the case and a small notebook and pencil. She wanted to take these next ten minutes and make the most out of them. If all went well in Oakwood Hills, she'd be back on the ten o'clock train, leaving plenty of time to ask Professor Henning for permission to use his surplus supplies for Ryan's battery and start her work day.

The tip of her pencil received the brunt of her front teeth as the train began to chug northwestward. Amber hardly noticed the rocking motion as she stared at one of the names listed: Pierce. An image of Christian Titus looking strangely at her when she'd introduced him to Ryan came to mind.

"Ryan Pierce," her new friend had said with a smile. There couldn't possibly be a connection. Ryan didn't strike her as someone who had anything to hide. And there were most likely dozens of Pierces in the area. No matter. Amber was confident if there was any relation between William and Ryan, she would find it. She looked out the window at the passing hills and occasional farm, feeling grateful that Trey's background was something that would never come into question. His family's reputation was impeccable. That's what she needed. Wanted. Had to have. Trey's roots ran deep which meant hers could, too.

Her attention traveled back to Christian's notes on Tabitha. *Maiden Name: Murray. Last known location: Near Oakwood Hills, Virginia.* Amber picked up the single sheet of paper that summarized what Christian had written of the woman. It was heavier than the others and just as she had last night, she turned it over and pulled off the envelope that was clipped to the back.

It was addressed to Christian Titus, Richmond, Virginia. A strange feeling came over her, like when she had been twelve years old and snuck into the orphanage's kitchen, standing on a stool to reach for the cookie jar even though she knew the treat was to be saved for after dinner. The childish inkling to look over her shoulder to make sure no one was watching was too strong to dismiss. Her glance revealed a man in a bowler hat and long brown coat who was holding a newspaper in front of his face. Across the aisle sat a mother and her two small children. Amber chided herself for the silly notion and pulled a folded piece of paper out of the yellowed envelope.

April 14, 1879
Mr. Titus,
It is with great sorrow I write to inform you that Tabitha has passed on to the next life. She endured an especially difficult labor yesterday and both she and the child perished.
Take heart that Tabitha will be buried in a reverent manner, and she will lie in rest to no more endure the struggles of this earthly life.
Biddy

It was unthinkable that Christian had lost his entire family all in one day. He had gone from being a husband and a father to completely alone. A memory came to Amber then, of she and the Tituses sitting before the cook fire on a cold December evening a few years back. Christian had shared about his father, an abusive man whose poor decisions had stolen everything good from the family. Love. Money. Trust. Christian had talked about turning his back on God after other tragedies had befallen him. Amber hadn't known at the time what he meant.

The train had slowed without Amber's awareness, and as she looked out the window for a second time, she could see the station coming into view. Oakwood Hills wasn't a destination for the *Richmond, Norfolk, & Waterford Cove Railway*, merely a small stop along the line, but for Amber, this could very well be where the mystery would begin to unfold.

◆ ◆ ◆

The sight Ryan had enjoyed for the last ten minutes was now blocked by his bowler pulled as low as it could go over his face. But in his mind's eye, he was still seeing Amber Graham's slight shoulders hunched over something in her lap, her shining hair pulled into a low knot. The woman had completely captured his attention—his father's file he'd seen poking out of her bag at the bank and her current quest for traveling to Oakwood Hills notwithstanding.

After Ryan had completed his transaction at Waterford Cove Holdings, he'd worked tried-and-true tactics to finagle Miss Childs at City Hall into telling him the nature of her interaction with Amber. The conversation proved to be more helpful than he anticipated. He had thought to find time later on that day to speak with Amber at the university; instead the clerk had put the cherry on top of his morning by telling him Amber was trying to catch a nine o'clock train to Oakwood Hills.

From where Ryan sat throughout the duration of the short ride, he had a clear view of Amber's hands. Whatever was in that file had certainly kept her occupied. Two competing questions assailed Ryan as he waited to ensure he was the last one to exit the passenger car. Dueling notions that vied for consideration in his already crowded mind: Am I following the girl or the file she carries?

Amber Graham was in no way linked to any law enforcement agency or private detective outfit. Of that, he was sure. She was innocence personified. An angel in a serviceable brown skirt and white linen blouse. An orphan who worked to keep the dark moments of her past from tainting the present. An intelligent mind with a bright future.

He stepped onto the platform and caught the tail end of her skirt rounding the corner of the depot. He ignored the calls of cab drivers and small dirty boys hawking bruised fruit and squawking chickens. In a moment, her sashaying skirt was directly in front of him. He chuckled to himself. The girl. Definitely following the girl.

♦ ♦ ♦

This can't be happening. William sucked in a deep breath, working to bring a sense of composure to his mind. He could do this. All except for the three cumulative years he'd spent in jail, he'd always been able to get out of a scrape. This is nothing, he told himself. Jelly Joe better watch his back.

It had been two days since Joe had spoken his ultimatum: find the money or else. William's out-of-date shirt that had been special-ordered from New York City was spotted with sweat as he sat down at his desk and pulled out a piece of paper. For the moment, killing Joe wouldn't solve anything.

Let Joe think I'm working for him. I'll turn the tables when he isn't looking and be the one laughing in the end.

It had been a foolproof plan from the beginning. Months of preparation leading up to Waterford Cove's hundredth celebration of the Fourth of July. Everyone in town too busy to realize what was happening right under their noses. The city's upper crust hobnobbing on the town square, leaving the bank safe completely unattended. A joker installed behind the combination lock, cleverly narrowing the sequence down to only three numbers. All William had to do was put them in the right order and the safe's contents were his.

Even Jelly Joe hadn't known the exact amount William had staked out. Joe would receive a minuscule portion, enough to shut him up and William would take the rest. The Waterford Cove Holdings Robbery of 1878.

According to Joe's theory, Tabitha had been birthing her own plan to rob the robber. The very idea that she turned against him at the last hour made William smolder inside. She had taken everything. If she was still alive today, he would see to it she would never again see the sun rise.

All he needed to do was write an orderly list of possible locations she could have taken the money. His pencil shook over the blank piece of paper. He would figure this out. If Joe was right and the little tramp had gone and gotten herself hitched before she up and died in childbirth, maybe that was the place to start.

William's hand came down hard on the desk, sending the pencil flying. His big brainstorming session had resulted in only one guess. Find the child. He straightened his collar and smiled. William Pierce was clever enough to outsmart them all.

♦♦♦

Gravestones never lie. Despite that consequential fact, in all her born days, Amber Graham hadn't dwelt for a moment on what lay beneath the carved monuments that succinctly documented a person's life. *Timothy Smith 1808–1809 Beloved Son. Anna Tennison 1811–1850 Rest in God.*

One after another, tombstones lined up in the grass like a game of dominoes played at the King's Castle on rainy days. Except these tributes to lives lived would take decades to begin to topple over. Amber shuddered as she stepped lightly down one row after another. It helped to remind herself why she was there. Tabitha Murray—if she had gone back to her maiden name. No Murrays to be seen. For that matter, no Tituses either.

Family names grouped together held the graveyard in place like clusters of shy children in a play yard. Jones. Quary. Smithers. Mothers and fathers buried next to both grown and infant children. Oakwood Hills may not be as prosperous as Waterford Cove, but no matter its economic status, family upon family had made it their own throughout the last several generations.

Amber bent to brush her hand against the cold stone of one marker. *Evelyn McPhearson, From 99 Years on Earth to Eternity in Heaven.* Gathered around the headstone of the matriarch stood at least a dozen markers, all joined in family name by marriage or birth.

Amber chastised herself for being jealous of a dead woman. Yet, it was hard to ignore the fact that this perfect stranger had physical proof of her legacy. She obviously had been surrounded by those she loved and those who loved her all the days of her life. Amber's heart faltered. It was time to move on.

A small but stalwart stone church shared a fence with the cemetery. Upon arriving in Oakwood Hills, Amber had walked the length of Main Street to the church's steeple at its other end. The building looked old enough to have been the Sunday home to most of the people buried nearby. Amber looked up at the belfry framed by small puffy clouds going by in a hurry, their destination unknown. Amber felt like that sometimes. Passing her days in a flurry of activity, knowing that nothing she laid her hand to held any real substance. Nothing she touched would last. Hers was destined to be a single gravestone.

She brushed a tear from her cheek as she climbed the first step to the church's door. It was then that a picture entered her mind, unsolicited. One of a young girl gobbling up pancakes for a birthday breakfast. Her only dress washed and pressed. A circle of interwoven clover adorning her head. Someone holding her hand as they approached a church's staircase. And inside the church, a man with a crown of thorns hanging sorrowfully in the stained-glass window.

The memory seemed as real as the hand she laid on her thumping heart yet as far away as the low hills surrounding the town. Amber lifted her foot to ascend another stair. As she did, she caught a glimpse of the edge of a brown duster at the side of the building. She was not alone.

Her quest momentarily forgotten, Amber hurried back toward the town, goose pimples breaking out on her arms. Purposefully turning her mind away from thoughts of whoever was behind the church wall, Amber recalled again the memory that had appeared out of nowhere. A strange sense of familiarity had come over her in that moment. Like she had somehow been there before. But the town was completely unfamiliar, its streets overrun with Monday morning happenings just like any number of places in the country. Oakwood Hills' clapboard buildings sagged in rows for city blocks on end. Perhaps someone here remembered a woman from twenty years ago. It was possible.

A cafe directly across from the town square seemed the best place to begin her inquiries but a quick glance at the wall clock of the bacony-smelling establishment told her she'd need to be quick about it.

"Can I start you off with some coffee?" a brown-haired, buxom woman wanted to know.

"Yes, please." Amber figured she'd have better luck getting some answers if she was considered a patron and not a dawdler.

The woman seated Amber at a table with a street view. She sipped her coffee quickly, hoping to get the waitress to come back soon to refill her cup. The train would be heading to Waterford Cove in less than fifteen minutes.

"Breakfast this morning?" the woman asked with a raised eyebrow when she returned.

Amber cleared her throat and touched her necklace. "No, thank you. But I do have a question for you. Have you worked here a long time?"

"Owned the place outright for eleven years now," she answered proudly. "Who's asking?"

"Forgive me." Amber smiled, hoping to win the woman's good graces. "Amber Graham. I'm not from here, but I am looking for someone who used to live in or near Oakwood Hills about twenty years ago."

"Well, deary," she said, putting the coffee pot down and crossing her arms. "I wouldn't know anything about that, but you could check with Reverend Buchanan down at Mount Hope Chapel." She clucked her tongue. "That man's been here so long he could tell you about drinking coffee with everyone buried in the churchyard. I'll check back with you in a bit. See if by then you've changed your mind about breakfast."

A wagon and team going noisily past jarred Amber's attention to the window. Passing it on the other side of the street was a motorcar, looking modern in contrast to what Ryan predicted would soon be an outdated means of transportation. She turned her head to watch the beautiful machine pass and as she did, noticed a man in the booth behind her, most of his face covered by a hat pulled low. A man with a long, brown coat. Just like the man on the train. Just like the man at the church. She was certain of it now; someone was following her.

◆ ◆ ◆

That was close. Ryan's overwhelming curiosity and thirst for Amber had nearly caused him to get caught. He'd worked too hard and too long to hone his skills to be undone by a little red head. And what good had all his sneaking around done? The only positive lead to investigate was that Amber might come back sometime and speak with the old reverend at the church next to the graveyard.

The next train that would depart after the one Amber had taken wouldn't get him to class on time but it would preserve his cover. He boarded this time with his hat in his hand, no need to hide. It felt good to not watch his back. So good that he dozed as the train rattled to Waterford Cove. The next few hours that lay before him would challenge him to maintain composure, constancy, and courage. Everyone in the Engineering Department had by now surely seen Paul Henning's announcement. Ryan knew an encounter with a fit-to-be-tied Trey Wright was inevitable. Perfect. All the more to please Mack.

Ryan shook his head as he took the stairs to the Modern Sciences Building two at a time. Mack was his kind of man. Honest, forthright, and not afraid to blow right past the gates everyone expected him to stay inside. Mack maintained boundaries, but they weren't ones that boxed him in; from Ryan's vantage point, they seemed more like ones that afforded an honest kind of freedom. Ryan wanted to be like that.

"You're a half an hour late, Pierce." His calculus professor called him out in front of the class. "See to it you don't show such disrespect for your instruction again. I'm not above docking your grade for repeated tardiness." The man went on lecturing while Ryan tried to get settled with his books as quietly as possible.

"Hey." A loud whisper came at Ryan from his right side. "Psst. Pierce."

"Shh. You'll get us all in trouble." Ryan never did care for Isaac Jennings. Ryan had been able to avoid him at the Valentine party, but Jennings was always lurking around places he didn't belong.

"You know they're limiting the Endurance Race to five participants?"

Ryan's heart slammed in his chest but he directed his features to appear disinterested. "Five, you say?"

"Yeah. You already in? Cuz if—"

"Pierce. Jennings." Professor Upton was not one to brook two disruptions in his classroom.

"Yes, sir. We'll save it for after class, sir." Ryan figured using terms of respect and offering a promise he intended to keep was the best way avoid two strikes against him.

Professor Upton looked stern but continued, addressing the room at large. "Page 236, please."

Hallway encounters with Trey in between classes, non-stop speculation from the senior class about the race, plus the ruffle of pages and the scuffle of pencils occupied Ryan for the next three hours. It would all pay off. Just a few short weeks of minding his p's and q's and Ryan would be in a prime position to bring his plans to fruition. The addition of Amber by his side as he entered the next phase of his life was more than he dared hope for.

"Pierce."

Ryan cringed as he halted his progress across the campus green and turned slowly toward the sound of a motorcar idling next to the sidewalk. Mack Wright's runabout.

"Not too bad, don't ya think? Father let me borrow it for the day so I could take Amber riding after classes." Trey's voice was more grating than usual.

"Wright," Ryan greeted Trey cordially. No sense stirring up mud by appearing put out or letting him know the runabout would be in his possession soon. "Nice."

"Nice? That's an understatement. It's gonna knock the socks off the girl. Not that it'll compare to the Packard that's coming. Maybe Father will let—" Trey paused in his self-congratulatory monologue to whistle sharply through two fingers.

Ryan turned to see the source of Trey's attention. Amber Graham was carrying what looked to be a heavy bag down the stairs of the Engineering and Modern Sciences Building. She looked their direction at the irritating sound Trey made and smiled. Ryan couldn't tell who the look was meant for, him or Trey. But as she made her way over to them, her eyes only flicked Ryan's direction once. It appeared she was fully engaged with Trey and what he had to offer.

"Hello, gorgeous." Trey's face commenced to put on what Ryan thought was a less than attractive grin. "I thought you might enjoy a ride in this fine machine rather than sitting behind smelly horses or walking home. What'll you say?" Trey hadn't bothered to get out to help the girl but motioned for her to come over so he could take her things.

As she passed off her heavy load, she caught Ryan's eye, a look of uncertainty and excitement on her face, as though she was asking his permission to go riding with the other man. Ryan shrugged one shoulder. "It's perfectly safe. Plus, Trey won't go too fast. Will you?" Ryan pierced his colleague with an expression of censure. He hoped his meaning was clear.

"Get on in, woman. Let's go." Amber hastily seated herself and Trey took the tiller. The vehicle lurched a bit then rolled smoothly away. As they rounded the corner away from the campus, Amber looked back. Ryan was sure she was out of sight before she saw him wave in farewell.

SEVEN

His boy was going soft. William stood to the side of the front window and watched Ryan walk in the direction of the orphanage. "Pah! Waste of time." William's voice echoed back to his own ears in the empty room.

Ryan had come home unexpectedly and interrupted William's work; now that he was gone, William marched down the hall to Ryan's study and, like he had done a few days before, reached to pull the paper from the bottom of the stack. He hardly needed to; the words were etched in his mind: *Endurance Race.*

If the stolen money couldn't be recovered, this was going to be William's ticket to success. At all costs, he needed to garner a win with the Chariot. No more would onlookers scoff or laugh at his creation. They would learn to bow in reverent awe. The only missing piece was a driver from Waterford Cove University's senior class, someone with enough ambition to want to get noticed. Someone who William could convince needed to win it for himself. William would simply be a generous benefactor helping a needy university student.

As William thumbed through to the bottom of the pile, trepidation washed down his spine. The paper wasn't there. Ryan had come in from school and gone straight to his desk, so he must have moved it in the two minutes he had been in the room. William tried the center drawer and found it locked.

He reached into his pocket to extract his ever-present lock picking set. Choosing the tension wrench, he made quick work of the wafer lock that blocked his access to whatever Ryan wanted to keep hidden away. The drawer was opened in less than a minute and it was satisfying to feel it slide out easily. Sure enough, the race flyer was there, but next to it lay two small yellow slips of paper fastened to a legal-looking form bearing the name *Waterford Cove Holdings*.

William's hand shook as he unclipped what he recognized as a bank deposit slip along with a detailed listing of past deposits. The truth was all too clear: Ryan had gone behind his back and opened an account at Waterford Cove Holdings. His most recent installment looked to be around $75, giving the little thief a total balance of just over $200.

His son's duplicity was mounting. It all began when he had undermined the meeting with Mr. Blake, spouting some promise about winning the race with something other than the Chariot. That meant he was conspiring with someone else. He had acquired this bit of money somehow and was clearly keeping it to himself when he knew full well that payment was due on the house. And this afternoon, Ryan was misusing his time by fraternizing with orphans when he should be taking action to keep the family afloat.

William put the papers back exactly as he'd found them and locked the drawer. "Gerrard!" he bellowed down the hall. He swore when he remembered that he'd fired the last of the household staff. "Well, never mind. I'll take myself."

As Waterford Cove Holdings came into view, William checked his watch. Almost closing time. Good. That meant he'd have the perfect excuse to keep this short and sweet. Unlike the withdrawal William had made twenty years ago, this time he would quickly cajole his way into extracting the cash he needed.

"Good afternoon, Mr. Pierce. How may I assist you?" A small young man with spectacles and ink-stained fingers greeted him.

"I need to speak with Garrett Cole immediately." When the teller's face appeared hesitant, William continued, "Don't even think of telling me he's not available. I saw him through his office window."

"Yes, sir." The man came around the counter. "I'll get him right away, Mr. Wright."

Garrett Cole, the bank owner's son, came into the lobby to personally greet William. Garrett shook his hand, saying, "Come on back, William. We can talk in my office. I've been meaning to speak with you, as well." Garrett led the way down the hall then seated himself and offered William a chair. "I assume you're here about your mortgage?"

"In a matter of speaking, yes," William put a conciliatory note into his voice. "You and I are both aware with both the holiday season and the Great Blizzard only just behind us that many in our community have struggled to keep up with their obligations."

Garrett cleared his throat and looked ready to launch into what William knew was a well-rehearsed speech. "Despite your own financial situation, Mr. Pierce, Waterford Cove at large is booming. When your son came to see me about the late payment, I told him what I'm about to tell you—"

"Is that a new picture of your lovely family?" William cut in before Garrett could get too far. Once the words were out of the vice president's mouth, they would be impossible for William to shove back in. "I haven't seen them around town for quite a spell. How old are the boys now?"

The diversion worked, for Garrett turned the photograph so it faced William and relaxed in his chair. "Six and seven, respectively. Less than a year apart, bless my wife's heart. But of course, it's not just Joseph and Josiah we're looking after. Got an entire house full of children who need our attention." Garrett smiled like a man who ate and drank satisfaction every morning for breakfast. William could relate, he just didn't get his fill from the same place. But he could play along for a minute or two.

"Yes, the King's Castle. Such fine work you and your wife have accomplished. As a matter of fact, my Ryan is there right this minute. Wanted to lend a helping hand if need be."

"You don't say? Must be his first time visiting." Garrett sat forward and grabbed a piece of paper. Here it comes. "Well, he's welcome any time."

"I'll be sure to tell him. Speaking of Ryan," William went on hurriedly, "I understand he opened an account here some time ago. Came as a surprise, I have to tell you. The boy is still under my roof. I have not granted him permission to detach himself from the family accounts until he turns twenty-one, which is not until this summer. Surely, this is your policy as well."

Garrett looked surprised. "Ryan is a man. Almost a college graduate. It didn't cross my mind that this might be an issue for you."

"It is," William said flatly. "I insist on the monies he deposited being placed within our family account. Have to curb poor behavior as soon as you recognize it, wouldn't you agree, Mr. Cole? I'm sure your boys try all kinds of shenanigans."

Garrett chuckled. "Yes, they do. Have to stay on them at all times. But as far as your home is concerned—"

"Do me this one favor, will you, Garrett?" William put on his best hangdog face. "Transfer the money from Ryan's account, an account you know full well I have legal right to, and put the funds down as my mortgage payment. Next month, I'll be early with the money. I've got multiple investors for the Chariot on the line. So much so, I'll be able to make several payments in advance."

"I've known your family a long time and I desire to continue to do business with you. But I'll need Ryan's signature before I can make the transfer."

"I saw the deposit slip from this morning. That money was meant to make our payment today, Mr. Cole. I gave it to him this morning and had no idea he'd go behind my back like this. Don't worry, though. I'll have a stern talking to him later, after we get this settled."

Garrett looked doubtful. "You gave him the deposit?"

"Sure as shooting. It was a down payment yesterday from the Chariot's latest investor. Said he'd be giving me another hundred next week. Maybe Ryan thought it was due him for all the work he's put in on the thing. You put that money toward the mortgage payment and trust me to give Ryan his just reward when the time is right." *I'll see to that myself.*

♦ ♦ ♦

Amber felt the springtime breeze running its fingers through her hair as she skipped toward the King's Castle kitchen door. Yesterday's ride with Trey failed to match the glory of this morning, however. She never wanted to get into an automobile again. At least not with Trey. Despite her heart residing in her stomach for the better part of fifteen minutes, she had exited unscathed, and Trey had kissed her hand in farewell. Fresh promises were arising, just like the daffodil sprouts along the path she took every morning. Buds of romance, germs of hope, sprouts she would water at every opportunity. This morning was going to be no exception.

Trey had invited her to the Seaboard Cafe in downtown Waterford Cove. Their first public meeting, where everyone in town could see with their own eyes she and Trey were becoming an item. Amber felt giddy when she considered her future's possibilities. She couldn't wait to find out more about this mysterious man who had come into her life.

Trey was proving to be inscrutable. One minute he seemed to be a jovial, joking companion, then he would clam up or change the subject right in the middle of a conversation. It was charmingly troublesome. Amber was certain that after they were married, he'd be comfortable enough to relax and just be himself.

"Hello, the house!" she called upon entering the empty kitchen. "I'll get started on the porridge!" It appeared neither Grandma E nor Summer had yet to arrive. No matter. The work was simple and the coming reward impending, causing the next ten minutes to fly by. If she was able to get this on the table in short order, she could dash out a bit early to ensure she was on time to meet Trey at the cafe.

The exterior door gave a creak and Amber turned to greet whichever of the two women had arrived first. "I'm just adding the brown sugar to the oatmeal—Oh!" Amber gave a small cry of alarm as a broad-shouldered man removed his coat and took a stool at the counter.

"Good morning," Ryan Pierce said as he sat looking as comfortable in the King's Castle's kitchen as she had always been.

Without regard for the clean-up she would have to do as a result, Amber set the sticky oatmeal spoon on the counter and tried to think of something to say. "Good morning" seemed most appropriate to the occasion, though it stuck in the back of her throat. "What are you doing here?" although blunt, was what ended up coming out of her mouth.

"Christian invited me."

"He certainly did, and we're glad of it." Summer had appeared unnoticed, and when Mirabel and Fiona came over to Ryan, he bent down to give them big hugs. "We all stayed up late last night playing games and eating popcorn," Summer said. "So we thought, why not continue the revelry this morning by having Ryan join us for breakfast?"

He winked at Summer's girls as he sat back down, leaning his elbows on the counter. "I only got about six hours of sleep, how about you?"

Mirabel played right into his hand while Amber stood by trying to capture the scene in her mind's eye so she could replay it again later, analyzing every angle. Mirabel poked Ryan in his side and whispered, "I don't know how to tell time yet, silly."

Ryan looked up and caught Amber's eye. His jolly expression turned somber for just half a second. "I don't have a pocket watch anymore. So I guess that makes us even. But," he said tugging on Mirabel's ear, "I could teach you how to tell time if your mama would like."

Summer clapped. "That would be wonderful, Ryan. In fact, if you wouldn't mind, there are several children here who could benefit from such a lesson. But I don't want you to say yes unless you feel comfortable."

"Pour me a bowl of that oatmeal and you've got yourself a deal."

"Amber, would you like one as well?" Summer offered as she took up a bowl for Ryan.

"Um, no thank you. I'm having breakfast in town today." Too late, she wished she had kept that bit to herself. Quickly she added, "I should go set the table and start the laundry. If you'll excuse me?" Amber nodded to Summer and didn't look back.

Shutting the kitchen door behind her, Amber leaned against it for a moment. Ryan had every right to be there, in this big house that she still considered home. In the kitchen where she prepared breakfast most mornings, the same place she often kicked up her feet at the end of a long day. In the Titus's good graces, a place she jealously wanted for herself. How had this man suddenly shown up in all the places of her life that meant the most? She drew in a deep breath and let it out shakily.

The sound of a door knob turning behind her didn't give Amber's mind enough warning to predict what would happen next. The solid wood gave way and she stumbled backward.

Strong hands were under her arms and lifting her to her feet again before she really had time to hit the floor. "Sorry about that, Miss Graham," said Ryan as she turned around to face him. "I didn't realize you were still around."

Over Ryan's shoulder, Amber could sense Summer and the girls watching the scene unfold, but her eyes were focused on Ryan's. She didn't want to look away from his caring gaze. "No," she said. "I'm the one who's sorry."

His calming hand reached out and stroked a thumb across her upper arm. "I'd gladly have you fall into my arms any day of the week. Speaking of, what are you doing tomorrow?" he said with a wink as he dropped his hand. "Or maybe more importantly, what takes you to town this morning. You said something about breakfast?"

Maybe saying the straight-out truth to this man who was always genuine with her was the best course of action. "I'm meeting Trey Wright."

Ryan took a step backward into the kitchen as she said the words. The motion was a good reminder she needed to pick up the pace. "I'd better get these chores done." She offered him a small curtsy before turning on her heel so quickly her new skirt fanned out.

Her thoughts created a jumbled torture for the next forty-five minutes until Amber stepped into the Seaboard Cafe. She wished she wasn't breathing so hard from her brisk walk or feeling conspicuous as she glanced from table to table. The fourth one down contained a frowning Trey. "I'm sorry I'm late," she apologized while taking the seat across from him. "This morning's work took me longer than I anticipated."

Trey leaned back in the booth and crossed his arms. "You'll find after you've spent enough time with me that I don't like to be kept waiting." Then he smiled, causing Amber's reservations about offending him to melt away.

"How are your sisters this morning? And have your grandparents and cousins stayed on?"

"You do jump right into conversation, don't you?" Trey motioned to the waitress and didn't answer Amber's questions until he had ordered for both of them.

She hated to mention the fact that she wasn't too keen on bacon, nor did eggs at this hour of the morning agree with her. It would be rude to mention she preferred a simple pastry or some oatmeal, but she didn't want to do anything else that might offend this man whose affections she so desperately needed to secure. So, she simply thanked him for the meal.

"You're welcome." Trey took a sip of his coffee while keeping his eyes trained on her. He set down his mug and answered, "The girls are doing fine. Fluttering about the house, talking nonstop about beaus and engagements and trysts. It's enough to drive a man to the sanatorium."

"And your extended family?"

"Oh, yes. Still occupying every room in the house and making it difficult to concentrate. This is my last semester at WCU and they know it, too. Wish they were more respectful of my time. I don't need another distraction." Here, he smiled at Amber disarmingly. "Except maybe you."

"I don't mind the distraction, myself," Amber said shyly. She was glad when the food she didn't like arrived at that moment. Was she ready to test another relationship? It would prove devastating if things with Trey got started only to not pan out in the end. She needed to see this all the way through, no matter what. Her future depended on this one single success. "But I know how you feel. This is a busy season for me as well. In fact, I can't stay too long. I have an errand I need to run before heading to campus."

Her breakfast companion was shaking his head, and Amber was beginning to recognize that look on his face, the one that said he didn't approve. "I think it's high time you stop fooling around with man's work. If you want to gain an education in an underhanded way, why don't you sit in on Mother's quilting group? Quit your job and act like a lady. In fact, I'll tell Mother to expect you at former Senator Wilson's home tomorrow at ten o'clock. They meet there once a week, and it'll be good for you to start rubbing shoulders with Waterford Cove's elite. See if living like the other half suits you."

daughter. Amber knew the circumstances of Summer's birth had not been ideal, but it grew her own faith to see how God could take an ugly, twisted mess and turn it into something beautiful.

"Yes, dear. Amber Graham here has been seeing the young man," said Harriet. "Amber, meet my husband, George Wilson."

Mr. Wilson buttoned his suit coat and pinned Amber with his clear eyes. "Watch yourself, young lady. Trey's a firecracker. I hear he wants to be mayor someday. And the sooner the better, as far as he's concerned. It's all the word around town."

Is this what an acid in the lab felt like? Placed under the microscope so everyone in the class could see all its minute details. Amber had never assigned emotion to an inanimate object until now. Poor little things. Nowhere to run and hide.

Sticking her needle into the fabric, Amber piled up her pieces and handed them to Summer. She could explain and apologize later. Her friend would understand. "Harriet, Sheila. Ladies. If you'll excuse me, I need to be leaving for the university." She stood and turned to the head of the household. "Mr. Wilson, thank you for your hospitality. It was a pleasure to make your acquaintance."

"I'll see you out," offered Sheila. Amber sighed with relief when she realized no one was going to try and make her stay. And having Sheila help her through this maze of a house was an added bonus. The older woman linked her arm with Amber's, and they were able to exit the room without too many more comments, teases, or predictions.

"I didn't know Trey wanted to go into politics," said Amber as Mrs. Wright fussed with helping Amber into her jacket.

Sheila shook her head. "Too true. But I'm surprised it hasn't come up in conversation. That just tells me the two of you need to spend more time together. Trey's always got some plan or another in motion. Between you and me, not many of them go very far. I think he needs to get his head out of the clouds and onto something firm and solid." Sheila regarded Amber with a peculiar look. "Like a permanent relationship with you."

EIGHT

He only had to make it another twelve weeks. Not even three months to graduation. And with the race breaking up the semester, Ryan could only pray the rest of the spring would go swiftly by. He hiked up his shoulder bag and stepped into the workshop at the end of the hall. Trey Wright was the only other person in the room.

Please let it go by quickly. Ryan's eyes widened as he settled in for his next class. Who was that thought intended to bounce off of? It sounded mighty close to a prayer. He was so used to the solitude of his home he often had conversations with himself in his head. Sometimes he even expressed his thoughts out loud. It was a way to think through things, to pretend his world was normal, that he lived a life just like anyone else.

This time was different. Ryan inclined the ear of his heart to hear an echo of response.

"You've got some nerve, Pierce." Trey interrupted his thoughts.

Ryan knew what was coming next. Trey had been trying to pick a fight ever since Monday morning. "Wright, don't tell me you're afraid of a little friendly competition." Ryan stated it with a slight incredulity to his voice rather than as a question. He had to remember Mack's reasons for sponsoring him. The man cared about his son and knew how to put a match to the kindling that was Trey's combative nature.

"How do you even expect to win without a car? My father isn't likely to just hand over one of his."

107

Ryan busied himself looking at a model engine that one of the professors had brought in.

"He's letting you, isn't he?" Trey huffed like a spoiled child then suddenly grabbed Ryan's bicep with iron-like force.

Ryan looked up in surprise and jerked his arm away. "Don't threaten me, Wright. You're only scraping by here. Everyone knows it. If anyone should be worried about their future, it's you. Your old man sees potential in me." Ryan stood to his full height and looked Trey square in the eyes. "What does he see in you?"

Two more of their classmates filed in, jostling each other good-naturedly. Behind them followed the professor who was already handing out the day's assignment.

"This isn't over, Pierce," Trey hissed in Ryan's ear, then his face took on a new look altogether. "And tonight while you're monkeying about in the carriage house with your silly ideas, I'll be holding little Miss Graham's hand. By the end of the evening, she's gonna be in my arms."

The picture Trey had painted splashed a messy mixture of dread and doubt in Ryan's mind for the rest of the afternoon. As soon as classes let out, he decided he'd had enough of that. He made tracks to Christian's house and knocked firmly on the door. This was something he needed and wanted to do. Some time with his new friend to shake loose thoughts of Amber and Trey together.

Little pairs of feet could be heard coming closer as he stood on the step. He turned slightly while he waited, trying to see any signs of life at Amber's cabin. Was she home at this time of day?

"Mr. Pierce! Mr. Pierce is here, Father!" The two Titus girls looked up at him, their faces freshly scrubbed with innocence. Even in the hubbub of their affectionate greeting, Ryan wondered when his own innocence had disappeared. He couldn't remember ever wearing hope as an accessory. And never had child-like faith in the goodness of another graced his mind. At least, not until recently. An unseen hand seemed to have perfectly placed unexpected people like Amber, Mack, and Christian into his lonely little world. It felt peculiar to consider the possibility that he wasn't chiefly in control of his life. Peculiar, yet comforting.

"Pierce," Christian came up behind his daughters and greeted him with a firm hand. "If you can shake these rascals off your leg, come on in. I've got coffee on."

Ryan pulled Mirabel's pigtail and swung Fiona in a circle, causing the littlest member of the Titus family to let out a squeal.

"Me next!" Mirabel got her turn, then the foursome headed to the rear of the home. Looking around at the comfortable chairs and smooth bedclothes they passed on the way to the kitchen, Ryan realized this wasn't a house where bitter words were spoken, where dishes were smashed against walls, where talk centered on how to best twist a lie into some semblance of the truth. The Tituses didn't possess wealth like the Wright's, but in this moment, that made little difference. It was the family that resided within, not the boards and beams, that made a house a home, all held together by the yeasty smell of bread and the camaraderie that hung about like a lovable Labrador.

"Girls, go on over to the big house to be with Mother while Mr. Pierce and I sit a spell. Mirabel, you take Fiona's hand and make sure you head straight over. No lollygagging on the way. Understood?"

Ryan wiggled his fingers, mirroring Mirabel's farewell. It was a comfort to his heart to know the world was still a safe enough place to send two little girls out alone for a minute or two, young though they were. Ryan wondered if his life would have turned out differently if he'd had a sibling to hold his hand and keep him safe.

His thoughts turned instantly to Amber and her guarded nature as she briefly shared pieces of her past. Ryan could still see the firelight reflected in her eyes, the pain from years of loneliness epitomizing his own childhood. She'd had no one to hold her hand either. But tonight that would change if Trey had his way.

"Grab yourself a cup. What can I do for you?" Christian cocked an ankle on a knee and threaded his hands behind his head.

"Just thought I'd pop in before heading home for the afternoon," Ryan said as he poured the black coffee. Dare Ryan share his real reasons for coming? They were adding up quickly. He felt comfortable with Christian, like being with an older brother. But no one needed to know he didn't want to go home. Wanted to avoid his father as long as possible. Hoped to have the chance to run into Amber. Ached to understand what made Christian's house so different from his own. And after learning his father was asking Miss Childs the same questions Amber was, the urgency to follow the line from Christian, to Amber, to his father.

"You're welcome any time."

A fact that somehow, I already knew. "I appreciate it." Ryan sipped his cup and looked around the kitchen, uncomfortable with the silence that followed his response. He wished for once he could have a simple conversation without some form of deceit seeping in. "The other night you mentioned you used to be on the police force here in Waterford Cove, Mr. Titus." Better to not lead out with a distinct question. Ryan knew most people took a bite when offered the right kind of bait.

"Sure as shootin'. A good four years spent." Christian set both feet on the floor. "But I told you the other night—it's Christian."

"Thank you, sir." *Keep digging, Pierce.* "Only four years, huh?"

"That's what the federal government will do to you sometimes." Christian wiped his mouth. "Passed a law saying Pinkerton Agents couldn't be police officers. I was able to hang on for a while since I wasn't a new hire. But I knew it was only causing tension at the station. So I stepped down with goodwill. Came home full time. Still work with their officers on cases now and again, but mostly I'm here at the King's Castle. Helping some of the orphans find new families and securing their adoptions. What really gets me charged up is when I get lucky enough to connect an orphan to one of their remaining extended family members."

An ex-Pinkerton. Interesting. "I can only imagine that brings you a lot of satisfaction." Ryan took a deep breath. The dots he was trying to connect were going from a straight line to a jumbled web. Now that he knew Christian was an experienced detective, Ryan would have to be more careful than ever. It was exhausting to always be in the shadows. He wished for the day when he could live his life in full daylight. He wondered if it would ever come.

♦ ♦ ♦

Spineless. William Pierce watched the jelly-bellied snake he used to call partner slither out the door without so much as a word. It was too much to be bossed around by the likes of him. Jelly Joe thought he had the advantage, but he'd better watch his back.

Despite his bravado, William's head began a steady pounding as he stood in his grand foyer and unfolded the note.

Report each Sunday at 8AM. Back door, 6 Baker Street. Due Date: April 2 or die.

Less than six weeks. Jelly Joe was out of his mind. The money had been missing for twenty years. But it was the way the crook signed the missive that made William's neck go hot.

Your Boss, JS

"I will not be taken to task like some schoolboy," William muttered as he crumpled the paper. Yesterday's trip to City Hall proved one thing: he couldn't go this alone. He needed power on his side in order to pocket the money that was rightfully his. He needed charm to graft back into his life what had been cut away. He needed a handsome face to pigeonhole that vermin Schneider back into the pit he crawled out of.

And by the sound at the front door, the answer to all of his problems was about to walk in.

♦ ♦ ♦

I think Amber might be in love.

The words rolling around in Amber's head seemed to bounce off of the dining room's coffered ceiling, onto the crystal chandeliers, and plop right back into her chocolate pudding. She knew Millie hadn't meant any ill-will by the comment, but for the remainder of the day, Amber had been able to think of little else.

Was it possible? Heart-thrumming, foggy-brained, this-is-for-the-rest-of-your-life kind of love? Since the night of the party, Amber had begun to fancy herself perfect for Trey Wright. And since she was eleven years old, she had imagined herself a perfect addition to the Wright family. Now, her chance had arrived. At last. She glanced at the dark-haired man on her right. He caught her look and sent back a coy smile.

When her heart hit her stomach, she knew. This was it. The name Amber Wright was a foregone conclusion.

I wonder when he'll propose.

The tinkling of a fork against glass interrupted the low and happy murmur of chatter around the dinner table. Grandfather Wright sat at the head of the table, his wife of fifty-two years at his side. "A toast and a thank you," he said, "to my son and his beautiful family for making us feel so welcome this week. Praise God from Whom all blessings flow."

"A toast, then." Trey stood and turned to Amber and lifted his glass. The heady feeling of finally being part of a family enveloped Amber all around like a protective covering. "But first, an opportunity has presented itself today." His opening words didn't sound quite like a proposal to Amber's ears, but something in her core began to quake, just a little. "It is with great pleasure that I would like to announce—"

Amber's eyes went wide. Maybe this was it. The culmination of the last nine years of dreaming.

"I would like to announce," Trey was saying, "that Professor Henning has graciously agreed to relieve Amber of her duties at WCU." He looked triumphant as he raised his glass higher. "Amber can put her labor to rest and aim her attention to new vistas that may well afford what she never thought possible."

Relieved of her duties. Relieved. It sounded like a word most would welcome. Relief usually brought freedom. But Trey's hand on her shoulder felt like a heavy coat of security smothering her plans for the future. Without asking her permission, Trey had handed her an ultimatum. Choose. Choose me or the silly job you love.

Didn't he know how many late nights and early mornings she had toiled to prove her worth at the university? How many insults from male students she had wrestled to roll off her back? How she had conceived a vision of sharing her knowledge and ideas with a country that seemed ready to burst at the seams with innovation and invention? Didn't Trey know that without her regular Friday paycheck she wouldn't be able to stay in her snug little home? It seemed like a cruel unfairness that with one hand she was being forced to let go of a precious dream in order to grasp onto a new one with the other.

"Here, here!" Ten glasses clinked to salute both the grandparents in the room and the newly blossoming love of the next Wright couple.

A counterfeit smile always made her cheeks hurt so Amber fished the words "I think Amber might be in love" out of her chocolate pudding and took a big bite, forcing her face to relax. The uncertainness of her belief in Millie's statement, the sweetness of the dessert, and Trey's meddling all mixed together to create something unexpected: boldness.

"Trey, I appreciate your intentions in speaking with the professor." Amber leaned her head close to Trey's. He smelled of Macassar oil that held a slight sickly-sweet odor. She went on, hoping that as she spoke, she would have the strength to continue. "I will have to get another job, though."

"What are you talking about?" Trey pulled slightly away from her.

"I live on a small income, Trey. I have to pay for my house. I have to buy food. Clothing. Things I need. If I don't have this job, I don't have money." Trey's brow furrowed as though none of these things had occurred to him. "Did you stop for a minute to think how this might affect every area of my life?" For someone whose father was a master at finances, Trey was alarmingly naive to the realities of having a budget.

A strong arm curled around her shoulders. A handsome face peered into hers. A pleading look took over her future husband's features. "My only desire is to provide for you. Give you the life you deserve. Remember what I said to you in the carriage the first day I picked you up from your little shack?"

Distinctly, Amber thought as she nodded. *How could I forget?* He had called her beautiful, had avouched the family's blessing on their attachment, reaffirmed her need for him. Three out of five reasons he wanted to be near to her.

"That's my girl. Such a good head on these pretty little shoulders," he said, rubbing his thumb along her arm. "I told you a woman shouldn't work. I stand by that. Her man should be the one to grant her every wish." Trey went back to his dessert, saying, "I'll talk with Mother. Maybe she'll let you move into the girls' room for a while." He winked.

Sleeping every night in the room next to a man who might be her fiancé before the year was through? It didn't seem congruous with her faith. Avoiding the appearance of evil and all that. It wouldn't really be unscrupulous, though, would it? They'd have a whole host of ever-present chaperones.

But could she give up everything she'd worked for just to see if this relationship experiment was the right combination? Amber gave one shake of her head. It was too late. She was in too deep. No job. A home soon to vanish. She was out of options. Plus, Amber thought with the slightest hint of a satisfied smile, once I cross that threshold with my suitcases in hand, I'll never have to leave.

♦♦♦

"Need some help with that?" Ryan wasn't sure where that question came from. He tried not to make it a habit of offering assistance of any kind to his father. But as he walked into the parlor and saw William hunched over, one hand on his lower back, the words came with ease. His father straightened up from trying to light the fire, turned, and for the first time, Ryan saw how the years of duplicity were starting to take their toll.

Without waiting for an answer, Ryan took the room in three strides and grabbed the bellows out of William's hand.

"I can get it," his father growled.

"Of course you can." Ryan added another piece of wood but didn't see any kindling. "But I'm here, so why not share the workload?" Ryan glanced around for something to get a quick fire going, his eyes landing on his father's other hand. "You gonna toss that? I need some tinder here."

His father's face went red as he threw the scrap onto the smoldering wood. "You can have it, as far as I'm concerned." He turned on his heel. "I'll get some more paper from the office."

Ryan squatted by the fire and regarded the wad his father had thrown in. If he moved it a few inches to the right, it would catch fire and he could get on with his evening. Long downstrokes of handwriting that didn't belong to his father's caught Ryan's eye as he used the poker to scoot the paper onto the hottest part of the log. The words *Your Boss* was all he could see.

Looking behind him to make sure his father wasn't coming into the room, Ryan plucked the paper from the heat and rapidly unfurled it.

It took only a moment to commit the words to memory before he pushed the scrap back into the embers. A job. A threat on his father's life if he didn't follow through. Someone with the initials JS, directing his father's next six weeks. The edges of the note caught fire just as the fringes of Ryan's imagination burned with questions. How did Amber fit this equation? It was more evasive than Professor Upton's toughest calculus problem.

"Here," his father said, thrusting the office garbage can at Ryan. "Get that fire going, would you? It's freezing."

"We need more wood," Ryan stated matter-of-factly as he added the extra kindling. "Know where we can get any?"

"This is the last time we should have to heat the house before the weather really turns."

Ryan used the bellows so he wouldn't have to look William in the face. So they were going to go cold for the next few months? It wouldn't be really warm until May. Maybe whatever job his father had taken would pay enough to keep them going.

The two men stood with their backs to the flames, now putting out much-needed warmth. Neither spoke for a long minute.

William broke the silence. "I refuse to forgive you for messing up the last investor for the Chariot. With your swagger, you stole much needed income for our family. You should be ashamed of yourself."

The blather coming out of his father's mouth was no surprise to Ryan. It wasn't as if he was used to being encouraged, built up. That had never happened. But the side effects hadn't been all bad. Being continually run into the ground had taught him to be a man who could stand up to whatever life threw at him.

"In short, son, you owe me. I've got an assignment for you."

"No." Ryan dared to turn and challenge his father directly. "I have to focus on this last semester. My senior project comes first this time."

A fist the size of a small cannonball came at him, directly connecting with his stomach. Ryan doubled over in pain. It had been several years since his father dared hit him. The last time it had taken Ryan a week to feel back to normal. He had been only eighteen and since then had no desire to be at the receiving end of William's abuse. He had said yes every time since, up until last Saturday. Now he remembered why.

"You will be in my study tomorrow morning before you leave for class." William jerked Ryan's chin up. "And if you need me to spell out the consequences if you don't comply, it'll be my pleasure."

NINE

Amber braced her knuckles to knock a little harder on the solid double doors of Mount Hope Chapel, the church that stood like a watchful grandfather at the end of Oakwood Hills' Main Street. While she waited for someone to answer, the back of her neck raised its tiny hairs. It wasn't possible anyone knew she was looking into Christian Titus's old case yet she couldn't help but peek around the side of the building.

Silly girl, Amber chided herself. Avoiding the dreaded moment she would step foot onto Waterford Cove's University campus for the last time to pick up her paycheck. Dodging the impending encounter she needed to have with the Coles and the Tituses, telling them she could no longer pay rent. Shaking off the fact that her life's purpose was about to drastically change from one of meaning and aspiration to sipping tea in decadent parlors deep in the heart of Waterford Cove's wealthy neighborhoods.

A short walk skirting the stone church brought her to the parsonage door. *This is where I should have started.* A Wednesday morning wasn't likely to find the Reverend Buchanan inside an empty sanctuary.

"Hello, pet." Instead of the pastor, an elderly woman greeted Amber. "What can I do for you?" Her voice quavered as though it needed rest from the millions of words it had spoken over the years.

"I'm looking for information on someone I thought might be buried in the church's graveyard. I can't find the headstone, but the owner at the cafe told me to come and talk with Reverend Buchanan. Is he here?"

"Out to see the Doyle's youngest. Be back after lunch, I wouldn't wonder. Won't you come in?"

Amber felt like she was stepping inside an old English country cottage as she followed the pastor's wife under the rounded, crumbling doorway. "You have a delightful home." She meant it. Home was home, no matter how humble.

"Been opening that front door to God's sheep for the last fifty-nine years, don't you know? Take your choice of chairs and I'll grab some tea."

The front room of the Buchanan home would have fit three times over inside the Wright sisters' quarters, but its low ceiling and welcoming furnishings made Amber feel comfortable. Pulling out the file, she read her latest note. According to Christian, Tabitha had arrived in America a mere three years before the postmark on the envelope he'd received from Biddy.

Amber knew from experience that sometimes the days are long but the years are short. This woman had traveled across the Atlantic to a strange new land. And in the brief span of time she had left on Earth, somehow had tangled herself with a gang of thieves, gotten married, run away from her husband, and had a baby. For the first time since Christian asked for her help, Amber saw Tabitha as a woman. A person. A soul. Someone who may have had a front parlor much like this one where she sat in the afternoons and took her tea.

But from what Amber knew, Tabitha had died without loving family near and that was the saddest part of all. Had she gazed into her baby's eyes before slipping into eternity? Had she hung her hopes on the child carrying on the Murray or perhaps the Titus family heritage?

Amber would never know how the last moments of Tabitha's existence had played out, but she did know one thing more certain now than ever: that will not be me.

The unfortunate outcome of Trey's underhanded meeting with Professor Henning and the uncomfortable feelings and repercussions it had produced seemed far away and unimportant. If difficult, momentary decisions dictated the fate of a person's life, then Amber would

the dark carriage house, but this time he had nothing to help guide him to the door. He couldn't seem to see any light, couldn't think of any way to escape the clutches of William Pierce. Graduation couldn't come soon enough.

Standing at the front room's wide window, Ryan ate his cold breakfast. A newsboy skipped past, throwing Waterford Cove's latest bi-weekly at the neighbor's porch. The morning sun highlighted the glossy coats of two chestnuts across the street as their owner boarded his buggy. An idea came to Ryan as he watched the world go by. He always thought better when he could see people going about their day, let the blue sky reign above him, stand at the ocean's edge and imagine that someone bigger than himself created it. Yes, he knew how to handle his father now.

Ryan wanted to feel the sun on his face with no glass obscuring even the smallest bit of its warmth. He flung open the front door and walked purposefully to the mailbox, breathing deep of air that smelled of soil just waiting to be turned up. Progress. Fresh ideas. Wide open spaces in his mind where he could sail unencumbered. He would not let his father pin him into a corner. *Just wait, old man.*

Even the mailbox's squeaky hinge made Ryan smile. It sounded like life, like a world going round. Three envelopes awaited and Ryan shuffled through them on his way back to the house. The third halted his progress. Return address, Waterford Cove University. He slid his finger between the flaps, pulling out a single sheet.

Spring Semester Tuition: Payment Notice
Amount Due Upon Receipt: $200
Interest of 2% per week will be compounded if payment is further delayed.
Please Note: Failure to remit by March 20 will result in termination of admittance to Waterford Cove University.

The day of reckoning was here. Two hundred dollars. Though he'd been counting on the family account to have enough to cover his final university bill, in a way, this was better. He would pay, not with stolen cash, not with his father's ill-obtained money, but with what he'd been hoarding away little by little.

Ryan stole back into the house, his plan of pretending to help William in order to find out what the man was up to flying right out of his head. His education came first. Ryan grabbed his hat and wallet and shut the door behind himself as quietly as possible. He walked purposefully toward Waterford Cove Holdings.

"I'd like to make a withdrawal. Here's the account number."

"How much, sir?" The same skinny teller who had helped him with his last deposit, the biggest one, raised his sparse eyebrows when Ryan told him he wanted to empty the account. "Don't hear that every day. You movin' away or something?" At the shake of Ryan's head, the young man said hastily, "I'll be right back."

Ryan removed his hat an undid the top button of his shirt while he waited. The folks standing on either side of him at other teller windows were just going about their day and probably figured he was, too. Doing some morning errands before starting to wrap up the work week. No one knew the monumental implications this one transaction meant to the rest of his life. No one would ever guess how, even though his heart was pounding, it felt buoyant and free.

Ryan didn't know until this moment that sacrifice could bring joy. He'd never thought about it before, but he supposed he'd been avoiding sacrifice all his life. It sounded uncomfortable. Painful, even. But thinking back on all the little deposits he'd made over the last year, the early mornings and late nights he'd taken odd jobs and then finally the sale of both his mother's heirloom gift and his bicycle, there he stood. Those small choices had led him to a place where he was not only seeing his dreams fulfilled, he was the one making them happen.

"You must have given me the wrong account number. What was the name?"

The floor seemed to tilt sideways as Ryan went through the motions of the conversation. But he already knew where this was headed. A zero balance. The steps Ryan retraced as he exited the building were deliberate like the ones he took upon entering Waterford Cove Holdings, but his purpose had dramatically changed. They were the steps of a man on a different kind of mission. One born, not of freedom but of red-hot fury.

As Ryan made his way to the university though, he slowed, his mind churning on what to do next. He didn't know how his father had learned of the separate bank account, didn't know how he had emptied it, but that hardly mattered now. The fact remained that William Pierce had stolen from his son. Stolen Ryan's future. Stolen everything.

The bursar's office was two stone throws across the manicured grounds from where his classes were held. Ryan stood staring at it for a moment, wondering what he would say. Was there a way he could fudge his way out of this?

Ryan sat on a bench and put his head in his hands. Everything he had worked for, gone. His mother's gift, his college education, somehow eaten up by William's carnivorous hand. "God," Ryan whispered so softly his lips barely moved, "help. I need You to help me." He cleansed his lungs slowly and realized he really did believe his prayer was heard. "God, I don't want to be like my father. No more lies. No more stealing. I don't want my selfishness or greed to rob those I'm closest to."

"Ryan?"

A feminine voice caused him to raise his head. Amber Graham stood looking down at him.

"Everything all right?" She cocked her head to the side.

He didn't want her to see him like this. Ryan stood quickly and worked to put a smile on his face. "Right as rain." But now that they were face to face, if he was reading her right, he wasn't the only one having a rough morning. He reached out a hand and ran it from her shoulder to her elbow. "What's wrong?"

Amber chuckled. "And here I thought I was doing a good job of hiding my feelings." She set down the large bag she'd been carrying and avoided his eyes. "I'm done at WCU. I'm just here get my things."

"Did you quit?" Ryan knew something big must have happened to cause her leave. She loved her job. Was good at it. Suddenly, a thought occurred to him. She was moving out of town.

"No, I wish it was as simple as that." Amber fiddled with her necklace. "I'd best not say what happened."

Ryan could clearly see Amber was struggling with this change, however it had been brought about. "You don't have to tell me if you don't want to." *But please say you're staying.* "Are you still free to collaborate on my senior project? With your expertise, together we've got what it takes to finish this project."

What if she said no? What if in leaving WCU she wanted nothing more to do with the place or anything that reminded her of her job? Ryan's heart hit his stomach. This was his only hope of finishing his degree. If he could win that prize money...

He didn't let himself finish the thought. Best not to jump to hope too quickly. If he didn't win, maybe in a year or two, he could come back and finish his classes, take the first step in his career. He knew even if that long shot came true, his chance at garnering an interview with Benz and Daimler would be past. It was a once-in-a-lifetime opportunity. That coffin would be sealed if he didn't enter the race and take the win.

"Mr. Henning gave me permission to use whatever supplies I needed," Amber said. "You were right when you guessed he's planning on teaching the concepts in the fall term. Said if we used some of the things he was planning on having on hand that he wasn't in a hurry to get them replaced. But he definitely wants to see what we come up with." It was easy to tell she was excited about the possibilities. A good sign. "So let's keep going."

"That's great. I think we'll do well together." *You have no idea how much I've been thinking that lately.* "Why don't I stop by your place tonight?" What a thing to look forward to after the day he'd had. By dinnertime, his soul was going to need some serious nourishment. Being with Amber would provide just the right nutrients.

"I suppose you wouldn't have any way of knowing this either, but I no longer live on the King's Castle property."

This time, instead of falling into his shoes, Ryan's heart gave a lurch. It was true then. She was leaving town. He felt suddenly desperate to find a way of keeping her near. "Where are you going?" *I have to know.*

Amber hesitated. "I'll be staying at the Wright's for a time."

Ryan's breath left in a silent whoosh and his shoulders relaxed. She was going to be around for a while. He still didn't know her final destination, but the fact that she wasn't taking a train out of town any time soon gave him some measure of relief. A bright spot in his day, even if she was going to be laying her head down every night in the bedroom two doors down from Trey's. Ugh.

"How about breakfast at the Seaboard Cafe early Monday?" said Ryan. "If you're free afterward, we can work in the lab for a couple of hours." He smiled. "Maybe I can even miss a lecture or two and we could get it finished."

After agreeing on a time, Ryan said goodbye to Amber and slowly made his way to the Engineering and Modern Sciences Building, knowing his father would be fit to be tied he hadn't shown up to his office this morning. William would just have to bide his time. Ryan's education was waiting. But although his studies normally proved to be a positive distraction from the debacle that was home, he knew he couldn't avoid the inevitable forever.

As he packed up his books later that day, he knew it was time to admit defeat. There was no way he could earn two hundred dollars by March 20 and victory in the Endurance Race wasn't guaranteed. William had won.

"I'm home, Father." The words sounded like a funeral call. The end of everything Ryan had put his hopes in.

William glanced up from his desk with a look of triumph on his face. Was he able to read his son so clearly? "If you're ready now, Ryan, come and sit. We've got a job to do."

That night, as Ryan tried to get warm enough to fall asleep, he whispered his second prayer of the day. "God, if You're there and You're listening, I'm afraid I have to go back on my word." A single tear slipped into his ear as he lay looking at the ceiling. "You didn't help. Seems I'm destined to become exactly like my father. Please forgive me." He rolled onto his side in the dark and shivered.

◆◆◆

"I wish you would have come to us first. You don't have to leave, you know."

Amber uncrossed her legs and was about to cross them the other direction when she realized her fidgeting was probably distracting those sharing her pew. The words Summer had spoken to her yesterday as they made the morning's meal at the orphanage still rung in her ears. They had stayed there long after she had hugged Mirabel and Fiona farewell and meandered back to the Wrights'.

"I appreciate you saying that," Amber had replied as she added more ingredients to Summer's pot, "but this is the door God has opened for me." Amber had steadied her voice before continuing. "I need to walk through it. Plus," she forced a laugh, "it's not like I won't be around. See, you already can't get rid of me." She'd stuck a finger in the cream and set the dollop on Summer's nose, but the lighthearted banter didn't last long.

"Amber, I'm concerned about you," Summer had said, wiping her face and sobering. "I know God has a plan, but I never saw it including you being shut out of your job. You love working at WCU."

The pastor was beginning the benediction and for that, Amber was grateful. Summer needed to understand God's ways didn't always make logical sense. It would be wrong for Amber to assume she could plan her future down to the letter and expect God to give it His stamp of approval. Amber was simply along for the ride.

Last night had been her first official night under the Wrights' roof as an almost legitimate member of the family. As she lay in her new bed, she could hear Trey walking in the hall as he left his room then came back. Amber drank in the little sounds of a household that had been empty from her ears for the last two years. Yet these were more homey, more elemental than a four-story orphanage filled with forty children.

She smiled to herself as everyone stood for the closing song, remembering how good it had felt yesterday to laugh a little and realize that her life wasn't so bad. In fact, it was a dream come true.

"Amen and amen," the congregation echoed the pastor before everyone began moving to say their after-church hellos.

Amber could feel Trey's hand at her elbow even though she didn't turn his way. His touch was an unspoken message to everyone at Waterford Cove Chapel that she was his. Amber had never been anyone's before.

Never anyone's daughter, never anyone's sister. She belonged now. And if Trey made this permanent, she would always belong. Parishioners milled about the sanctuary as Amber and the Wright family made their way out into the spring morning. The family had brought two carriages to accommodate everyone, including Grandmother and Grandfather Wright. Having them there only served to warm Amber's heart further to what life would be like with this family. A big family. A forever family.

"You'll soon learn what Sundays look like at our place," Millicent was saying as she took a seat across from Amber in the enclosed carriage. It was just the girls of the family, with the sisters sitting opposite of her and the two older women hemming Amber in between their skirts. Not once in her life could she remember feeling so cozy and safe.

Winnie picked up where Millicent left off. "Maybe a little different from what you'd expect. Everyone fends for themselves in the kitchen." She gave her mother a quelling look.

"We've been over this a hundred times, haven't we, girls?"

"Yes, Mother," the three sisters dutifully replied.

Sheila patted Amber's knee. "You don't mind scrounging for a bite to give our household staff a day of rest, do you dear?"

Amber didn't want to come between Sheila and her daughters in this subject of contention but also didn't want to appear as though she was taking sides. Thankfully, Amber didn't have to respond, for Yvette stuck her hand out the carriage window to wave to her new beau. This caused Sheila to launch into a speech on proper etiquette, and it appeared the topic of lunch had been forgotten.

A movement to her left caught Amber's eye as the carriage began rolling. She peered past Grandmother Wright and saw Ryan Pierce duck between two houses across the street from the church. He was gone from sight in less than a moment. Amber felt a twinge of guilt at having promised to meet him tomorrow for breakfast. Should she have talked with Trey about it first? She knew he didn't want her working. He had made that crystal clear. And if their destination was a wedding, she ought to start acting like they were a married couple.

But yesterday on the campus green, Amber had caught something in

Ryan's posture, almost identical to what she had witnessed just now. As if in unison, his body and spirit were head down, shoulders hunched. Not the typical demeanor of the friendly, confident man she was beginning to call friend. She had wanted to say yes to his request. And she would help him, no ulterior motives in sight. Trey needn't know.

Ryan was still on her mind when she and Grandmother Wright stood at the kitchen counter making a few sandwiches for whomever might want one. Amber had never felt like a tall girl, but she had a good foot of height on the elder woman. Despite her petite size, Grandmother Wright's heart was proving to be larger than life.

"What did you think of the pastor's message today?" The older woman placed a thick slice of cheese over the meat on each portion.

Amber was glad her hands were busy. It gave her an excuse to not meet Grandmother Wright's eyes. Amber truly didn't remember much of what the minister had said. Something about Romans chapter one. A general comment would have to suffice. "It was a lovely church."

"But that's not what I asked you." The older woman brushed off her hands and turned to Amber.

Amber cleared her throat, unable to do anything but put aside her work for a moment. "I admit I was a bit distracted during the service." She smiled sheepishly, hoping she was off the hook.

Grandmother chuckled and went back to making lunch. "I noticed." She was putting each sandwich on a baking pan and then loading the entire thing into the oven.

Baked sandwiches? "That's one I've never seen before."

Grandmother shut the oven door almost all the way, but not quite. "A little heat will melt the cheese and bring out the deeper tones in the bread and meat. Trust me. Heat is a good thing sometimes." She winked, causing the wrinkles around her eye to scrunch together. "In our lives, too. When God turns up the temperature, you can bet we'll come out of it better than before." Grandmother used thick cloths to remove the pan. "Mercifully, sometimes it doesn't take long at all. These are ready."

The double-meaning behind her words wasn't lost on Amber. The heat had been turned up on Amber's life to near boiling at times, a mere simmer at others. Now, for the first time she could remember, she could rest in the fact that everything was at just the right temperature. The only heat she could think of was what she felt when she looked at Trey; a handsome man who would soon be hers. She wouldn't get burned this time.

Millie and Winnie came into the kitchen then, closely followed by Sheila. Suddenly she and Grandmother's conversation was over. But that was all right. Amber had a feeling there were many more to come.

◆◆◆

Two lives. Ryan Pierce was going to have to keep up the appearance of two lives, both of which were a direct result of his father's misdeeds. At the university, Ryan would do his best to preserve his honor and attend classes as though nothing was amiss. When he wasn't at school, he'd bow to his father's unrighteous demands.

But inside, where no one could see, Ryan had drawn a line down the middle of his heart, keeping what he had to do and what he wanted to do on opposite sides. There would be no bleed-through, no overlap. On the compartment being forced upon him by his father, Ryan had installed heavy doors of duty and ambiguous detachment.

Six Baker Street was two blocks over from Waterford Cove Chapel. Ryan went between two close-together houses and around to the back stoop, if it could be called that. A couple of rotten boards had been placed directly on the ground, a failed attempt at helping visitors up off of the mud. Ryan's best shoes would be covered by the time he was done. Now that he knew his Sunday morning destination for the next five weeks, he would dress more appropriately for the occasion.

A man with a belly that wasn't quite covered up by his shirt jerked the door open. "Where's William?" the man growled.

"My father sent me instead." Ryan stuck out his hand. "You can call me Pierce."

"Your pa never could stand to do his own dirty work." The man looked him up and down then spit tobacco juice into the trodden grass next to the stoop, ignoring Ryan's hand.

It was clear that on this, the last job Ryan would ever do for his father, he wouldn't be rubbing shoulders at parties with city council members or prominent business men like he sometimes did. Those who most knew as family men. Either criminals in tailored suits or those easily swayed by deception. Judging by the filth of the room and the smell of burnt toast coming through the open door, this time he'd be dealing with the other half of the criminal world.

Ryan would need to be diligent to counterbalance the other side of his heart whose entrance was guarded by a door of hope. At the moment, the compartment stood mostly empty. His education had been stolen. His chances for an interview with Benz and Daimler were slim. Any aspirations of leaving home would be put on hold unless this job delivered the cash William promised. But in the far corner was a hallowed place, a hope that Amber would not truly fall prey to Trey's attentions. Ryan decided he would need to visit it often, feeding the fantasy of spending his life with such an angel.

Joe motioned him inside and Ryan gladly shut the door. Covering his tracks this time was going to be just as much for his father as it was for himself. Not that anyone was watching.

"Sit yerself down, boy. Can't say as I'm surprised to see ya, but gee whillikens." Here Joe let out a whistle through his stained teeth. "You look just like William."

That was about the last thing Ryan wanted to hear at the moment. "So people say. But I'm not here to talk about him. I'm here to do a job. Tell me everything."

Joe sat on a worn divan and rubbed his belly. "Tabitha Murray. Our old partner. That's where you need to start."

Tabitha. The same woman Amber had been looking into. To get to the bottom of this, he'd need more to go on than a name. "What money are we talking about?"

Joe laughed mirthlessly. "Didn't your pa tell you? The Waterford Cove Holdings gig from 1878. Ten grand gone."

Ryan kept his face neutral while his heart went wild. It wasn't possible. Yet everything was lining up. Tabitha Murray. Waterford Cove Holdings. Amber's file and his father's missing money were one and the same. Looked like William hadn't been man enough to speak his crimes out loud. "You say Tabitha has the money?"

Joe smirked. "Not unless it's in her coffin. Tabitha's been gone many a year. But the way the job went down, the talent it took to steal from a thief such as your father, it had to be her. She had a good thing going, really. Get inside a gang. Learn their strengths and weaknesses. Spend just enough time working the jobs to gain their trust, then skedaddle. Wait until a big score went down. Hang back like a scared dog while your old man and I did all the hard work. Then…boom. Yes siree, find Tabitha and you'll find the money's trail."

"So, what's up with the short timeline? April 2, I heard. Seems like if it's been gone for, what, almost twenty years, there's no fire under it now."

"Don't worry your head with stupid questions. Just get crackin'. Cuz if that cash ain't in my hands soon, everything you have will be mine. Including your father's life."

TEN

The Wright home was large enough that each person could have their own bedroom two times over. Normally, Amber would have shunned the thought; sharing space with the Wright sisters was to her the ultimate recompense for all the years of wandering and cold nights she had spent alone.

This morning was different. She wished she could pace the halls or even go to the carriage house and look at Mack's new automobile without disturbing anyone else's sleep. It hardly seemed possible to lie there in her new bed, listening to the breathing of the sisters. The peace they had wasn't fair. Last night, none of them had to turn their head to the side when their new beau tried to kiss their lips. They hadn't had to squelch their enthusiasm for a job they were passionate about just to appease someone they were trying to impress. They had nothing to disturb their perfect little world.

Amber decided she couldn't lie there another minute wondering if she had done the right thing, wondering if she should have welcomed Trey's embrace instead of trying to struggle out of it. He liked her. Of that she was certain.

She set her bare feet on the floor boards, hoping they wouldn't creak and pulled out the bag she kept under her bed. Fluffing up two pillows, Amber settled back with the Waterford Cove Holdings Robbery file on her lap. If she had to stay still for a little while longer, she could at least let her mind roam the backroads of the adventure that was before her.

Even though she knew another trip to Oakwood Hills was unlikely, when she had been downtown last Friday depositing her final paycheck, she had paid Ms. Child's one more visit. Something had continued to niggle at Amber as she mulled over the circumstances regarding Tabitha and Christian's marriage.

Tabitha was a gal who had a criminal background then turned around and married a law man. Christian had indicated on more than one occasion that until some things started to come to light after his wife left, he'd never had any inkling of Tabitha's past. He admitted he fell for her beautiful face and jumped into the marriage without looking.

Perhaps something happened that propelled Tabitha to alter her lifestyle, start fresh with an upstanding husband like Christian. Amber wouldn't fault anyone for that. Even so, Amber shook her head. This mother-to-be had run out on her husband, never to be found.

Then again, there might be more to it than that. Amber brought to mind all the times she had fudged her own name for the sake of keeping herself hidden. Safe. In the dark alleys and alms houses, it was better to be forgettable than to do anything that would make her stand out. Wasn't it entirely probable Tabitha had done the same? She'd married a very smart man who, if he knew her real last name, would have eventually rooted out the truth. Why not change it to something random, move to a different town, and go untraceable?

The clerk had agreed to look through the immigration records for the month and year Christian said his wife had come to America from Scotland. Miss Childs had found three Tabithas from 1876 and then the young woman had an ingenious idea: why not see who was listed above and below each of the Tabithas she had found? Those folks could have been possible traveling companions or even family members who might lend a clue to finding Tabitha Murray.

Amber tucked her uncombed hair behind her ears and scanned over the names Miss Childs had included. Blacketer. Gore. Lorimer. McLachlan. MacDonald. Westwater. Wondering where to even begin, she sighed, causing Millie to stir. Amber shuffled the list of names back in with the other papers and put the folder in her bag. The more Amber thought about it, the more it sounded like chasing the wind.

The sun was dressing the window sheers with its cheery yellow light, inviting Amber to join the day. It was late enough now that if she woke Winnie or the others, they wouldn't be too grumpy at her. Still, she grabbed her dress and underthings as quietly as she could and slipped into the hall.

"Good morning, beautiful." Trey was just coming out of the washroom. "I would have thought you'd sleep in today after our late night together." His gaze was depthless. Intimate.

Amber smiled and tried to smooth down her hair with her free hand. "Morning." She swallowed. As much as she liked imagining greeting this man every morning for the rest of her life, it would have been better if she could have snuck away unseen. Trey would not approve of her meeting with Ryan. "I didn't sleep well last night."

"You poor dear. Come here." Trey took her in his arms before she knew what was happening. He laid her head on his shoulder and caressed her hair. "Why don't you go back to bed? You deserve a day of rest after all those years of working so hard."

That might be tempting to some, but Trey didn't know how restless she felt inside. Crawling back under the covers was the last thing she wanted to do. Breathe the fresh air, let the sun soak into her skin, talk with a friend, feel useful. That's what she needed. Somehow she knew if she tried to explain how she felt, Trey wouldn't understand. "Thanks, but I think I'll head out for a short walk this morning." Not an untruth. It was a short walk to the cafe.

"Suit yourself, Red." Trey chucked her under the chin, then frowned. "There are lots of other men who would love to claim you as their own. While you're out and about, just remember you're mine."

His words brought to mind the same feeling she'd had at church when he had silently yet publicly proclaimed her as his. They were a couple. Lord willing, they would always be a couple. She finally had a place to let her roots run deep.

Amber's thoughts kept her company as she made fast tracks to the

Seaboard Cafe where Ryan was waiting at the same table she and Trey had sat at last Tuesday. Ryan stood and greeted her, offering to take her coat. His eyes were friendly yet bore new lines since the last time they had spoken.

"Thanks. I don't know about you, but I'm starving." Amber seated herself but didn't pick up the menu. "I know exactly what I'm going to get."

"Do you come here often?" Ryan asked, placing his elbows on the table. His relaxed demeanor reassured Amber this meeting was a good decision. Ryan was a friend. And she needed a friend during this time of transition. All of the familiar cornerstones had been knocked out from her life in less than a week. But the rapport she felt with Ryan smoothed out some of the rocky places. It felt wonderful to relax and be herself.

"Usually I'm at the King's Castle making breakfast for everyone else. This is only my second time here." Amber paused to greet the waitress and ask for a cinnamon roll and a glass of water, the cheapest breakfast Amber knew to order.

"I'll have the same." Ryan handed his menu over and turned back to the conversation. "That's right. I should have guessed. You seem like the kind of person who's always looking to help others."

"It's my duty and my pleasure. Serving the least of these, you know?"

Ryan's brow furrowed. It was charming and reminded Amber of one of the little boys at the King's Castle who was concentrating over a multiplication problem. "I'm not following. I've never heard that phrase before. Sounds like something from a Tennison poem or something."

Amber smiled. "Not exactly. It's from the Bible. Jesus said it. I think it's near the end of the book of Matthew."

The food arrived and Ryan took a drink of his water and cut off a big chunk of pastry. The smell was making Amber's mouth water, but she knew where her provision came from. Best to stop and thank the hand that fed her. "Do you mind if we bless the food first?" Her breakfast companion's face turned a shade darker, which only caused his black hair and pale blue eyes to look even more dashing.

"Quoting from the Bible and praying over meals." Ryan smiled and set down his fork. "When I asked you to collaborate on the battery, I

was the question he'd been mulling over all night. If she knew he was the kind of man to skulk in back alleys trying to find stolen money, a man with no future, the likelihood of having her as his own would dwindle to nothingness.

His chances were already slim to none now that Trey had her in his sights. It wasn't as if his classmate was going to let him stop by to see Amber's fair face, smell the lavender that drifted from her clothes, watch the sunlight brush across her beautiful hair. Yet if he couldn't be near her now and then, the world would turn too dark, too quickly.

"Absolutely. And I picked up the Westinghouse motor I was telling you about, so after today, I'll be all set. But let's not spend the rest of our time talking about the project. I have you all to myself," Ryan decided to test the waters, "and I'd love to get to know you."

A look of pleasant surprise chased away the confusion that briefly skimmed its way across Amber's features. "I've already told you about my past—" Amber left her sentence hanging between them. She wasn't grabbing her purse or trying to catch the eye of the waitress so she could pay. It looked like Amber was comfortably settling in for a long talk. Even better.

"You can tell me about what you've been working on for Christian. Since you are no longer at the university, I wondered if this was a paying job. Maybe enough to float you for a while."

Amber shook her head, her bun coming undone just the slightest bit. The look it gave her was more Amber-like. Soft and unassuming. Touchable. "Christian didn't hire me. He had something he wanted me to look at."

She didn't offer anything more. It would be up to Ryan to bridge the gap and get her talking. That, he was somewhat confident, he could do. "When I was at the Titus's last week, Christian told me he used to be a Pinkerton." If he was reading Amber right, he would say she looked relieved. Her shoulders didn't look so rigid and her face had relaxed a bit. "I put two and two together and figured he asked you to look at an old case of his. He told me he tinkers with them from time to time." Ryan knew it would be hard to avoid the direct question, especially when he was giving Amber the added bonus of knowing Christian had brought Ryan into his circle of confidence.

"He told you he was a Pinkerton? Well, he is very proud of that fact. I was over there a few weeks ago, and he had all these papers spread out in front of him. Told me it was a case that had gone unsolved for twenty years. Can you imagine? It must eat at him to still be trying to figure out the clues. The Pinkertons dropped it a long time ago, but Christian knows me well enough to suggest I toy with it a bit. See where I could maybe find another lead."

"And? Have you?" Ryan put his arm on the back of the booth seat, hoping to appear relaxed and interested, but not too interested. He wanted Amber to trust him. Open up to him. Tell him what she knew about this case concerning his father. He could even steer the conversation if he was lucky, buying himself time to gain her affections. If only.

"A little. Mostly dead ends."

"You look upset." Ryan felt the opposite. She wasn't really working for law enforcement. She didn't have incriminating information about his father. He could see it clearly now. Amber was a girl who liked to solve puzzles, figure out solutions. Her answer confirmed why she had gone to Oakwood Hills, asked questions around town. Yet it didn't answer who she was searching for in the graveyard. "Want to tell me about it?"

Amber had the same look on her face that Miss Childs did when he asked after what Amber and his father had been looking into. Slightly embarrassed. Mostly disconcerted. Likely hoping to not hurt his feelings if she admitted his father was the key suspect. "I really don't know if I should."

It was time. "Amber," Ryan leaned forward and spoke in a softer voice, "remember when I was at your cabin and you had been working on the floor in front of the fireplace? Well, when I helped you pick up the papers, I saw my father's name on a suspect list for a crime. Must be the one you're looking into."

"Goodness." Amber's face was coloring quickly. "You weren't supposed to see that."

Her hands were clasped together and resting on the table. Ryan reached over and encompassed them in his right hand. Gosh, but she fit so nicely to him, like when they danced together at the party. Maybe one day he'd get the chance to put his arm around her shoulders and tuck her up against him. "I didn't mean to. But I did. Amber," Ryan said her name so she would look up from his hand covering hers, "it's okay. I know my father is not an upright man. Never has been, as far as I can see. Let me help you. Help Christian." Ryan removed his hand but kept his imploring tone. "Do you trust me?"

Amber looked to the side, as if someone were watching them. Ryan looked too but nothing seemed out of the ordinary. Outside the restaurant's windows, horses and buggies were going down the Waterford Cove thoroughfare just like any other day. Stores welcomed shoppers. Barbers swept their steps. A trio of women crossed the street.

Ryan's heart gave a jump when he saw the Chariot stop to let the ladies pass with none other than Trey Wright behind the tiller and William in the passenger's seat. Ryan wasn't even aware the two men knew each other. Despite Ryan taking the Chariot out of the running for the Endurance Race, it looked like William had somehow managed to weasel back in. He gave a shudder to think of William training up another young soul to carry out his evil whims. And his classmate was just reckless enough to jump without looking.

Until Ryan was able to investigate further, all of his questions would have to wait. Amber's response was more important than Trey Wright's shenanigans, more important even than if she let him in on the case.

It wasn't possible for a girl like Amber to truly put her trust in a man like him, was it? When he looked at who he really was, heavy doubt weighed down his heart. Ryan risked a glance at Amber to see if she had noticed the spectacle outside. What he found were shy blue eyes meeting his across their empty plates and an answer that made him believe he just might one day be worthy of love without counting the cost.

"You know, Ryan Pierce, I believe I do."

♦ ♦ ♦

"You're doing a fine job, son." William slapped his new protege on the back as the Chariot took to the streets of Waterford Cove.

"Thanks, Mr. Pierce. It's a mighty fine vehicle you've got here. Wouldn't mind taking my new girl out for a spin in this beauty."

Trey Wright, the charmer. The natural charisma cloaked as complimentary humbleness was almost comical to watch. Those were some of the same tricks of the trade William had taught Ryan over the years. From the first moment Trey had shaken William's hand, this had felt right. Trey was already shaping up to be more than twice the man Ryan ever was.

"I take that as a compliment." William pointed to the crossroads ahead. "Turn right. That'll take us to downtown. I want everyone to see that Trey Wright is the best driver Waterford Cove University has ever seen. Partner with me, and you'll have that competition in the bag."

The Chariot had received a loving once-over last night after sudden inspiration struck. He'd put on his best suit and sweet-talked Professor Henning into telling him who needed a sponsor and a car for the race. William had been at the Wright's front door before breakfast, worked his magic and there they were.

"You add your little modification and then all you have to do is drive. Then you'll have that interview you've been salivating over."

Yes, now that he'd pinned Ryan to the wall, literally and figuratively, giving the ne'er-do-well no choice but to find the money, William could focus on the next piece to building his empire: the Chariot.

That fool schooling had the boy so distracted he couldn't see straight. Well, not anymore. With no more money to pay for tuition, Ryan would chase William's rabbit until it was caught. He had to. Let Ryan think if the money was found that he had a ticket back into WCU. It would keep the cretin motivated. And if the money was never recovered, Ryan's life could be traded for it just as easily as William's. That ought to appease Jelly Joe.

Just as he hadn't been around for Ryan's birth, William determined he would not be around for Ryan's hasty exit from which there would be no return. William cordially waved to curious onlookers as the Chariot's sleek body wound its way through Waterford Cove's downtown streets. Easter would be William's day of reckoning, standing at the finish line of the Endurance Race, ready to have his picture taken with the car that would become an overnight success. He'd have more investors and buyers than he would know what to do with. And Trey Wright was going to help him get there.

◆◆◆

Amber stood outside the Engineering and Modern Sciences Building and waved goodbye to Ryan while deciding her next move. A walk to the King's Castle would do triple duty—her mind could clear and her heart could pray while she let the spring-like sun warm her all the way through.

Trust. Amber's steps tapped out the rhythm of the word as she made her way west and a little north. Ryan didn't know the magnitude of what he was asking. Trust someone she barely knew. Trust him with her knowledge of the robbery. Trust him with her time. Her friendship. That last part would be the easiest to give after spending a few wonderful hours working shoulder to shoulder next to Ryan. The design she suggested turned out better than expected, and their shared excitement over the project created a sweet harmony between them.

Still, Amber's lips twisted to one side. Trust. It was a question she usually didn't answer lightly. There weren't many to whom she had granted that request without getting burned. Growing up without family or home, she hadn't been able to afford letting her guard down. After many years in the loving presence of the Coles and the Tituses, letting others into that protected place came a little more easily. Still, skepticism tended to play tug-of-war in her mind more often than not.

Currently, the Wrights were in the testing lab. Looked like Ryan was about to join them.

Rounding a corner and leaving downtown behind, Amber picked up the pace and swung her arms freely. The movements gave her a confident feeling, like she had made the right decision. Ryan may not come from the best stock, but she could not condemn him for that. He wasn't to be faulted for his parentage. Whenever they were together, she felt seen, like she wasn't simply another face in the crowd. Most importantly though, Ryan always made her feel as though she had really been heard. Beyond that, he was generous and honest. Yes, she would give him the benefit of the doubt. Innocent until proven guilty.

Still, it wouldn't be right to bring him in on the case without Christian's permission. The information in the file was only on loan to her; she had no right to divulge what wasn't hers to begin with. She had a feeling Christian wouldn't be too keen on her doling out crucial details to the son of a suspect, even if the case had been closed years ago.

"Lord," Amber said under her breath, "thank you for putting me with the Wrights, with Trey. You knew what You were doing by joining me to that family. And Lord, I pray for Ryan. I think he's hurting. Seems he doesn't have anyone to be with, anyone who's looking out for him. I can tell he's anxious to get away from his dad. Meet him where he's at. Show him that You love him."

As the Titus's home came into view with the King's Castle as its backdrop, Amber could see the family was putting the nice day to good use. The adults were on hands and knees in the flower beds, pulling out winter's weeds with the girls nearby making mud pies. "Hello!" Amber called, causing Summer to sit up and put her muddy hands on her thighs.

"Well, isn't this a nice surprise," Christian said as the girls ran to greet Amber. "Been wondering how you're doing but didn't want to behave like an overprotective father."

Christian might not know it, but Amber actually welcomed it when he did just that. She needed someone to watch out for her, tell her when she was steering in the wrong direction, make sure she was safe and cared for. It had definitely been the right choice to come and visit today.

"You can be as overprotective as you'd like, Christian." Amber smiled at him over Summer's shoulder as her friend gave her a hug. "Do you guys have a minute to chat? There's a couple of things I'd like to run by you."

"Any time. You know that," Summer said, leading the way inside after she wiped her hands on a towel. "Girls, you can play out front for a while longer. Amber, have you had lunch yet? We've got some leftover soup."

"That sounds perfect. Thank you."

"What's on your mind?" Summer poured hot coffee for the three of them and set a bowl of potato soup out for Amber. "Judging the look on your face, we might need more than one cup."

"It's not as bad as all that," said Amber, adding enough sugar to take the sting out of the flavor.

"Things not going too well at the Wright's?" Christian asked. "Or do you just miss us so badly you had to stop by?" He said the last with a twinkle. What a kidder.

His jovial ribbing made Amber feel more at ease. Still, what she had to ask wasn't easy. "The Wrights are wonderful people, though I do miss you all. Terribly, in fact. But that's not why I'm here." Amber wished she had the case file with her. Then she could ask Christian to look at the names listed next to each *Tabitha* who had immigrated in 1876 and see if they rang any bells for him. For the meantime, she would stick to the subject at hand. "You remember my friend Ryan?"

"Of course we do. The girls are crazy about him," said Summer. "Comes by the King's Castle more than I would have expected a full-time student could. Always ready to jump in where needed. Why do you ask?"

"A couple of reasons. One I can talk to you about later and the other I can't ask in his hearing." Amber hesitated. Now that she had to put the request into spoken word, it sounded illogical. But the Tituses were hound dogs when it came to not letting her off the hook. Once the cat was out of the bag, it never got back in. Better to plunge ahead. "You see, I learned two interesting things this morning. Number one, Ryan is interested in collaborating on that file you gave me, Christian."

"Is that a fact?" Christian didn't look too disconcerted, which gave Amber confidence to carry on.

"Yes, he seemed quite keen on helping. But here's the other thing you need to know: he's the son of the main suspect for the crime. William Pierce is Ryan's father." Amber held her breath. What would they think of Ryan now that they knew? For some reason, it was important to Amber they maintain a good opinion of him. Just because his father might be nefarious in character didn't mean Ryan was. No, instead he had a steady way about him. Amber knew she could count on him when it mattered.

Christian slapped his knee. "No need to look so nervous, Little Bumble Bee. I already knew that. Knew it from the first time I laid eyes on him in your cabin, even before he said his last name. Looks like his old man. Talks like him too. Has the same mannerisms."

"When did you meet William?" Summer asked the question that was on Amber's mind.

"I didn't meet him at first. Staked him out, learned his habits, his trademarks. But when I finally had the chance to interrogate him face to face, I wanted to put him away so bad I could barely keep from pulling out the cuffs and slapping them on his wrists right then and there."

"Did you know he was guilty?" asked Amber.

"Nah. Just a hunch. My instincts on the man were one of the reasons I've kept my thumb in the file, so to speak, all these years. I've got details about other crimes he was implicated on. Many other crimes, a couple he even spent time in prison for. But this one, he weaseled out of. Had an alibi even I couldn't refute."

By now, Amber was on the edge of her chair, lunch forgotten. "What was it?" She had to know.

"Attending his son's birth," Christian said matter-of-factly. "The night of Waterford Cove's one hundredth anniversary of celebrating our nation's independence. July 4, 1878. Of course, up in Philadelphia, the Declaration had been signed in 1776. The very next year, bonfires and fireworks and bells marked the first celebration of our new freedom. But other towns, like ours, didn't begin the commemoration until 1778. Your friend Ryan made his grand entrance as Waterford Cove celebrated a very special day."

Amber made a mental note. Not knowing exactly when her own birthday was caused her to be acutely aware of celebrating her friends' milestones. "Why did you still suspect William if you knew he wasn't there?"

"Someone thought they saw him near the bank that night, but it could never be proven and none of our other leads ever panned out. Then one day, Tabitha went missing. When I went looking for her, my

Pinkerton nose started sniffing out leads, and I found a small connection between her and William Pierce. The scent grew stronger, and it seems they used to run in the same circles; Tabitha exactly matched the description of one of Pierce's criminal acquaintances. That, and I remembered she was forever trying to get me to pass off the assignment to another agent. She always looked uncomfortable when I had to make the trip to Waterford Cove."

While Christian spoke, the rest of the world disappeared for Amber. She was caught up in the picture he was painting with his words. By hook or crook, Amber knew the mosaic pieces of this case must be put back together. Tabitha and even William may very well be innocent. Even more reason to bring Ryan into the search. Proving William's innocence could give Ryan a chance to put faith in his father again.

"So, what do you think? About Ryan, I mean." Amber's hand went to her necklace, her thumb stroking the golden wings of the bee. Please say yes. Talking the case over with Trey or his sisters was incongruous with how she wanted them to perceive her. Millicent would roll her eyes and Yvette would laugh her out of the room. Winnie would agree with her sisters, and Amber was fairly certain she knew what Trey would say—women had no place mucking up their hands with something that wasn't their business in the first place. He'd tell her to box up her ill-considered ideas and throw them in the trash heap where they belonged. Amber sighed.

Christian drained his mug and looked over at his wife. She lifted one shoulder nonchalantly, apparently giving her husband her blessing because Christian continued, "Ryan's a good man. He's a seeker. I can tell from the questions he asks that he's searching for what matters in life. Lord willing, I'll be able to help steer him to his Maker and the life He has planned for him." Christian leaned back in his chair, lifting the front two legs off the floor as he regarded Amber. "You're good for him. You're straight as an arrow. He needs your influence. So, yes. Go on ahead. Tell him what you know. See if he can aid in bringing this thing to a close."

Amber got up and gave Christian a quick hug. "Thanks. It's been fun to poke around. I've even made a couple of trips to Oakwood Hills.

Money's tight again, so I don't know if I'll be able to do that anymore, but now that I'm not using my brain for anything worthwhile, this gives me something to fiddle with."

ELEVEN

Where have you been all day?"

Amber walked into the Wright's parlor to find Trey rapidly pacing its length. His hair was mussed and there was fire behind his eyes. "Hello to you, too," she said, hoping to show him with her words he was being rude.

Trey pulled up short in front of her and jerked her hand from her necklace. "Who have you been with?"

Sidestepping him, Amber went to the hearth where Emma was keeping watch over her pups. They were two weeks old now and a few were starting to open their eyes. Amber squatted down and cooed to the mother while she picked up the smallest of the litter, purposefully avoiding eye contact with Trey. "If you really need to know," she said, trying to maintain composure, "I've just come from visiting with the Tituses. They had me in for lunch and we sat a spell."

Trey stalked over and sat beside her. "Give me that thing." He plucked the puppy from her arms and plopped it back into the box. "I missed my classes today not knowing where you were or who you were with. Everybody's talking about us." That thought seemed to make him happy, for suddenly Trey's expression completely changed and he rocked back on his heels, arms around his knees. "I'm gonna be mayor one day, and I intend on working my way up after that. If we're a couple, we need to act like it. Look like it. And if you're out wandering around town, doing who knows what, it reflects poorly on me." He frowned again. "Understand?"

Amber stood and Trey followed suit. Seeing the distress on his face and hearing him refer to them as "us" caused her heart to soften. She hadn't meant to worry him. Her absence had obviously been a torment. "Please forgive me, Trey. In the future, when I am away, I'll make sure I tell you when I plan on returning." She gave him a sweet smile, hoping to dispel any further rebuke.

Trey gathered her into his arms and sighed. "I would appreciate that. Thank you. And by the way, I wanted to ask you to accompany me to a dinner and dance to be held this weekend at the Wilson's." With his arms still around her, Trey inclined his head toward hers. His eyes were on her lips. He was going to kiss her. Trey Wright was about to give Amber Graham her very first kiss.

"Afternoon tea is almost ready, you two," said a voice from the foyer.

Amber turned to see who had spoken but not before she caught the annoyed look on Trey's face. The more she was with this dynamic man, the more she realized he couldn't be pushed around. Trey was someone who appreciated being at the tiller of each situation, a natural leader. What excellent qualities to have in a husband.

"Stop smoochin' and come out back. We're going to take our snack al fresco." said Millie. "Cook made chicken pudding. Your favorite, Trey."

Late that night when Amber had some moments to herself, she thought about that almost-kiss. Would she have let Trey follow through with it? Her heart hit her stomach in anticipation of what it would be like and when it would happen. Somehow though, she was glad their brief moment had been cut short. It didn't feel right for their first taste of intimacy to directly follow a moment of intense conversation.

Amber sighed happily. But it will come. I know it will and when it does, it will be perfect.

Despite her dreamy thoughts, Amber couldn't drop off to dreamland. Clearly, she would have to be discreet when she met with Ryan or was researching the case. That undeniable fact gave her an uneasy feeling about her future with Trey. She wanted to be with someone who partook in every facet of her life. In his defense, however, Trey had finally shared about wanting to be mayor of Waterford Cove. He was opening up to her. That's what counted. In matters of consequence, they were headed toward being a real couple, even if they weren't there quite yet.

Before long, one of two things would happen. Amber would find more clues to give to Christian or she would hit dead ends and that would be that. Either way, in a matter of days or weeks, working with Ryan would come to an end as would sneaking around to dig up twenty-year-old evidence.

Putting the details in tidy mental columns settled Amber's mind, and she snuggled down into the soft covers. Trey was only being watchful of their future. This weekend she'd be in his arms again at the Wilson's dance, if not sooner. Lord, let it be sooner.

◆ ◆ ◆

A faint knock at the front door roused Ryan from his deep concentration. Papers were spread all across his desk, the summation of four years of ideas. Ideas that at one time, he thought would take his career far and wide. Give him sure access to an open vista of possibilities, a good long way from this hateful house.

Meeting with Amber and putting the battery together had in some strange way given him the courage to look out on that horizon again. The darkness that shrouded him at his father's command would come to an end. In four weeks' time, Ryan would toss it aside and when he did, he wanted to be ready for what was next, even if it wasn't working for Benz and Daimler.

"Coming!" Ryan knew his father was in the carriage house working on the Chariot, but even so, Ryan took a moment to shuffle the papers into a pile and place them in a drawer. The knock came again, just as Ryan was turning the knob.

Framed by the morning sunlight at her back, there stood Amber Graham. She had left her hair down and it shone like a fire halo around her shoulders. No one could have looked more ethereal, more out of place on his doorstep. This angel didn't belong anywhere near the bottomless pit that was the Pierce residence. She needed to leave. And quick. "Hi there. Wasn't expecting to have the privilege of seeing you this morning. I'm glad you came." *Please go away.* Ryan leaned around the doorjamb to ensure the carriage house doors were shut. They weren't.

Amber gathered her hair and brought it to one side, letting it hang in front of her shoulder. She was purely wholesome and everything he needed. And he had to get her out of there.

"Hi. I tried to find you at WCU, but one of your classmates told me you wouldn't be in for a while yet. So I asked him where you lived. I hope you don't mind."

She was so alluring, looking at him with her innocent eyes. If she only knew how much he needed her. Ryan closed the front door behind him as he said, "No, I don't mind. Why don't we walk a bit?" Not waiting for her answer, he took her elbow and led her in the opposite direction of the carriage house.

"First day of March," she said.

Amber had linked her hand through his arm, her small fingers encircling his bicep. This was an independent woman who had lived alone for the last two years, who had raised herself on the streets until she had come to the King's Castle. A woman who Professor Henning knew was smart enough to efficiently carry out work usually reserved for a man. And now she was rooting out clues from a decades-old Pinkerton case. She certainly didn't need assistance navigating a level walkway, yet there was her delicate hand gripping his arm.

Ryan felt his chest swell. He knew people. Had been raised to read their quirks and idiosyncrasies in order to coerce them into doing what he wanted or into telling him what he needed to know. That left only one conclusion—Amber Graham wanted to be with him. He didn't know why, didn't know how long it would last, but for the moment, she was there and didn't look in any hurry to get away. They rounded the corner, out of sight from the house and Ryan breathed deeply. *Thank you, God, for the amazing gift of this friendship.*

"I know, right? Always my favorite time of year," Ryan responded, looking up at the naked oaks that stood sentinel along their path. "Winter almost gone. Spring just weeks away. I can't wait until the trees start putting out their leaves."

"Same here," said Amber. "I always start looking at the bushes first. See?" She stopped and fingered a lilac's long twig. The first signs of life showed the promise of what was to come.

Rather than continuing their walk, she looked up at him, her eyes scanning his, back and forth. What was she looking for? What did she see?

"Christian said I was welcome to discuss the Waterford Cove Holdings case with you," Amber said unexpectedly.

Eyebrows against his hairline, Ryan wasn't sure how to respond. In one move of trust, Amber had made herself, his father's past, and the details of the robbery accessible. His initial shock diminished and he smiled. "That's fabulous, Amber. You know I'd love to aid you in any way I can."

Amber started to walk again and Ryan fell into step beside her. She had removed her hand from his arm and was looking at the ground. Quietly, she asked, "Why do you want to see your dad charged with a crime he committed so many years ago?"

An honest question that deserved an honest answer. Not that he had to tell her everything. "William Pierce is many things, but innocent isn't one of them. Other than squandering other people's money he's managed to take from them, I've never seen him commit a crime. All I have to go on is rumors."

"What have you heard?"

"Theft. Embezzling. Scams and long cons. Just speculation, really. He's never held a job for any length of time, as far as I can remember. Been working on that pile of rubbish he calls the Chariot for a while now. Roped me into helping him get investors. Couple of weeks ago, I drew the line." Ryan sliced his hand through the air. "No more. I plan on being my own man from here on out." Guilt severed his convictions the second the words were out of his mouth. Hypocrite, a voice whispered in his ear.

"No wonder you want to get a place of your own," Amber said as she looked up at him. "Have you talked with the Tituses or the Coles about the cabin yet? I'm sorry I forgot to mention it when I was there."

So this is what it felt like to be on the receiving end of someone's concern. It was astonishing Amber felt even the smallest hint of remorse for her oversight. It had been fifteen years since anyone had made him feel cared for. When Mother went away, it had meant the end of all the niceties a relationship could bring. Ryan became his own watchdog that day. "It's not your responsibility," he told her.

"I know," Amber said as they came to an intersection. "You really should talk with them though. Even if you think you can't afford it. And those rumors about your father, they may be truer than you know. Christian said he has some files on William." She paused at the street's edge. "We'd better turn around here. I'm going with the Wright ladies to a sewing circle at the Wilson's."

"Why don't I walk you back then? It's not too far from here."

For the first time that morning, Amber looked uncomfortable. Still, she acquiesced and they turned at the corner. Ryan decided to steer the conversation back to more lighthearted topics. "I didn't take you for the kind to be fond of feminine pastimes. No offense I hope."

"Trust me," Amber said with a laugh, "I'm not going there for the joy of sewing. But I can tell you this—some well-placed questions can go a long way in a group of older ladies who like to talk, if you know what I mean." Amber winked at him and his heart took a dive.

This girl. Oh, this girl. "I need to stop by and talk with Mack Wright later on today. When I'm there, why don't you tell me what you find out at the Wilson's?"

Amber looked distressed again. It wasn't beyond Ryan's notice that each time it was in reference to the Wrights. "Hey," Ryan said, stopping along the way, "what's wrong? That's the second time you've gotten that look on your face in less than a minute."

Her expression strained, Amber said, "It's Trey. He won't like me talking to you."

Ah. That he should have inferred. If she and Trey had even a hint of an understanding between them and if he was in the other man's shoes…

well, Ryan figured he wouldn't want anyone near his girl either. "Listen, Amber. The last thing I want to do is make it awkward for you at the Wrights'. Where a person lives needs to be a place they feel like they can rest. A place they can be themselves. I don't want to wreck that for you."

What Amber did next was the last thing Ryan anticipated. And it would occupy his dreams for many a night to come.

♦ ♦ ♦

William leaned his shoulder against the splintered wood of the carriage house, watching Ryan and the red-haired girl walk toward town. Whoever she was, William could easily read in Ryan's body language his attraction for her.

"I'll call her Red," William said to himself as he went back to adjusting the Chariot's valves. The fool thing hadn't been able to stay running for more than a couple of miles, which proved embarrassing Monday morning with Trey. Pushing it home the last hundred feet had almost cost him Trey's acceptance of his offer. Almost, but not quite.

"Red. Gorgeous." William pulled a wrench out of his toolbox, mentally replaying the scene when she had turned her head to speak to Ryan. Her hair had swung to her other shoulder, revealing half of her face. There was an aspect of familiarity about the girl. The set of her shoulders, the curve of her cheekbone, the lilt to her gait. Almost as if he had seen her before.

"Don't worry, Red," William said, returning his attention to the Chariot. "Sooner or later, I'll find out who you are. Don't you worry."

♦ ♦ ♦

Amber could now add why she kissed Ryan on his cheek to her list of questions about the man, although some of her curiosities were slowly being answered. It made sense now that he couldn't afford rent on his own place if his father had squandered, to use Ryan's term, their investors' money. What didn't make sense was the way Ryan could discern her heart. The way he anticipated what she really needed, deep down where no one else could touch.

"You're awfully quiet this morning," Sheila remarked as the tree-lined drive leading to George and Harriet Wilson's estate came into view.

"She's probably daydreaming about her kiss with Trey," teased Millie. Yvette squealed. "Really?" She squeezed Amber's hand. "I want to know the second he asks for your hand. I can't wait till you're our real sister."

"Don't embarrass her," Winnie chided. She turned to Amber as the carriage pulled up in front of the grand entrance to the home. "You don't have to tell us a thing. What you and Trey have is special, and it's just between the two of you." This time she turned to her sisters. "Right, girls?"

Yvette and Millie looked at each other and giggled. Amber figured they were still whispering about the new romance as they climbed the steps with their heads together and shoulders touching. Amber sighed. She wouldn't correct them and tell them it had been an almost-kiss. Let them gossip. Having them in her corner wasn't a bad thing.

"Don't pay them any mind," said Sheila. "When my peers were announcing engagements and planning weddings, that's how I was, too. Couldn't get enough of the latest because I couldn't wait until it was my turn."

Amber settled herself in the same seat she had taken last week when she couldn't wait to leave. This time would be different. Her agenda had changed from attending to please Trey to ferreting out as much information as she could about that fateful night so many years ago. She felt certain with well-timed statements and inquiries she could stitch together a few more clues.

A natural break in the conversation came sooner than Amber expected when she asked the women what they planned to do with their quilts once they were finished.

"We usually give them to local churches," Grandmother Wright said. "They may have someone come their way who needs one."

"Have you ever thought about having an auction at a community event and giving the proceeds to the orphanage? At something like the Fourth of July picnic in the park?" Amber tried to say it as casually as possible. She knew from what the Wright sisters had told her that some of these women were on the annual picnic's organizational committee.

"That's a great idea, Amber," Justine Cole said.

Both Justine and Summer were in attendance today, with Mirabel at her mother's side. Amber gave the little girl a wink as Summer picked up the train of thought. "Most of us have a history of helping to plan the event anyway, so why not make the quilts a part of the celebration?"

Amber let the conversation take its natural course as the women took the bait she set out, hook, line, and sinker. It didn't take long before everyone was in agreement about the auction for the King's Castle. "I've never been to the celebration. What's it like?"

The response Amber received was exactly what she had intended. Once the older women in the room began reminiscing, Amber knew she had perfectly executed her plan. Ryan would be proud. Now for the next opportune opening. "Sounds splendid. I bet in years past, this large of a community event has been a boon to the entire town. Maybe even bringing in a boost to the economy." Amber tried to look casual as she watched thread chase needle through the calico fabric.

Grandmother Wright spoke up. "It hasn't been all roses." She looked knowingly at another older woman in the room. "Remember that one year, Theresa?" Grandmother shook her head. "What a pity. So much lost that night."

Justine Cole's lilting English accent danced across the room to Amber's ears. "My father-in-law still speaks of it. Of course, that was long before I came over from East Wharf. It took the bank years to recover."

"And they never found the cads who pulled it off, if you can believe that." Sheila looked up from her stitching.

"Do you think more than one person was involved?" Amber asked.

Justine shrugged. "Could have been a one-man job. We'll never know. From what Garrett's father told me, there was no one injured, no dynamite used, no trace of evidence left behind. Just years of people's hard-earned cash gone. The bank worked hard to repay every single customer back. Thankfully, the vault wasn't as full that night as maybe the thieves banked on. A southern railroad tycoon had made a large withdrawal the day before and many locals were splurging on Fourth of July celebrations."

"They got away with enough to make things miserable for Waterford Cove for many a day," Grandmother Wright said. "But we have to remember, 'There is nothing covered, that shall not be revealed; and hid, that shall not be known.'"

The women dropped the topic of the robbery and altered the course of their conversation to the pending party in the Wilson's conservatory. Amber kept quiet, her thoughts on what Grandmother had quoted from the Bible. Her breakfast on Monday with Ryan disguised as a walk wasn't something she wanted to be revealed, especially to Trey. It would take extra effort to keep their meetings an absolute secret, but it would be worth it.

TWELVE

Thank you, Mack." Ryan held out his hand at the Wright's front doors, his feelings of confidence in the older man verified in his firm handshake. "I'll stop by Saturday morning and pick it up."

"See that you do, son," said Mack. "I have a feeling you've had a rough go of it, but don't let that deter you from keeping your eyes where they should be. The Lord's got something special planned for you."

Ryan adjusted his hat and put a foot on the first step down. Mack Wright had the unique ability to make Ryan feel humble and proud within the space of a few words. No, that wasn't all together true. Christian Titus had the same effect on him. The commonalities Ryan could see between the two men were growing. Both could claim success in business and life, love, and family, but Ryan had a feeling none of what they possessed had been gained by dishonest means.

"I hope you're right about that, sir. Good day." Ryan descended the rest of the porch stairs much differently than he had come up them twenty minutes before.

A whistle escaped his lips as he made his way back home on foot. Saturday. Only three days from now and he'd be behind the tiller of the Wright's gasoline-powered automobile. Not exactly the response from Mack that Ryan had in mind when he set his pride aside and told Mack that Waterford Cove University would soon be a thing of the past. Mack hadn't asked too many questions; a fact for which Ryan was beyond grateful. In the end, however, Mack seemed to understand funds were tight and opportunities had been lost. The man must be an eternal optimist, for rather than show Ryan the door, Mack had not only given him permission to alter the runabout but also welcomed him to take the car on a jaunt to get a real feel for it.

For the first time in his life, Ryan was being offered someone's trust. Three people's, to be precise. Amber and Christian both knew William Pierce, the alleged criminal, was Ryan's father. Yet, they were allowing him access to details that, if he chose, could be used to William's advantage. And now Mack's insistence that Ryan use and modify his car came at a time when Ryan felt like he was only picking up breadcrumbs. It was like a miracle.

Turning on Fifth Street, it dawned on Ryan that if he asked them, Christian and Mack would probably agree it was a miracle. They seemed like the kind to believe in acts of God. Like the Great Blizzard of 1899, Mack and Christian and especially Amber's trust in him were an unseen hand that covered all his mistakes with a blanket of white absolution and all-forgiving grace.

Whether fortuitous or miraculous, it had been quite the morning. His only grief was not seeing Amber when he visited with Mack. But Ryan would make that sacrifice again and again to avoid causing his girl even a hint of pain.

His girl. No, Amber Graham wasn't his girl any more than Mack Wright's runabout was his car.

Ryan opened the large carriage door, wanting to shuffle some of the larger items that were stored there to make room for Mack's vehicle.

"So, who's the redhead?" No greeting. Nothing cordial. Cold and to the point. That was William Pierce.

Make that two griefs yet today. This one he didn't want to repeat.

"Hello, Father." Ryan busied himself by grabbing a small crate and positioning it in the far-left corner of the structure. So, William had seen the two of them this morning after all. Somehow, Ryan would have to relocate his father's interest to something else, anything but Amber. "I'm making room for another car in here." There. That ought to do it.

"You're what? What kind of scam are you running that you'd be able to afford an automobile?" William set down the rag he'd been using to shine the body of the Chariot and came to stand in front of Ryan. The dance had begun again. "You work for me, Ryan, and every penny you earn goes to keep this family afloat."

"Actually, you work for Joe, and I'm only helping you out so you don't lose everything." Ryan grabbed the edge of a rolling wooden bin and pushed it to the back wall. "Don't get your dander up. The runabout's not mine. Just making some modifications for a friend. And don't bother asking me who. You don't need to know."

"Sure as shooting I need to know. Your time is mine, son."

Ryan's scalp prickled. *Don't call me that. I don't want to be your son.* He breathed in deep as he picked up a broom to create a smooth surface for the runabout to sit on. Ryan couldn't change his name, couldn't put new blood into his veins. But after this infamous money was found, he would make his life as dissimilar to William's as humanly possible.

"I'm working as hard as I can. My little project isn't going to hinder me helping you in any way. If you know me at all, you'd remember I think best when I'm not pacing the floor. I need to keep busy to think straight."

"Does this girl have anything to do with keeping busy? Because if she's a distraction of any kind, I can take her out of play."

Ryan's heart hit his stomach. More and more, he was grasping just how much this money meant to his father. William didn't let things get in the way. Ryan needed to do what he could to keep Amber from looking like an obstacle. He would need to find out what she knew and protect her at the same time. It would be an interesting assignment.

"Leave her out of this. Everything is under control."

"I once knew a girl who looked a lot like Red." William laughed when Ryan's head snapped up. "Yeah, already gave her a little nickname." His smile turned into a sneer. "Don't underestimate the power of a woman to get you off your game. She'll bait ya when you're least expecting it and take everything you've got."

◆◆◆

"I'd like to see Mr. Cole, please." Amber answered the receptionist's friendly inquiry in the lobby of Waterford Cove Holdings.

"Garrett or his father, James?"

"James, Mr. Cole Sr., please. If he's available." Amber steadied her nerves but figured she wasn't the only one who would be jittery speaking to a bank's founder and president, even if she'd had many interactions with him throughout the years at the King's Castle.

"And may I tell him the nature of your visit?"

"It's about—" Amber faltered. She wasn't a detective. Had no formal training. Was only a former resident of this man's son's orphanage. A girl who was about to ask a silly question. "Can you tell him Amber Graham is here to see him?" Hopefully that would suffice.

"Certainly."

Within moments, she was seated in one of James Cole's rich leather chairs and feeling more relaxed as she looked into his aging but handsome face.

"What can I do for you today, Amber? A new account? A loan, perhaps? Maybe a mortgage?" James always had been a bit of a teaser.

"No home loan for me. I wish. No, I'm here on an entirely different matter than personal banking." Amber scooted to the edge of her chair. This might turn out to be a far-fetched idea, but she wouldn't know unless she tried. "Mr. Cole, you know Christian used to be a Pinkerton, right?"

James's eyebrows raised a tad. "Certainly. Used to speak of it often. That's what first brought him to Waterford Cove."

"That's right," said Amber. "He may not have mentioned it to you, but the robbery of your bank is still on his mind even though the Pinkertons closed the case a long time ago." Amber brought her courage to the front. "It's been more than twenty years, you know, and I think he's anxious for some resolution. He even asked me to do some investigating in my spare time. I'm not at WCU any longer, so lately I've had plenty of that."

"I'm sorry to hear about your work situation." Mr. Cole stroked his short beard. "But it thrills my heart to know someone still cares. Nothing was damaged that night—no windows or locks broken, nothing blown to pieces. The money simply disappeared. Took many years and most of my family's personal savings to pay everyone back." James's eyes drooped a bit at the sides as he said the words.

"The fact that no evidence was left behind compels me to think that one of your employees may have been paid off to give someone access to your bank." Amber held her breath, wondering if she'd made her statement too boldly.

"Young lady, that's a stone that was turned over before you were ever born. Every one of our employees was questioned thoroughly. The Pinkertons are very meticulous."

Amber felt put in her place, even though she knew James well enough to understand he hadn't done it out of meanness. He was simply stating the facts. And he was right; the Pinkertons were the best in the game. Still...

"True enough, sir, though I got to thinking the other day and wondered something. Was there an employee that came to work for you shortly before the robbery? Or was there someone who quit not long afterward? It might be worth looking at who came or left within a year on either side of the crime."

"You mean, someone who became an employee to gain access to the vault after hours?"

"Yes, or someone who felt they had to leave either out of guilt or fear of being connected to the theft in some way."

James smiled. "I like the way you think. Reminds me a lot of Christian. No wonder he's taken you under his wing." Mr. Cole paused for a moment. "I don't have any recollection of the Pinkertons asking for those kinds of records, especially up to a year after the fact."

He stood and Amber followed suit. "Let me see what I can dig up. If I find anything, would you like me to give the details to Christian?"

Amber walked to the door. "I think he's having fun watching to see what I come up with. I'll just stop back in a few days or you can send word to Mack and Sheila Wright's house. That's where I'm staying for the time being."

"Oh? Not at your little cottage anymore, eh?"

"No, I moved out a little over a week ago," Amber said with a forced smile as she bid Mr. Cole farewell. But if I keep up this detective work, Amber thought amusingly, the police station may just consider putting me on the payroll.

◆◆◆

"Give this to Amber, would you?" Ryan handed a folded slip of paper to Winifred Wright as he passed her in the hall outside Mack's office.

"Certainly," she replied, not looking certain at all.

"You promise?" Ryan prompted the girl. "And don't say anything to anyone else." Ryan said both statements quickly, knowing from experience if she said yes to his first question that she was automatically complying with the second without really thinking it over.

"Sure," Winnie looked up at him timidly. "I promise."

Ryan gave her a winning smile and made his way to the Wright's carriage house. He was thankful Trey and Amber weren't home even though that meant they were presumably out and about together. No matter. Trey couldn't heckle Ryan for borrowing Mack's runabout and upon seeing Ryan, Amber wouldn't be caught in the middle of her loyalties.

Even as he dreamed of how marrying gasoline with electricity could revolutionize the auto industry, Ryan's thoughts were on Amber. The runabout motored down the road toward home, and he wondered if Trey had cornered her yet and taken what he wanted. He thought about her kind words, her sunshine smile, her passion for life. But most of all, he thought about her faith in him. Tomorrow was Sunday. That meant only four more weeks until he could be himself again. No more dividing his heart in two, wearing deception like a well-tailored coat. He could shed it forever and become the whole man he was meant to be.

Reporting to Joe Schneider tomorrow morning ought to prove interesting. As he pulled up to the carriage house, Ryan formulated a plan for what he would tell the man. There were no records at City Hall for a Tabitha Murray. He figured she and Christian had met and married in another county, and the woman must have been buried somewhere else as well.

His lack of knowledge didn't let him off the hook, nor did Ryan figure Joe was joshing in his threats against his father. Ryan had bided his time for the last three days, giving Amber space, not wanting to appear too eager. But today, he would make his move. He knew from Miss Childs that Amber held six names which somehow might be connected to Tabitha. Joe wanted a report; Ryan would deliver, and an afternoon ride with Amber would afford the perfect opportunity. If Winifred Wright carried out her promised duties, Amber would meet him at the corner of Fifth and Chestnut at one o'clock precisely.

Over the next couple of hours, Ryan's hand went to his pocket more than once. No watch, only the sun outside the carriage house window to indicate if he needed to start heading that way. Of course, a look at the mantle clock was an option. Not today. No more run-ins with William for the time being. Ryan would avoid him until after his meeting with Joe in the morning.

Finally, it was time. The runabout's engine didn't turn over easily. Conceivably, that would soon be a thing of the past. Again and again, Ryan grabbed the crank handle, giving it a jerk in a circular motion. Finally the motor chugged to life. Adding an electric motor and a well-suited battery would be the solution to the problem every driver encountered. A quick start until up to speed, then a simple switch over to the gasoline motor to go the distance. And if the driver had a reason, the two motors could be run simultaneously for a burst of power no one had ever seen or felt before. Ryan's blood pulsed faster and not merely with excitement and apprehension about seeing Amber. If he could unify the two designs and somehow sell the concept to a manufacturer, he'd have the ability to support himself for a long while. He owed Mack Wright an eternal debt of gratitude.

Ryan could tell the moment Amber spotted him. Even from a distance, her face lit up with joy. "Hi there, beautiful." Immediately, Ryan wanted to take back the words. Amber didn't need him fawning all over her. It would, in fact, put a damper on his efforts to garner information. To cover his discomfiture, he tipped his hat low and hoped down, making his way around the front of the automobile. "The project just took leaps and bounds. Mack Wright saw to that." He gave what he hoped was a carefree smile. "Can I help you up?"

"If you're implying we'll be riding this lovely machine, I'd like to see if I can manage better than the last time when I rode with Trey. After all, the goal is to cater to women drivers too, isn't it?"

"By all means, then." Ryan watched as Amber blithely seated herself and grinned down at him.

"Mack told me to take it out for a long jaunt. Get a feel for its peculiarities." He pulled the tiller to the right and turned at the corner, glancing at Amber. "You up for a drive?"

"Absolutely. Lead on, conductor."

Heading northwest, the city dropped away behind them while the road opened up to country with low hills on either side. Despite the tires hitting a rut every now and then, Ryan could tell Amber was enjoying herself. Her eyes were closed and her chin was jutting out a bit, like she was trying to feel as much of the wind in her face as she could. She looked happy. Lit up inside. No wonder Trey was staking his claim. Ryan had never met another girl like her.

"How far do you want to go?"

"Forever!" She raised her hands to the sky and laughed.

"Forever it is, then." No demands on his time. No William in sight. William. Ryan sobered at the thought. It was time to get down to the business at hand. He slowed, making it easier for them to converse. "We've got all the time in the world. That is, unless Trey is expecting you back soon."

Amber slowly ran her hand along the seat's smooth surface. "No, I told him I'd see him later this afternoon when we leave for a party at the Wilson's. He's with his father right now, working on some financial things, I think."

"Good. That'll give us plenty of time to chat. What did you learn at the Wilson's the other day? Anything interesting?"

"Yes, as a matter of fact, several things." She reached into a bag she had set on the floorboard and brought out a folder. The same folder he'd first seen at her cottage. The same folder that had peeped out of her bag at the bank. Bringing it with her today was a good sign. Amber was about to tell him everything she knew about the Waterford Cove Holding's Robbery. He wouldn't have to pry the details out of her or skirt around each question, trying to get to each answer covertly. She was going to hand him everything on a platter.

"Looks like you have a couple of pages there. Must have been quite the sewing circle," he said, fishing for what she would present first.

"Well, this isn't all from society gossip. Everything here is what I've compiled over the last couple of weeks, from Christian's original notes to a meeting I had with James Cole at the bank. There's also a young lady at the City Hall who's been very helpful and given me some new leads to check out. I admit I haven't done anything with the latter yet. Maybe you could help?"

From the sound of things, Amber didn't have much to go on. That meant neither did he. Best to see for himself. "How about we pull off the road and have ourselves a look at what you've got?"

Amber pointed to a place in the road that widened a bit and he brought the car to a stop. From her bag, she pulled a thin blanket and some cookies. "Looks like you've been busy in the kitchen," he said.

They each grabbed two corners of the blanket and laid it under a tree. Amber settled herself against its trunk and took a big bite of her snack. "Grandmother Wright and I whipped these up this morning. I brought plenty, so don't be shy."

Ryan hadn't eaten since his measly breakfast that morning and his stomach rumbled to let Amber know.

"Have you had lunch yet?" she asked while wiping a crumb from her lower lip.

"You caught me. Nah, didn't get around to it." More like, didn't get around to finding some money to buy it. The small stockpile of canned goods in the cellar of the Pierce home would hopefully get him and his father through this slim time. Missing a meal now and again would help ensure their supply would last.

"Here," she said, handing over the uneaten portion of her cookie, "have mine."

There were times when Ryan knew it was best to accept hospitality rather than make excuse. This was one of them. "Thanks. So, show me what you've got."

As Amber explained each piece she had uncovered, Ryan's realization that there wasn't much to go on grew. Oakwood Hills may be a dead end, unless the reverend came through. She mentioned her suspicions about an ex-employee at Waterford Cove Holdings and showed him the names of the other two suspected criminals besides his father, along with the names of six people Miss Childs had given her for possible immigration companions. That was it. But at least now he had a handle on everything Amber knew. From there, he could make a plan, being extra cautious not to let any connection to Joe Schneider or his previous knowledge about Tabitha come out.

"Show me those names again from the clerk at the courthouse. What did you say her name was again?" he asked casually.

"Miss Childs."

Ryan snapped his fingers and stood, offering Amber a hand up. "You know what I think?"

"No, what?"

"We've got all afternoon and we're already halfway to Oakwood Hills. I've got an extra gas can right here. That, and I'm ravenously inquisitive. Why don't we go the rest of the way? You may not have had any luck finding Tabitha in the graveyard, but what about those other names the clerk gave you?"

Before he could blink, Amber threw the blanket and her bag onto the seat and stepped up into the automobile. "Ryan, you're the best. Somehow, you always know just what I'm thinking."

With one foot on the running board, Ryan froze. He couldn't do anything different, for Amber's eyes were dancing with his. No one had ever looked at him like that, not even the girls who over the years had tried to catch his attention. A look that said "I know you and I like you anyway." Ryan also caught glimmers of adventure. Friendship. Acceptance. He realized that never before had he known what it meant to be truly free and alive. Now that he did, he never wanted it to end.

◆ ◆ ◆

Amber wanted to reach across the seat and squeeze Ryan's large hand that rested on the tiller. She didn't. Instead she looked out at the expanding hill country that led into Oakwood Hills. Life and time had been cruel in her early years and even though she had been surrounded by other children at the King's Castle, she was well aquatinted with going solo. A solitary existence was doable. Familiar.

Then Trey Wright had changed it all. Being included in the Wright family had opened up a new world to Amber. Going to sleep every night after chatting with Winnie and Millie and Yvette. Baking with Grandmother Wright. Dinners and church with the whole family. Parental figures in Mack and Sheila. Somehow though, even in the fullness of all those gifts, Ryan's friendship outshone them all.

It was as if he could see to the core of her heart, what she was thinking, what she was feeling. Amber was too rooted in God to believe in magic, yet she questioned Ryan's uncanny ability to read her. Did something show in her face that gave her away?

"One thing I forgot to tell you," Amber said as the Main Street of Oakwood Hills came into view. "I spoke with Reverend Buchanan's wife last time I was here."

"How many times have you come?"

"Twice. The first time, it was on a whim, kind of like this. I had just gotten the file from Christian and saw that letter I showed you. The one written by Tabitha's friend. There was no return address, but the postmark was from Oakwood Hills. I thought I would start looking for Tabitha there."

"And what did Mrs. Buchanan tell you?"

"Turn here," said Amber. They drove by the cafe where the waitress had told her to visit the reverend. "She didn't have much to say. Said the last name didn't ring a bell but that Tabitha sounded familiar. Told me to come back and speak with her husband. I never thought I would get the chance."

"Why not?"

Amber blushed slightly as she looked at Ryan out of the corner of her eye. It was hard to admit she was almost penniless. "I don't work for the university anymore."

Ryan's face took on a knowing look. "Ah. I should have drawn that conclusion on my own. Seems I missed my cue on that one. Evidently I don't always know what you're thinking." He smiled.

It was so easy to smile back. This was a man who cared, deep in his heart. That couldn't be disguised, no matter his bloodline. "The church is just straight ahead there. See it? Let's check the graveyard first, then see if the Buchanans are home."

The afternoon sun was taking a bit of a dip in the western sky as they disembarked at the deserted graveyard. A few of the daffodils had opened their sunny faces, and Amber breathed in the scent of moist soil. The rake and garden tools leaning up against a tree made it clear someone had tended the grounds recently. Everything felt different to Amber. Being there with Ryan and seeing signs of life in this place of death reversed her qualms 180 degrees.

She found the headstone that had made her sad the last time— *Evelyn McPhearson*. So much had changed in the last two weeks that looking at the matriarch's headstone surrounded by her children and grandchildren didn't bring with it the same heartache. Amber's life had been filled up to the very verge of overflow.

Ryan came up beside her. "Let me see those names again."

She turned her head and found his face only a breath away. Like a child from the King's Castle, hugged for the first time by new parents, Amber felt surrounded by Ryan, even though he wasn't touching her. She wished he was. Even if it was just a hand at the small of her back. Trey and the entire Wright family seemed as distant as the years she'd spent going from one bad situation to another. Her thoughts were completely on the man beside her. His blue eyes shone luminous in the sunlight and seemed to meld with hers as they stood eye to eye.

A loud but musical note sounded from above their heads and they both turned to look. Two tones from the church's belfry declared it was time to make the most of what was at hand.

Ryan lowered his head at the exact moment Amber did and they shared a smile before Amber pulled out the list of immigrants.

"I'll take Westwater, McLachlan, and Gorrie," he said.

"Good. I'll try to find Lorimer, MacDonald, or Blacketer." Amber decided to start at the back of the property and let Ryan take the front. A little space was in order. Amber walked slowly, noting each engraved name and once in a while found herself glancing up to see if Ryan was watching her. Had he savored the unspoken connection between them?

Her reverie came to an abrupt end as she reached the middle of her second row.

THIRTEEN

Bridget MacDonald April 12, 1885. No sweet endearment or words of remembrance had been added to the small wooden slab that had been beaten by the elements. It tilted to the right as if shying away from the hardy stone markers of the Tackett family by which it presided.

"Ryan! Over here!" Amber ran her eyes over the crudely engraved markings. No other clues indicated if this was the person for whom they searched. Could Bridget MacDonald have been a travel companion with Tabitha? Maybe the name would trigger a memory for Christian. She would see him tonight at the Wilson's party. "Look," she said, pointing at her finding.

"Interesting. What was the last name of the Tabitha that was listed next to Bridget MacDonald on the immigration list?" Ryan asked.

Amber's finger trailed across the page where Bridget's name had been printed and said, "Grantham. Tabitha Grantham. By the way, we'd better keep an eye on the time."

"I don't have a watch." Ryan's face took on a melancholy look.

"I've seen that look before." Amber hoped he would open up to her if she asked the right question. "It's the same one you had on your face the day we ran into each other at WCU. The day I had to leave my job." She tilted her head. "Want to talk about it?"

Ryan ran his hand across the back of his neck and looked everywhere but her face. "My mother gave me a watch for my fifth birthday. I had to sell it recently."

"Why?" Ryan's family was well-to-do. It didn't make any sense. When he didn't answer, she said, "I only ask because we should be heading back soon. I know the drive is going to take some time, and I need to be ready by five o'clock at the latest. Trey will be waiting."

"Don't worry. We can manage." He crouched and ran his hand over the wood. "So, do you think this is our next clue?" he asked.

"Could be a connection to Christian's Tabitha," she said as Ryan turned his head to look up at her. "Or it could be a coincidence."

He straightened and they stood side by side, Amber lost in thought. MacDonald. The name brought to mind her childhood. The woman who had cared for her, given her the special necklace. The woman who had disappeared from her life, just like so many others. Not anymore. From here on out, there wouldn't be any more leaving. The Wrights weren't the leaving kind.

She shook herself from her woolgathering. "Maybe Christian will have a lead on the name for us."

"What about talking to Reverend Buchanan?"

She looked at the sun. It had moved a little lower in the western sky. "I think the Buchanans are the kind that like to sit a spell."

He tipped his chin in the direction of the parsonage. "I'll just check to see if they're home. I didn't see any smoke from their chimney, which most likely means another trip to Oakwood Hills for you and me." His eyes twinkled down at Amber. "Why don't you finish these last few rows and then we'll head back home?"

Ryan disappeared around the side of the church and suddenly, Amber felt very much alone. She made quick work of the remaining headstones and went to join Ryan. But as she passed the church steps, she paused and bowed her head. "Lord, I'm getting weary somehow in here." Amber put her hand over her heart. "I don't have any reason to feel this way. Everything is going well for me." She squeezed her eyes shut and an unexpected tear rolled down her cheek. "Why do I feel so torn when there's nothing to feel torn about? You've given me so much. Please help me to be grateful. And thank you for Ryan, Lord. Amen."

Amber's eyes opened in time to see Ryan's brown duster come around the corner of the church.

♦♦♦

Candles reflected on the glass ceiling and walls that encased the Wilson's conservatory. The ethereal light drew Amber onto the gravel-strewn paths that wound between citrus trees, palms, and ferns. Women wearing silks in every color of the rainbow competed with the natural beauty of orchids and bougainvilleas.

The dozen or so men who were in attendance made their way more slowly into the conservatory to join their womenfolk. Amber had been listening to snippets of conversation throughout dinner and was beyond grateful to have Summer and the Wright women nearby. It still felt foreign to be transferred so easily from being an outsider to the inner circle. She needed something familiar and at the moment, Summer provided that.

"You know, it was on this very property where Christian and I first met and started to have feelings for each other," Summer was saying. "That was nine years ago, if you can believe that." She chuckled and what Amber saw was a woman still in love with her husband.

"How did you know Christian was the one for you?" Amber asked with open curiosity. It was obvious she and Trey were meant for one another, but it would be interesting to hear Summer's answer.

Amber was startled when Christian jumped from behind a large fern and swung Summer in a circle before setting her back on the ground.

"I'll tell you how," Christian said teasingly. "I forced her to marry me."

Summer swatted his arm playfully. "I would marry you every day, and you know it. No forcing necessary."

"Good to know, woman." Christian turned his attention to Amber. "We'd better stop fooling around. The dancing is going to start soon and Amber looks like she has something on her mind." Christian's smile could be seen under his short reddish-brown beard.

From the first day she'd met Christian, he had taken on a kind of paternal role in her life. Though he'd never said so, Amber guessed he prided himself in being both her friend and her protector. His fatherly demeanor had never seemed odd, even when the other children from the King's Castle looked to Garrett and Justine Cole as surrogate parents.

"You're a mind reader, that's for sure," said Amber. "And you're right. I wanted to ask you if Tabitha ever—"

"There you are." Trey rounded a curve in the path and joined their little gathering. He came to stand next to Amber and proceeded to put his arm around her shoulder. "Don't go running off like that. We need to be seen together tonight. This is an important evening for me."

Trey had said as much several times over the last couple of days but Amber didn't understand what was so critical about this particular get together. George and Harriet Wilson were excellent hosts, and it was certainly an entertaining evening, but Trey seemed inordinately pre-occupied with the night's outcome. "Mind letting me in on the secret?"

Trey squeezed her shoulder. "You'll find out soon enough, little lady. Now, ready for some dancing?"

Christian raised an eyebrow. "In a minute, young man," he said. "We were just finishing up here with Amber. I promise to send her your direction when we're done chatting." He gave Trey a friendly look with a hint of authority behind it. Trey seemed to understand.

"Come and find me as soon as you're done. My girl should always be at my side." Trey put two fingers to his brow and gave them a mock salute before walking away.

"Goodness, but that man goes after what he wants," Summer said.

"Not unlike me when I met you, my love. But Amber, please finish what you were saying."

Her heart rate speeding up, Amber drew a breath. Finding a con-nection between Bridget MacDonald and Christian's Tabitha could be her one shot at untangling this old Pinkerton case, one that at first had been merely to appease Christian and maybe just a little to satisfy her curiosity. A case that somehow her entire being had become very invested in. "Did Tabitha ever mention someone named MacDonald? Bridget MacDonald?"

Christian's face went white.

At that moment, the quartet in the far corner of the conservatory struck up a tune, and all around them couples began their practiced steps. Trey appeared again and with a hand on her elbow, pulled her away from the Tituses.

"You'll excuse us, won't you?" Trey didn't wait for an answer. He locked eyes with Amber and started a simple box step. Three beats in, she stepped on his foot. "Ow!" he said under his breath. "Just follow my lead, okay?"

Trey looked slightly perturbed as they brushed up against other couples in a clearing near the middle of the atrium. The foliage and density of the plants made for close quarters, causing her to step closer to Trey to avoid bumping into the Wilson's on one side and Millie who was dancing with Mack Wright on the other.

Trey smiled at her as she did so. "That's more like it." His eyes held an intimacy that frightened her.

Don't run away like a scared rabbit. This is exactly how you want him to feel about you. Be brave and just go with it.

But she didn't feel brave. She felt as if there was no air in the room, so paradoxical to her drive back to Waterford Cove with Ryan. In the passenger seat of the runabout, her chignon had come loose in the wind and she took out all the remaining pins. Abandoning propriety, Amber had closed her eyes and let her hair whip her face at will. Ryan had laughed, a light, friendly laugh that curled its way around her heart and gave a great big squeeze.

It didn't surprise Amber that never once over all the miles they traveled did the conversation stop flowing. Amber learned a lot about Ryan, even catching glimpses of how much William had hurt him over the years. When she asked about the Chariot, even though his eyes had clouded over and his jaw clenched, he told how his father had pieced it together with parts and ideas stolen from other inventors.

Looking into her dance partner's eyes, Amber knew she needed to reach that level of familiarity with Trey. It was high time to stop wondering if the man was going to open up to her. Time to take matters into her own hands. "Trey, tell me about your senior project. I know—"

Trey's eyes narrowed and he leaned close to her ear. "Why would you ask such a thing here? Just keep quiet and dance with me." Trey pressed his cheek to hers and took her through a series of steps she was unfamiliar with, causing her to crunch his toes more than once. She couldn't wait till the music stopped.

As though the band understood her chagrin, the strings played a final note and the couples broke apart, clapping politely. Amber looked at Trey from the corner of her eye. He had not passed the test. Amber knew the Endurance Race held a lot of weight for Ryan; she had assumed it did for Trey as well. If he wasn't willing to talk about something of consequence, the question remained as to what he would tell her. Thus far, Amber felt she had only seen a sliver of who he really was.

That will come in time. Give him grace and be patient.

Unexpectedly, Trey continued to clap, even after the others had stopped. But it didn't sound like applause; this was a clap to call others to attention. "Everyone, listen here." Trey held a palm up to the musicians. "If you'll indulge me for a moment, I would like your attention."

Amber began to take a step back but Trey pulled her next to him. "As many of you know, Amber Graham has come into my life. And for that, I am beyond grateful." Here, he smiled down affectionately at her and she felt warmed all through. He seemed genuine and earnest, the kind of man she could spend a lifetime with. It was too soon for him to propose, but Amber felt an important announcement was about to be made.

"It's with her next to me that I would like to share some news. After graduation, I plan to run for mayor of Waterford Cove." Trey raised his hand to check the polite clapping. Amber was more certain than ever this man could command an army if the need arose. Everything and everyone bowed to his wishes. "My first act as mayor will be to infuse Waterford Cove's economy with new jobs by means of a manufacturing plant featuring automobiles made by Benz and Daimler."

Amber was unaware he had connections with two of the biggest names in the automotive industry. She would ask him more about it when they were alone. Trey was someone who appreciated his privacy, although from the way he was eating up the praises and well wishes of those around him, she could certainly be convinced otherwise.

"We all know there are homeless adults and children on the streets of our fair town. Building a new factory where they can be gainfully employed will solve that problem. Amber here is intimately acquainted with the hardships of not having a family or a place to lay her head at night. She was on the streets until she found a place at the King's Castle, which we all know is overrun by the street urchins we call orphans. Entry-level jobs are needed so we can take pride in Waterford Cove once again. "

The humidity in the conservatory seemed to seep into Amber's skin. Shame burned her face and neck as the past she had worked so hard to leave behind was laid out in plain sight for all these people to see.

Men were slapping Trey on the back and congratulating him for his philanthropy and ingenious idea. When the dancing resumed once more, Trey pulled Amber down a graveled path and into a secluded spot between two ferns.

He held up his hand and pulled back his pinky finger. "You asked, I'll answer. You just heard reason number four. When I run for mayor, you'll be a hit with the members of the community. Shake up the status quo, that's what I say. Give them what they didn't know they wanted." Trey loomed over her and before she knew it, had planted a kiss on her lips. "And that, my dear, is number five."

♦ ♦ ♦

"I've been tracking some people who I think used to run with Tabitha," Ryan told Joe early Sunday morning. "If I can find them, I can get closer to where she may have spent her last days. I know it was in or around Oakwood Hills. At least, that's the lead I'm going off of right now."

Joe Schneider's face held a contemptuous look. "It's not enough, Pierce, and you know it." He crossed his arms over his ample stomach and stood his ground. "Come next Sunday with something better than that or you'll be sorry. I've been watching and I'm drawing a neat little bullseye on the back of some people you care about."

"What do you mean?" Ryan had to ask even if he wouldn't like the answer. There were only a few people in his life he could lay even the smallest claim to. *God, don't let Amber be in Joe's sights.*

"Let's just say you might want to warn the folks over at the King's Castle that one of their little girls may go missing sometime soon. One of those little blonde girls who live in that cottage." Joe snapped his beefy fingers. "Oh, that's right. You can't tell them that. If you did, they'd know you're a criminal and would never let you near the place again. Or near Amber Graham. That's right. I know all about Amber."

It's not enough, Pierce, and you know it. Joe's words rang in his ears as he walked away from Schneider's hovel. Was it ever enough? No. Never. The story of his life. Crowded between a rock and a hard place by his father's demands and their family's lack of financial wherewithal, Ryan was always forced to choose between the least of two wrongs. This time though, lives hung in the balance. Part of him wanted to find another way to get the cash. Pay Joe off and be done with it. Rob a bank or something. No, if he stooped so low, he'd be no better than his crooked father.

Hands in his pockets, Ryan took the same route home he had last Sunday. The street was quiet as he passed by the Waterford Cove Chapel. Sunlight bathed the stone staircase, and even though God seemed irrelevant and far removed from reality, Ryan sat down on the top step and put his head in his hands. He didn't know why he was even there. If he strained his ear, he could just make out the pastor's words. Maybe he wanted to hear a shred of truth to somehow find a way out of the box he'd been shoved into. Maybe he needed to hear how holy God was so he would stop entertaining thoughts of being good enough to come near.

Whatever the reason, the result was not what he expected. A tear escaped the corner of his eye as he heard the Holy Scriptures being read. "I call heaven and earth to record this day against you, that I have set before you life and death, blessing and cursing: therefore choose life, that both thou and thy seed may live:

"That thou mayest love the Lord thy God, and that thou mayest obey his voice, and that thou mayest cleave unto him: for he is thy life, and the

180

length of thy days: that thou mayest dwell in the land which the LORD sware unto thy fathers, to Abraham, to Isaac, and to Jacob, to give them."

The tear brushed away, Ryan stood and began walking slowly home. He wondered how those people the verse mentioned had responded. Had they chosen life or death? And was it really up to them? Ryan had never been given a vote. The death of physical comfort, the death of warm relationship, the death of a future. That was his heritage.

He is thy life. The words resounded in Ryan's head. If they were true, the people could obey and love their God and then they would find life. God was their life. And if they had God, death would have to stay away.

If only that were true for himself. Even if Ryan could somehow choose that path, he wouldn't know the first thing about loving God. Maybe Christian would have some answers.

"Well, don't leave me hanging, boy," William said when Ryan walked in the front door. "I need to know everything. That goes for what evidence you've dug up to what you and Joe talked about."

What little strength Ryan had left seeped out of his bones, and he sank onto the nearest chair. He ran a hand over his face and let out a long breath. Just get it over with, he told himself. You've got work to do out in the carriage house.

Ryan made short work of telling William what he knew about Tabitha thus far, leaving out all points concerning Amber. She was already being tracked by one low-life criminal; she didn't need William breathing down her neck. "Joe finished the conversation by threatening to harm some people I know. I need to come back next week with a whole lot more information. To be honest, I don't know where I'm going to get it. I need more time."

William was pacing in front of the barren fireplace, stirring up cold ashes each time he passed. "You don't have time. Joe's not the giving type and neither is Waterford Cove Holdings. Everything is on the line."

Ryan didn't reply. He sat slumped in his chair, letting his eyes glaze over. He couldn't lie or charm his way out of this tight spot.

"There is one option—" William's tone caused Ryan's head to snap up.

"What?" Dare he ask?

Bending down, William picked up a handful of ash. Without looking at his son, he said, "If Joe Schneider was out of the way, at least half of our problems would be over." He spread his fingers and let the ash fall back onto the cold grate.

♦♦♦

It was as if some great secret was just beyond Amber's grasp. A kite flying barely out of reach. If she could only catch it, she could be comfortable in her mind.

In the background of her thoughts, the pastor of Waterford Cove Chapel was wrapping up his Sunday morning message. She wished he would hurry it up. She was sandwiched between the memory of Trey's imposing kiss on one side and Yvette's overly exaggerated bonnet on the other.

If only she could get over to the Titus's today to finish the conversation she had started with Christian at the Wilson's party. She knew there was slim chance of that. After Trey's announcement last night, he planned an impromptu get-together with some of his comrades. The afternoon was to be food and cards and good times. Amber felt desperate to escape and hear whatever Christian had been going to say; she was positive it would lead her to the next step, whatever that may be.

Had Tabitha known Bridget MacDonald? Her mind created a vision of the two women packing up their few belongings and setting off toward a new life. Yesterday's ride with Ryan mirrored the freedom Amber had felt the many times she'd been out on the cove with Summer and Grandma E. The open waters brought a sense of freedom, and Amber wondered what dreams Tabitha and Bridget may have held close and if any of them had come true.

The humble wooden grave marker was the only line from the book of Bridget MacDonald's life she could read; its only footnote the day her life had ended: May 1, 1885. She considered for the first time what was so obviously missing. Whoever had buried Bridget must not have been a family member, nor a close acquaintance. The rudimentary markings bore no knowledge of her date of birth.

"Please rise for the reading of God's Holy Word." A deacon had taken the lectern and was bringing the congregation to their feet. Amber's contemplations would have to wait.

"From the book of Romans, chapter twelve, verse two. 'And be not conformed to this world: but be ye transformed by the renewing of your mind, that ye may prove what is that good, and acceptable, and perfect, will of God.' And now, the closing hymn."

The song was one Amber was unfamiliar with so she pretended to follow along in the hymnal while her mind spun back to the question of Bridget MacDonald. A shiver slid down her spine when she thought again of the year Bridget had died: 1885. The same year Amber had been sent out into the world alone with nothing but her mother's necklace to connect her to her roots.

FOURTEEN

The almost three-week-old puppies were proving to be the perfect excuse for Amber to not join in on the Sunday afternoon festivities. Nearly a dozen of the Wright siblings' friends had gathered in the front parlor and were spilling across the foyer and into the library. Amber wasn't in the mood to analyze whether or not Trey would try to get her alone again nor did she feel like hanging on his arm simply for the benefit of his friends.

The churning in her mind was becoming inescapable. She eyed the front door from where she sat with a wiggling puppy on her lap. Ever since last night when Trey had pulled her away from Christian and Summer, Amber could feel the panic rising higher in her chest.

"Hey, Amber, come here." A friend of Trey's was motioning her to join a group of four who had gathered at a corner table to play euchre.

"Yes, please come and join us," said Yvette. "You can take my spot the next hand." The trap had been set.

Amber snuggled the puppy one last time and went to put it back. The entire litter had been taking steps on their own for several days now and most had been trying to wander off, so Mack and Grandfather Wright had used tall crates to create a makeshift pen near the dogs' original spot near the fireplace.

"You know, I think I'll pass this time, but thank you for the offer," Amber said as politely as she could while inside she felt like climbing the walls. "I'll just check in the kitchen and see if there are any more treats to set out."

Thankfully, the kitchen was deserted and the food trays empty, but the door that led to the backyard stood open, letting in the cool spring air. Breathing deep, Amber decided enough was enough.

She began walking in the direction of the Pierce house, not even knowing why. Halfway there she decided to ask Ryan to accompany her to the orphanage. He could be present when Christian answered her questions about Bridget MacDonald.

The glorious sun shining on her face and the thrill of adventure gave her the courage to know she could hold her own when it came time to face the music with Trey tonight.

◆ ◆ ◆

Murder. That's what his father was threatening. Choose life or death, the Scriptures had said. Unfortunately, it wasn't always that clear cut. It was almost certain now a life would be lost, death would be chosen. God, let it not be Amber's. But whose? Joe Schneider's? William's? One of Christian's girls? His own?

William had left after his cryptic suggestion about Joe. Ryan didn't know where his father had gone; all that mattered was that he wasn't there now. Ryan wrapped his housecoat more tightly around his middle as he climbed the attic stairs. Maybe there was something up there he could burn for fuel. The middle of the day always seemed to be the worst, even though Ryan knew it wasn't the coldest. In the dark of his bedroom, his blankets and thoughts of Amber kept him warm. Mornings seemed to go by in a hurry and evenings he stayed out of his father's way as much as possible. But after a cold lunch from the basement, the chill always made a concerted effort to permeate his bones.

After this small errand, he would make a weak cup of tea. He thought he'd spotted some in the back of the pantry the other day. And water was free, right? So was abandoned furniture to take the bite out of the air.

The entire attic held the feel of a time and place of long ago. Cast away items that had once held value to their owners lined the walls and took up space in the middle of the wooden floorboards. Being in the shadowy room that possessed a certain smell unique to untouched places reminded Ryan of the day his father had forbid him from ever going up there again. Ryan had been around ten years old that year, and when William found him, he was kneeling in front of a big chest that had been pushed underneath a window facing the front of the house. It must have been afternoon because Ryan remembered dust dancing in and out of the rays of sun.

Before his father had interrupted, Ryan had looked over his shoulder then slowly lifted the trunk's lid, silently commanding the hinges to keep his secret. They obeyed and Ryan saw what his eyes had hungered for—his mother's things. She had been gone five years then, but he still remembered the brightness in her eyes and the feel of her gentle touch when she laid her hand on his shoulder.

On the very top lay her wedding gown, a cream-colored dress with lots of lace and buttons. Ryan wondered if it was still there today. He had just been lifting the dress to hold it to his pre-adolescent nose when William had come in, shouting obscenities and throwing whatever he could get his hands on. Ryan had scrambled down the stairs and after many bruises that night decided to heed his father's command.

That had been more than a decade ago. He let his heart grow all the calluses it needed to not bear the pain of two parents who had deserted him. Mother didn't have to go. She chose to. William didn't have to treat him like he was a paid steward, but he did. Whether Ryan liked the facts or not, there they were. Forsaken by one parent, used by the other.

He sighed and went to the side of the room opposite Mother's trunk. What looked to be an old shipping crate had been broken into separate pallets and was stacked against a wall. As he glanced around the room, he decided that would be as good a start as any. If he carried the wood down bit by bit, he could further break it up by the fireplace and if they used it sparingly, he and his father would be warm for at least a day or two.

Every time Ryan made the trek to carry the wood to the top of the ladder, he glanced at his mother's trunk. A lifetime packed into one container. It was a little humbling to think the length of his own days would one day be dwindled down to a few meager earthly belongings. Would his future son or daughter go digging in his things to learn more about their daddy? Then again, it was entirely possible he would never marry and have children. Who would be left then to mourn his loss or celebrate his small victories? No one. The answer was that simple. Unlike the verses the pastor had read, there was no inheritance promised to him, and he had nothing of the sort to give to the next generation. The only thing holding this family up were spoiled, rotten roots. And it looked like they were about to crumble into dust.

Setting down his last load of wood, Ryan brushed his hands together and knelt at the trunk. Within moments, his mother's dress was pressed to his face, just as he had wanted to do so many years before. He would never know what had prompted his mother to marry William Pierce. Had she been the kind of woman to applaud William's lifestyle? Amber mentioned Christian had other files on William. Crimes he had committed. Maybe some people were destined to be crooked.

Gingerly lifting out the dress, Ryan set it to the side and began rifling through the other contents. A perfume bottle held enough lingering scent to transport Ryan to another place—a Christmas tree at a church, Ryan sitting on his mother's knee, his father smiling beside them. Singing hymns and gazing with wonder at the candles and presents. The memory gave him pause about his father. Maybe there had been a time when William was a decent man.

A rectangle-shaped wooden box was brought out next. It's carved top looked familiar and when Ryan opened it, he knew why. His mother's jewelry box. The inside was large enough to hold a dozen rings plus several bracelets and necklaces. But only one item remained. A wedding ring. Ryan guessed that over the years William had sold off the other pieces. It chafed Ryan to think his father had a shred of decency within him. William was black, through and through. He didn't have the right to force Ryan to give him any benefit of the doubt.

One by one, Ryan made his way through the rest of the items. As he went to shut the lid, he noted its curve from the outside, yet on the inside, blue silk had been laid to make a flat roof for Mother's things. He ran his hand along the edges of the fabric and noted there were clasps on two sides; the silk was meant to be pulled back.

The clop-clop of hooves could be heard out front and even if it wasn't his father coming home, he noted the sun's position and knew it wouldn't be long until he was found out. Quickly undoing the clasps, Ryan discovered what would prove to be the greatest treasure his mother left behind. Two journals had been tucked away into a little alcove. Ryan flipped the first one open to somewhere in the middle, noting the date: 1881. Written when Ryan was about three years old. He put them inside his housecoat and took pains to make the area look like he had never been there.

A knock on the front door surprised him as he came down the stairs. Father never forgot his key. Then he remembered that sometimes on Sundays, one of the neighboring families passed along newspapers they would have otherwise thrown out. Ryan was still holding the last piece of crate when he opened the door. "You can just leave them on the st—"

"Hello, Ryan." Amber. "Did I come at a bad time?"

♦ ♦ ♦

Amber peered past Ryan into the interior of the Pierce home. From where she stood, the place looked dark and deserted.

When Ryan didn't answer her first question and only pulled his housecoat tighter, Amber tried again. "May I come in?"

He looked hesitant but finally said hello and motioned for her to follow him into the front room.

Beautiful wood casing the numerous doorways and windows spoke of the money it took to build such a place, but the unlit fireplace and drawn draperies made the Pierce home feel void of any life.

Ryan set down the pallet he'd been carrying and put two books on a dusty end table before removing his robe. "Believe me," he said, laying the garment on a sofa and running a hand through his hair, "I don't normally go about like this. It was just the most convenient thing at the moment that looked warm."

Amber's hand went to her necklace. "Yes, the evenings can still be a bit crisp, can't they?" But it wasn't evening. And by the feel of the house, it hadn't been heated in quite some time. A quick look at the hearth revealed no chopped wood waiting to be burned. Was William Pierce so poor a provider that Ryan was resorting to burning pallets for heat?

"I was wondering if you'd like to come with me to the Tituses? I want to ask Christian if Tabitha ever mentioned having an acquaintance with Bridget MacDonald." Amber stroked the bee's wings absentmindedly.

Ryan's face relaxed and he smiled for the first time since he'd opened the door. "Sounds good to me. There was something I wanted to ask him, too." He picked up the books he'd been carrying. "Let me put these away and freshen up. Have a seat and make yourself at home. I'll be back in a couple minutes. We'll have to walk though. I spent last night tearing into the runabout and there are parts and pieces everywhere."

That's good, thought Amber. *I'm not in a sitting kind of mood.* She felt like starting that walk now, and since Ryan would need a minute or two, she decided to look around. Amber went back to the foyer where three doors led to places unknown. Behind door number one lay a library devoid of all but a couple dozen books. The second door held cleaning supplies, but the third swung to reveal a kitchen at the rear of the house, a kitchen to rival many of the places she had stayed as a child. All the cupboard doors were either open or hanging on broken hinges. But that wasn't the most alarming thing; all but one was empty. In haste, she backed out of the room and went to stand by the front door. Ryan would be mortified if he knew what she had seen.

Amber was beginning to get a good picture of life at the Pierce house. No household staff. No heat. No food. She doubted they were making mortgage payments. Any bank, no matter how amiable the president, would demand payment before long.

"All set," said Ryan, coming down the hall and opening the front door. Amber smiled but could think of nothing to say. The harsh reality was clear though she didn't yet know the full story—Ryan was about to be homeless. Amber wanted to take him in her arms and tell him everything was going to be all right. But was it? She didn't have enough money to fix what must certainly feel like a desperate situation. Money. That's really what this boiled down to. The Pierces needed money.

Amber could hear Christian's voice that first day she'd taken home the file. *A grand total of ten thousand dollars was stolen,* he had said. *It was never recovered. It's still out there somewhere.* Handled correctly, it was enough to float a family for years and years.

Given the family's current situation, it seemed to Amber one of two things had happened. Either William had wasted the money on lavish living and hadn't taken his future or his son's welfare into consideration, or he'd never had the money in the first place. As she and Ryan walked and chatted as if nothing awkward had transpired, a third scenario came to mind. Someone could have stolen the money from William, someone who knew him well, knew how he worked, knew all his weak spots. Someone on the inside. Someone like Tabitha Murray or Joe Schneider.

"Wish we had something to bring Fiona and Mirabel," Ryan was saying. "These'll do." Ryan didn't miss a step as he picked two daffodils that hadn't yet opened.

Amber turned her head to study Ryan's face as an uncomfortable thought crossed her mind. If the money still existed, she didn't know anyone who had more motivation for finding it than…Amber didn't let her imagination finish the thought.

"That's so thoughtful of you," Amber said, still looking at him. His handsome face was joyful and serene, such a contrast to his dark and barren house. It was hard to believe a man without proper upbringing could illuminate the world from every pore of his being. "Tell me, how's the runabout coming along?"

"Not too bad. I've got a plan for going forward with the conversion. But let's not talk about that right now. I suspect you're just as anxious as me to find another clue to our little mystery. Will you follow up with the bank this week?"

"I was thinking of giving Mr. Cole a few days to do some digging. Why don't we go there together on Friday around noon? In case that doesn't lead anywhere, I also want to crack open another door. You're giving me insight on your father and we're chasing Tabitha's trail, but what about the third name Christian gave me? Joe Schneider. Seems like it would be shortsighted to not at least find out if he's still living and if he was somehow involved."

"No," Ryan said with a bit of an edge to his voice. Then his tone changed. "I mean, why don't you let me look into him. We know Tabitha's gone, so checking into her isn't likely to put you in any danger. But what if this Joe character is still alive, and he learns you're wanting to turn over his rock?" He shook his head. "Nah. If there's any heat to take, let me feel it, not you."

The King's Castle came into view and Amber trained her eyes on the children playing in the grassy area between her old cottage and the orphanage's front door. What she wanted to do was look at her companion in amazement. From the day she and Ryan first spoke, he'd been a safe harbor for her visionary ideas. When others shunned her creativity, Ryan encouraged it. Times when she felt no one understood, this man shot that theory to pieces. His understanding manner and keen insights perpetually wrapped her in their embrace.

"Thank you, Ryan," she said as Summer and Justine spotted them. She waved back but continued softly, "I don't know what to say."

A smile as bright as sunshine took the place of words as Ryan looked down at her. Their eyes locked and Amber didn't want to look away, even when Fiona began to pull on the edge of her shirtsleeve.

"Hello, you two," said Summer, who had made her way over to them. She patted the bottom of a baby who was sleeping on her shoulder. "You haven't met Birdie, have you?" Summer turned for a second, giving Amber a view of the baby's face.

"What a sweetheart," Amber said, laying a hand on Fiona's shoulder. "What's her story?" Amber knew that no matter the love a child was guaranteed at the King's Castle, there was always a past. No matter the bright future the Coles and Tituses could provide, history would work to overshadow it. For some, it was easier to not look back. For others, like Amber, the timeline of life couldn't be completely filled in. Questions would always remain.

"She was left on the doorstep yesterday. I went to answer a knock on the kitchen door and there she was. Can't be more than a few weeks old. Garrett is having Christian check with the police and the coroner to see if we can find any leads to her family. But you know how that goes."

"More so now, than ever," Amber said to Summer, then glanced at Ryan. He gave her a nod. "Speaking of that, Ryan and I have some questions for Christian on the Waterford Cove Holdings Robbery. Is he around?" Amber couldn't see him from where she stood.

"You still looking into that? I thought you'd have a quick peek and be done with it." Summer looked from Amber's face to Ryan's and back again. "I see." She cleared her throat. "Well. I'll just go check for him at the house. Come on, Fiona. Come with Mother."

"First, let me give you these," Ryan said, bending down to the little girl's eye level. "If you put them in some water and wait a few days, they'll open up. And you know what?" Ryan tweaked Fiona's nose. "What's inside will be a surprise."

"Really?"

"For sure. Some daffodils are all yellow. Some white with yellow centers, some even pale yellow with orange in the middle. You watch close and tell me what kind you get, okay?"

Fiona wrapped her skinny arms around Ryan's neck, and Amber watched him return the hug. "Thank you, Mr. Ryan!"

"That baby is lucky," said Ryan after Summer and Fiona walked away. He stood and watched the kids play their Sunday game of annie over. "No matter that someone gave her up, she'll be wanted here."

Amber could hear a wistful note in his voice. "No doubt there's enough love to go round, but she'll never be whole."

Ryan turned toward her. "Why do you say that?"

"Because these aren't her people," Amber said matter-of-factly. "She'll have no link to her past, no way to know her heritage. Her family tree will start with her. And that's only if she marries and has children."

"Knowing your relations doesn't mean you'll be happy," Ryan countered. "Look at you, for example. You don't know your folks but you've got the Tituses, the Coles, now the Wrights. What more could you ask for?"

"What about family traditions? Learning at a father's knee or being so interconnected to siblings, aunts, grandparents, cousins that wherever you turned, support and love and care were all around." Amber could feel her passions rising. "There's no substitute for a legacy. Links to your past give hope for the future. I would give anything to have a forever family."

"I disagree. I'd rather have grown up an orphan than live every day knowing I wasn't important enough to my mother for her to stick around. Knowing I'm just a means to my father's latest end." Ryan looked down and rocked back on his heels. "Better to be thrown out and loved by someone else than to be chewed to bits by your own father."

Suddenly, the three thousand days she'd spent pining for the life the Wright sisters were afforded sounded paltry at best. The sum of Ryan's days both in time and length of misery far out-weighed her own torment. For the second time that day, Amber wanted to reassure this man that everything was going to be all right. Instead she kept quiet, regarding him as the conversation died away. There was little in the way of comfort she could offer when he was clearly bearing so much pain. They stood side by side, and it was the most natural thing in the world to slip her hand into his and give a little squeeze.

◆ ◆ ◆

Over my dead body. Ryan squeezed Amber's hand, a silent promise to keep her far from both his father and Joe Schneider. He liked to imagine he could keep her away from Trey as well, but that was a battle he could never win. Hadn't he just stated that so clearly? Amber had been taken in by the King's Castle, by the Wrights. She had everything and Ryan had nothing. Nothing to give because there was nothing left. Maybe he'd never had anything to give away in the first place. Sometimes he thought he saw a glimpse of what he could be, what he wanted to be. Lately it seemed the fleeting image drifted away like smoke before he could even think about reaching out to grasp it.

"You ready to go find Christian?" he asked Amber. If he was lucky, she would keep her hand in his as they walked. When she turned her blue eyes his way, he didn't like what he saw. Pity, perhaps. Definitely consternation. Maybe even a little commiseration. It struck him like a blow to the stomach that Amber wasn't holding his hand because she saw them as a couple. She had other purposes, and even if they were noble, Ryan wanted more.

Rather than experience yet another rejection should she break their link, he smoothly tucked her hand around his arm and began leading them to the Titus's home. Summer was coming out the front door, the baby no longer in her arms, followed closely by Christian.

"Good afternoon, you two," Christian said, hugging Amber and shaking Ryan's hand. "I'm guessing you're here to finish what you started to ask me last night." He ran a hand down the back of his neck and shook his head, smiling. "I had a feeling your inquisitive mind would have some fun with this one, but you've taken this further than I expected. What've you come up with?"

Amber looked at Ryan and he took the hint. "We really just have one question for you," Ryan said. Amber squeezed his arm, her touch making this seem more like a playful adventure than a hunt where lives were on the line. "Did Tabitha know a Bridget MacDonald?"

Christian whistled low through his teeth. "I thought that's what I heard you say last night, Little Bumble Bee. Where'd you hear that name?"

"Little Bumble Bee?" Ryan asked.

"Oh, yes," said Christian. "She's been buzzing around since the moment she came to us. Going from one activity to the next. Busy as a bee, I've always said. But I need to know, where'd you hear that name?"

"Since there was no record of Tabitha Murray in the city records, the clerk had the idea to see if there were any Tabithas who immigrated the year you said your wife came over from Scotland. She found three Tabithas and gave me the names of other passengers who were listed above and below in the roster. Ryan and I took a trip to Oakwood Hills, where the letter from Tabitha's friend had come from and went searching the graveyard for the six names we had to go by. Bridget MacDonald was the only one that matched. Did you know her?"

Christian drew his wife near. "Haven't thought of that name in years.

I remember Tabitha mentioning her several times, though I never met the woman. Tabitha always said if it weren't for Bridget, she'd never have stuck it out in America."

"Sounds like they had a good friendship," Amber was saying when a child squealed behind them and the four adults turned to look.

Ryan never could tell the difference between a cry for help and a child's sound of delight. Maybe that was because he'd never really let out either of those noises himself. Growing up, he had learned it was best to keep quiet and after Mother left, there were no more moments of pure joy. Mirabel had the ball and was trying to tag a member of the other team with it. He sighed.

Fiona stepped out of the house then, holding a vase she'd put the daffodils in. She set it on a small outdoor table and began pulling her mother and Amber toward the game. Ryan took their leaving as his cue to speak with Christian alone. "You've certainly given us a lot to think about," he said.

"I hope you and Amber know I don't expect any of this to bring us to an arrest. When I asked for her help, I must admit it was more for my own pleasure than hers." Christian looked thoughtful. "She's held a special place in my heart since the first day we met. Maybe it's because I see some of myself in her. Her ability to take a situation and dissect the pieces one by one or to come up with a strategy no one else thought of. Or maybe it's because she reminded me of Tabitha in some small way. The red hair. The blue eyes. The zest for life." He shrugged. "I guess I wanted her to see what she was made of. And I wanted to see it too. For myself."

The men took a seat on the Titus's front porch step, facing the game. "Christian, where do you go to church?"

The older man looked curiously at Ryan. "Summer and I have attended Christ's Church since we got married. Why do you ask?"

Not Waterford Cove Chapel. If Christian had heard the same sermons Ryan had caught pieces of, it would have made it easier to start the conversation. Either way, though, the verses were burned on his heart. Life or death. He was caught in the middle. Could anyone truly decide or were they all simply victims of chance in an invisible gamble?

196

Ryan felt nervous on how to begin. But this wasn't an assignment from his father to swindle someone. Christian was his friend; Ryan had no obstacles preventing him from getting straight to the point. "I'm not exactly sure how to say this, but it seems everywhere I turn lately, I hear another Bible verse or prayer. Each scripture cuts me right down here." Ryan rubbed a fist across his belly. "And the prayers seem like the person is talking to Someone who's real, Someone who's there, who cares." Ryan lifted his head and looked out across the King's Castle's acreage. "But when I pray, it doesn't feel the same. God doesn't answer."

He swiveled his head to catch Christian's reaction and was surprised when his friend grinned and clapped him on the back. "About time, my friend. I've been praying for this."

"You've been praying for me?" Ryan asked incredulously. "Why?"

"Because I'm well-acquainted with the torment of not knowing Christ as my personal Lord and Savior. I know how dark life can seem when you're trying to be your own source of light."

That was about the best description Ryan could have come up with himself. He'd meticulously laid out his plan to step into the light he'd created for himself.

Unfortunately, it hadn't worked. He was still stumbling around, trying to find his way. *If anyone knew how dark it really is inside my heart*...still, something was off in what Christian had said. "Why do you say 'Lord and Savior'? Isn't a lord a master? I hope God doesn't expect me to be His slave or something." Ryan didn't welcome that idea at all. He'd spent the last ten years being at his father's beck and call. He wouldn't knowingly sign up for anything resembling that.

"Yes and no." Christian laughed lightly. There wasn't anything funny about it, as far as Ryan could see. "The Bible tells us we're slaves to whatever we obey. And we all obey something, whether it's our own sinful wills or God's perfect will."

Ryan stood, keeping his back to Christian. His friend had no idea how this conversation confused him even further. It was hard enough to go to sleep at night without more questions of torment rolling around his head. He needed to get back to what was real, tangible.

What he could feel with his own two hands. His senior project was the perfect solution. Every time he was underneath the runabout or working on his design, he felt alive, useful, full of purpose.

"Well, I'd best be heading back home. Let me go find Amber and see if she wants to walk with me." Ryan spoke quickly, not wanting to give Christian the chance to speak about God again.

"Hold on just a second, will ya?" Christian said, going inside. He came back in less than thirty seconds. "Here." Christian thrust a leather-bound book in Ryan's hands. "The first Bible I got when I started to come back to God. I had been reading it pretty regularly but when I got shot, I remember Summer bringing it to me in hospital. It was water to a thirsty man."

Ryan couldn't help but raise his eyebrows.

"Oh, yes, don't let my life now tell you I haven't been through the ringer. Raised by an abusive father, left by my wife, lost a baby I never got to meet. Abandoned by everyone. I even thought God had deserted me. Struggling to keep my head up and convince myself I was good. That everyone around me needed to change, but I was exempt."

"Then what happened?" Ryan's need to flee began to dissipate.

"God happened. Like God calling out to Adam and Eve after they'd sinned, in His love, He never stopped pursuing me. It took a while, but finally I understood I'd been trying to hide from Him, do things my own way, be self-sufficient." Christian put a hand on Ryan's shoulder. "He showed me He was the only way to life. It's all in here." Christian tapped the Bible with his other hand. "Take it. Read it. Start in the gospel of John. You'll find it about two-thirds of the way in. Then read the book of James. That's toward the end. Ryan, Jesus can be your Savior, if you'll only admit you need one."

Through countless situations and conversations, Ryan had been belittled, put down, made to feel like the lowest of all mankind. What he felt now was a different kind of lowliness. It was a humility that made him feel small yet significant. What Christian was saying fed the hunger that was already inside him.

"Thanks. I'll start reading tonight—"

Loud honking cut off his words. Screaming down the road came a vehicle he recognized just as he well as he knew the look on the driver's face. Mack's new Packard sped to where the road stopped in front of the King's Castle and in the blink of an eye, Trey Wright marched into the middle of the game and grabbed Amber by the elbow.

FIFTEEN

Would you like to join me and the other girls for a walk outside? It's such a nice day." Amber could hear the gentle pleading in Winnie's tone as her friend came into the big bedroom.

"Maybe in a little while." Amber turned her face back to the window and gazed out over the expanse of lawn bordered by trees. It was the same view she'd been looking at for the last four days. She felt like Rapunzel, locked away in the tower, unreachable by anyone. The children's story she'd read so often to the little girls at the King's Castle took on new meaning. She was trapped. Shut away. Alone with her thoughts.

But Amber had to admit, those things weren't all together true. Every night, her long-held dream of being one of the Wright sisters was being realized. Grandmother was teaching her how to cook some new recipes, and everyday Amber took her meals with the family and played with the puppies. Throughout the hubbub of activity, though, she had kept quiet.

Even when Trey tried to draw her out or Yvette worked hard to make her laugh, the most she had to give was a small smile. Like a wild western pony that was used to roaming the countryside at will, when Trey had hauled her home, she knew the gate to the pen had been permanently shut.

On the drive home, Amber had clutched the door tightly with one hand and the seat with the other as Trey careened around corners until the car spluttered to a stop in front of the Wright's carriage house.

That's when Trey first spoke. "Ryan Pierce is only trying to get your attention by weaseling his way into what should be rightfully mine. I should be the one driving the runabout at the race. Or at the very least this car. Stay away from him, you hear?" He turned to face her as they sat in the sunshine. "And if you ever ruin my reputation again like you did this afternoon, you'll be sorry. All my friends were forced to leave because of you, and it was an embarrassment to have to tell them you ran away from me. Thankfully, I knew right where to look."

He had sighed and his shoulders sagged visibly. "Amber, Amber, Amber. You don't know what it did to me when I couldn't find you this afternoon. I looked all over the house in a panic." He had reached for and removed her hand from her necklace. "You told me you'd let me know where you were so I wouldn't worry, remember?"

She did remember. Amber shut her eyes and leaned her forehead against the glass of the bedroom window. She'd been selfish and impulsive and look where it had gotten her. Ryan on the other hand was just the opposite. He had nothing yet he was so giving, so generous. There was no way he could possibly be after the missing money, even if his family was clearly in need of it. Guilt pricked her heart that she'd even had such thoughts.

The long look she and Ryan shared last Sunday and the feel of her hand in his scared Amber more than any danger investigating this case might possibly bring. She had relived those moments with Ryan and her kiss with Trey countless times in the last quiet days.

A thought hit her then, so hard that she stood up straight—her mind had been so filled with Ryan and their two shared adventures she hadn't given Trey a fair chance. Trey was a good man with a bright future, a future he was trying to include her in yet she kept pushing him away. She shook her head forcefully. Well, no more. It was time to take with both hands what God had handed her on a silver platter. Everything she wanted was within striking distance and it was time to seize the day.

She smiled genuinely at her reflection in the vanity mirror as she freshened up. She had much to smile about. The time had come to put pettiness to the side. She had been too busy looking at Ryan's qualities to invest completely in Trey, acting as though Ryan was one of her romantic conquests. Trey had the big picture in mind; Ryan was living moment by moment. Trey's long-term plan was secure; Ryan didn't know where his next meal was coming from.

Walking purposefully from the room, Amber decided she would still meet with Ryan tomorrow at the bank, as planned. They would speak to Mr. Cole, and Amber would politely ask if Ryan had found out anything about Joe Schneider. Both the leads would be dead ends and that would be, as they say, that. She would make herself available for consultation on Ryan's little school project, but on the whole, Amber's time and attention would be on Trey. She would learn all his likes and dislikes, how he preferred his eggs in the morning, even ask to hear his testimony and how he came to know Christ as his Savior. And one day soon, she would be the wife of the future mayor of Waterford Cove, Virginia.

Yes, Amber thought as she descended the stairs and headed toward the library where she could hear Trey speaking with his father, it's high time to win the heart of the man God intends to be my future husband.

♦♦♦

July 5, 1878
Yesterday was a day I'll never forget, for more reasons than one. Most importantly, I got to hold my son in my arms. Little Ryan is as hale and handsome as I could have dared hope for. Black hair, dark eyes that might be blue someday. But hopefully he'll take after me so every time I look at him, I don't see William. I don't think my heart could take it.

Placing a bookmark in the diary, Ryan set it beside him on the bed. A deep breath kept the tears at bay as he lay looking at the ceiling. Truth be told, it wasn't the first time he'd read those words his mother had written. Once he realized the journals were dated, he had flipped directly to her last entry, written only a week before she left. When that revealed no significant clues to her departure, he tried to find solid answers for his mother's desertion by looking for what she'd written around the time he was conceived or born. And he had found his answer. Ryan looked like his father. Always had, unfortunately. Tall, broad-shouldered, a commanding jaw line, and instant smile. Like she'd said, dark hair and yes, his eyes turned out to be the same light blue as William's. No wonder she had left. She couldn't stand the sight of her own son.

Even with the shameful truth in hand, Ryan continued to make his way through the other missives from his mother. They were words not meant for his eyes, yet he devoured them. With each page, this woman whom Father had refused to speak of was becoming less of an enigma. It seemed she had a love for music and art. Her pregnancy had been a difficult one, hence her relief when Ryan was born healthy. She had married William after a short courtship and lamented her haste time and again. Like a moth to a flame, Ryan picked up the journal again.

I could have saved myself much heartache by simply expecting to be alone on such an important occasion as the birth of my first child. Only my personal maid was there to comfort me in my distress and help celebrate the arrival of my son. William left sometime before supper the day before yesterday and didn't return until past three this morning. He took the room next to mine and has yet to wake. Even now as the sun begins to rise, he doesn't know his son has come into the world. If Mother were still alive, she'd tell me it would have been better for Ryan and me if William had never returned.

I won't argue with that. He rolled onto his side and grabbed the Bible Christian had lent him. Ryan's promise to his friend had been taunting him for days, but it had been easier to peer into his mother's past than to deal with what he might find within the pages of the Word of God.

Never before had the Pierce residence housed such a manuscript. The best works of noteworthy authors such as Emerson and Thoreau had once occupied the library shelves alongside as many scientific journals as Ryan could get his hands on. Even though most had been sold long ago, they were some of the compelling impetuses on which Pierce family decisions were made. Books that fueled the fire of self-reliance and gave knowledge to ensure success in the best of cons.

The calfskin leather felt supple in his hand and he brought it to his nose. He breathed deep of the warm earthy smell and thought of what Christian had said. Water to a thirsty man.

If there ever was someone who qualified for that description—Ryan let the thought trail off. After a moment of familiarizing himself with the layout, he flipped to what was called the book of John. Evidently, the Bible was made up of many separate books all compiled into one volume.

The preconceived ideas Ryan had about what he would find written there flew out the window as the words poured over his soul like a freshwater stream. Deep and clear, they revealed Jesus Christ as both the Son of God and son of man. Jesus was called the Lamb of God who takes away the sin of the world, yet at the same time, He overturned the money tables in the temple and wasn't afraid to speak what was true. It was astonishing that even though Jesus knew the secret thoughts of each person, He still extended the same offer to everyone—all people were invited to become children of God. Most shocking of all, it seemed belief was the only prerequisite to receiving eternal life.

Did God see what was in his heart right now like He saw the true motives of the Pharisees? If the words of John were true, then both Ryan's pain as well as his shortcomings and failures were plain as day. He wasn't too certain he wanted to be known that well. Christian said he had tried to hide from God for years, yet God pursued him, a thought that left Ryan feeling both comforted and uncomfortable. It didn't sound so great to be chased down until he was caught. He'd worked too hard to be removed from William's clutches to get into Someone else's so quickly.

Stacking the journal and the Bible on the bedside table, Ryan turned down the lamp and closed his eyes, conjuring a picture of Amber's face in his mind. He fell asleep quickly and dreamed of being so close to the angel that all her virtue and goodness became his own. He woke with a smile on his face, knowing she was everything he'd ever need.

◆◆◆

Last night had gone better than Amber had expected. Trey's wrath took flight when Amber gave him her undivided attention and made it a point to either hold his hand or his gaze throughout the evening. As the night wore on and a lively game of old maid ensued between them, Trey's frustration seemed to evaporate all together. More of the same was all that was necessary in order to protect her destiny.

Amber sighed happily as she sat down on the Wright's porch swing and sipped her after-breakfast coffee. Trey had promised to meet her in a few minutes after he had a short meeting with his father. She couldn't wait to continue the happy feeling that had begun when she'd made the decision to step all the way into this new relationship. Keeping her eye on the front door, it was all she could do not to go looking for Trey, to let him know how she desired to be his and his alone.

A movement at the end of the long curving drive broke into her happy thoughts. A young man on a fast-approaching horse cantered up to the porch.

Amber stood and set her coffee on the railing. "May I help you?" She felt proud to be there, greeting visitors, almost the lady of the house.

The man removed his hat and stroked his horse's neck. "Looking for a Miss Amber. I've a message to deliver." He patted his coat pocket.

Her poise faltering slightly, Amber walked down the steps. "I'm Amber," she answered, looking up into his honest face.

"Here," he said, handing her a white envelope. "From Mrs. Buchanan, if you please."

Amber took the letter and checked to ensure the front door was still closed. It wouldn't do for Trey to catch wind of this. "Thank you, sir. Please give my regards to the Buchanans." With a tip of his head and his hat back in place, he turned his horse and proceeded back down the lane.

Setting the porch swing in motion once more, Amber wished she could calm her heart into such an easy-going rhythm. "How in the world did she find me?" As Amber turned the letter over in her hands, she remembered. Right after the reverend's wife had asked her that dubious question about Jesus being Lord or servant, Amber had spoken of where she was staying in Waterford Cove.

But that wasn't the most compelling query at the moment. What was inside the envelope demanded to be revealed. Dare she open it there? Trey would most certainly interrogate her if he saw, perhaps even take it away. He had made it clear he didn't approve of extracurricular pursuits that took her away from him.

Maybe just a peek. The words were written with a hand that shook as much as Mrs. Buchanan's voice, but the message was clear: return to Oakwood Hills. A conversation awaited; Reverend Buchanan had information Amber was looking for.

The timing couldn't be more fortuitous. In a few hours, Ryan would be waiting at the bank for her and she could share with him this latest development. Yet after yesterday's renewed commitment to be single-minded, it seemed unwise to delve back into what had originally stolen her attention from Trey in the first place.

She sighed again, this time out of resignation rather than joy. Before she could be found out, Amber folded the letter and stuffed it into her pocket. At the eleventh hour, too.

"Hello, gorgeous," Trey said, joining her on the swing. "I wanted to ask you something at breakfast but I can't stand nosy sisters. May I accompany you to the King's Castle this morning?"

This was a surprise. Amber struggled to keep her face passive. "Why the change of heart?" she couldn't help asking. Trey had all but forbidden her from working there, and she knew she was on thin ice when she mentioned at breakfast she wanted to pay the children a visit. Maybe her affections over the last day had helped to change his heart. Perhaps he would even apologize for hauling her away in front of her friends.

The soft look in Trey's eye was all the explanation Amber needed. Still, he said, "I want to be in every part of your life. No secrets between us." He squeezed her hand and kissed her cheek, pulling back with a smile.

"What about your classes? I don't want you to miss them on account of me."

Trey shot her a sideways glance. "Oh, hadn't you heard? No, I guess you wouldn't have any way of knowing since you don't set foot on campus anymore. Starting today, it's WCU's spring break until the big race next Sunday."

Amber felt her nose rubbed in her past but only just a bit. Plus, she told herself, that certainly wasn't what Trey had intended. He was simply giving her facts she was not aware of. How kind of him. "Well, in that case, it would be lovely to have you along. Why don't we head over right now?" Amber was anxious to do what Trey just said—share every part of their lives together.

"Sounds good to me, my darling. Let's take the carriage."

They walked to the barns and while Trey arranged transportation, Amber smiled to herself. *My darling.* As in precious and dear. That was the first time he had used the words. A good sign. A sign of things to come.

Her face turned sour though as she thrust away the next thought, one as unwelcome as memories of sleeping in a cold church basement. Her mind was trying to plant a seed of doubt she refused to water; a hint of misgiving she had to work to ignore. As she kicked at a tuft of hay near the barn door, Amber remembered what Trey had said the other night at the Wilson's party. Orphans were dirty little urchins that needed to be cleaned up off the streets of Waterford Cove. It was a difficult truth to look in the face. Trey was lying. He didn't want to spend time with the kids. He wanted his eyes on Amber to keep her under his thumb.

After a silent few minutes in the carriage, Justine Cole greeted them at the wide double doors and ushered them inside. "So nice of you to come by. The older children are upstairs doing their schoolwork and the young ones are out back in the garden for some fresh air." Justine's curly chestnut hair bounced as she nodded to them. "If you'll excuse me, I'll be heading back to my work. Make yourselves at home, you two."

"Stay right here," Amber told Trey as Justine sashayed down the hall. "There's someone I'd like you to meet." This would be the first of two tests. Amber came back a few minutes later with little Birdie in her arms.

"Would you like to hold her?" Amber didn't wait for a response.

"Whoa, whoa. Not so fast." Instead of looking down into the cherub face of the newest addition to the King's Castle family, Trey handed the baby directly back to Amber. He brushed off his sleeves and the front of his shirt as if the baby had left some sort of filth behind.

A definite fail. What would he do with their own children someday? Leave the childrearing up to her? Inside, Amber fumed, but she bounced the infant until Birdie's eyelids drooped closed once again. "Why don't I take you through the rooms? You can see where I spent most of my growing up years."

The second test. His mouth looked like he had recently sucked a lemon as he said, "Sure. No problem. Lead the way."

But she could tell it was a problem. Trey's reaction as she showed him her old room and introduced him to the older children clearly showed he didn't want to be there. Her hunch had proved true. He had no intention of sharing this experience together. He simply didn't trust her enough to let her out of his sight.

For now, she would use his discomfort to her advantage. Tonight, she'd go back to winning his heart. "Trey, the kids are going to need to eat lunch in a little bit. Why don't we go help Grandma E in the kitchen? You can peel and cut the potatoes if she hasn't already. Or maybe you could play with the little ones outside while I help in the kitchen?"

Trey tugged at his ear. "Er, ah, I think we should be heading back home, don't you?"

"Oh, do we have to? I'd like to spend at least an hour or two here. If you stayed, you could really get to know the children. We're just getting started."

"*You're* just getting started. I need to head back. Why don't I pick you up later on today?"

He'd fallen right into her trap. "Well, go if you must. But I can find my own way back. I'll just take the baby to Summer, then head to the kitchen."

"Suit yourself, Red."

She had never seen Trey look so relieved or move so fast. He gave her a quick kiss on the cheek and made a beeline for the front door. Perfect. Now she could meet Ryan at the bank without prying eyes. Amber pushed open the door that led to the garden and saw Justine sitting on the grass with the children circled around her as she read from *Mother Goose in Prose*. Summer sat on the fringes with a curly-haired toddler on her lap.

"Mind if I give you Birdie back?" Amber asked her friend quietly so as to not disturb the story. "I'm going to help in the kitchen for a bit then head out."

Summer directed her charge to join the others on the grass and took the baby. "Hello, little Biddy. Are you just waking up from your nap?"

Amber's heart did a peculiar sideways lurch. "Did you just say Biddy? I thought her name was Birdie."

"Bridget just seemed too grown up for such a wee one and between Justine and me, we couldn't decide on which would make a better nickname. I'm partial to Biddy, myself."

Birdie. Biddy. Both pet names for Bridget. "You know, on second thought, I don't think I can help in the kitchen today." Amber bent to give her bewildered friend a quick hug and waved to Justine. It was time to head to Ryan's and then it was on to Oakwood Hills.

◆◆◆

"Bridget MacDonald sent the letter to Christian. She's the one who told him of Tabitha's death."

Ryan looked down at Amber, standing at his front door, all breathless and rosy.

"Bridget is Biddy. Biddy is Bridget," she went on. "And I've received a letter." She pulled something from her skirt pocket. "I know we weren't supposed to meet until later but I couldn't wait any longer. Here," she said, starting to hand it to him. Then she folded it and put it back in her pocket. "No, there's no time for that. We have to go to the bank to find out what James Cole knows. Then we have to go to Oakwood Hills. Reverend Buchanan has information about Tabitha. Come on!" Amber pulled on his hand.

Ryan laughed out loud. He'd never heard Amber talk this fast or seen this side of her passion. It fueled his own for her exponentially. "Hang on a second, Little Bumble Bee." Now he could see why the name fit her so well. "I'll just grab my things and we can take the carriage."

"No. I've got a little money. Let's take the train."

Grabbing his coat, Ryan shut the door behind him. "You sure?"

"I've got just enough. I can feel it, Ryan." She smiled up at him, her blue eyes beaming rays of light that shot straight to the dark places of his heart. She took one skip ahead on the walkway leading to the street and spun around. "I can feel it. We're just about to crack this case wide open."

"What are we waiting for then?" he teased. "Come on!" They walked quickly to Waterford Cove Holdings, each with speculations on what James had come up with in the last week. His answer didn't disappoint.

"You'd be amazed," James said after Ryan had shaken the bank owner's hand and they had seated themselves in his office, "as to how accurate you were, Amber. The Pinkertons should hire you." He chuckled and pushed a piece of paper across his desk. "A Mr. Stanley Petty came on as a janitor about three months before the robbery. Quit about five months later. Smells pretty suspicious, don't you think?"

Ryan rubbed his chin and sat back in his chair. "An inside man. Makes sense."

"There are only two people who still work here that were employed when the robbery happened. I asked both of them about Petty. They each said he was a heavyset man who kept to himself. Neither could remember much else."

"Is there any speculation of how could he have accessed the safe? A key, perhaps?" Amber said.

Even before she had finished speaking, James was shaking his head. "No. No key. A combination lock had been installed earlier that year. I was the only one who knew the numbers. I never wrote it down or told a soul." James tapped the side of his head. "Kept it in here, even though it was often inconvenient to be the only one with access. But I was determined to make good on my promise to my customers. Keeping their money safe and helping them to grow interest was my utmost goal. A lot of good that did."

Amber gave James a sympathetic look. Ryan wanted to do the same, but his mind couldn't get past how the thieves had done it. "I see an old address for Petty. Do you mind if I take this and show it to Christian? Have him follow up on it?"

"Not at all. Take it with you, but promise me you'll let me know if this leads anywhere."

"You can be sure of that, Mr. Cole. We'll be in touch again soon."

Walking out of the bank next to Amber made Ryan feel like they were a couple. She was so lit up inside today, so on fire to find the truth. "What else are you this passionate about, Little Bumble Bee?" Ryan teased as they stood outside in the sunshine. She ducked her head self-consciously, but Ryan wasn't sure if it was from the use of the name or her obvious zest for this case.

"Truth be told, I had all but given up on this." Amber turned solemn for the first time that day. "I haven't been a very good friend to Trey, and I was going to tell you today that I couldn't spend time with you anymore on our projects. He's not been very happy with me lately. Doesn't want me to taint his reputation in any way."

"I see." Ryan made a split-second decision to tell Amber how he felt about her, right then and there. She was about to cut him loose, and Trey would garner the win. He already had. It was time. "Amber, I—" His words were cut short by the blow of a train's whistle, and Ryan let the matter remain unspoken. Maybe it was for the best. He couldn't very well start a serious relationship while he was in the middle of a long con. *Soon, though, my sweet girl. I will tell you everything when this is all over.*

"Why don't we go see Christian and tell him about these new developments. It shouldn't take too long," he suggested. "I have a feeling he'll get further with this lead than we will."

"Yes, let's." Then she surprised Ryan by picking up on his first question. "Well, first and always, I'm passionate about my relationship with God. Hopefully more than I am about anything else."

"I can see that," said Ryan as they strolled in tandem. "You're compassionate and thoughtful, always looking to do the right thing. I admire that in you."

"I hope you're right. When I last saw Mrs. Buchanan, she asked me if God was my King or my servant. I admit sometimes I do act as though He's the latter, expecting God to answer my every whim rather than let Him be Lord over my life and ask Him to lead me."

"I'm not so sure I want to have a king ruling over me." Ryan felt like he could be honest with Amber.

"But it's not like that at all," she countered. "It's my honor to serve God with my life. He's my Creator and my Savior. I owe Him every-thing." She looked down as she said, "And I know how things turn out when I try to make them go the way I think they should. Been there too many times to count."

"But you're so good at everything you do. I can't see God being dis-appointed in anything you've done."

Amber turned her head and caught his eye. "You're wrong, Ryan. I was born a sinner, just like everyone else. We all need a Savior. Someone who never sinned, someone to die in our place so we could have eternal life."

"It's still a mystery to me, but I think I'm finally starting to see things a little more clearly. Thanks for helping me understand even this. See, you're always trying to make things better for everyone else. And that in-cludes all you've done to help on my senior project. You made it possible."

"Kind of like a worker bee who brings pollen back to the hive so it can be turned into something useful." Amber shrugged and fiddled with her necklace. "That's me, I guess. I like being a piece of the bigger picture. Hopefully that's helpful to someone in some small way." She kicked at a stone and sent it scurrying. "Helping makes me feel like I'm part of something since I don't have any family of my own. Probably doesn't make any sense to anyone but me."

"No, I actually understand perfectly. I think that's why I'm such a big dreamer. I want to make an impact, a difference. See new inventions take off, knowing I was part of the process." Ryan smiled at her. "We're more alike than you know. Amber Graham, I get you." He took her hand and held it tight. It was beginning to feel at home there. She didn't pull away and instead set their hands swinging gently between them.

"We've got some news for you," Ryan told Christian when he'd opened the door to them.

"Come on in then. Can't wait to hear it."

After they were settled at the kitchen table, Amber began. "Remember how you were sure Tabitha traveled to America with Bridget MacDonald?"

"Yeah, that's why she was so sad when she died," Christian replied unexpectedly.

Wait a minute. Something wasn't quite right. "We just made the connection today that Biddy, the name of the person who signed the letter, is a nickname for Bridget. We think Bridget MacDonald sent the letter. It was dated 1879," Ryan said. "But her headstone said she died in 1885. So unless there were two Bridget MacDonald's, I'm sorry to say, but I think your wife was lying to you."

"It wouldn't be the first time, let me tell you."

The news of his deceased wife's deceit seemed to be hitting Christian very mildly. Or perhaps he was the kind to bottle things up and one day when his family was least expecting it, he would unleash his emotions. For the moment, Christian was stalwart, unwavering. If possible, his face even looked at peace.

"So, what do you know about Bridget?"

"Not much that I can recall. Tabitha didn't like to talk about her past. What was the last name of the Tabitha who traveled with Bridget MacDonald?"

"Grantham. Does that ring any bells?"

"Nope. Not a one."

"You said Tabitha told you Bridget had died. When did she tell you that exactly?" Amber asked.

"Let me think. It was actually one of the last conversations Tabitha and I had before she ran off. I remember her sitting on the bed with her head in her hands, her hair all around her shoulders. She had beautiful red hair like yours, Amber. When I asked her what was wrong, she looked up and told me her friend had died and she needed to go to the funeral in Waterford Cove. We lived in Richmond, about ninety miles away. She left on the morning train and returned a couple of days later."

"If Bridget was still alive, then it seems to me she had another reason for leaving," said Amber. "Do you happen to remember when that was?"

"Sometime midsummer of '78," Christian said.

If what Christian said was true, and Tabitha had traveled to Waterford Cove, that would put her there around the time of the robbery.

Ryan looked at Amber meaningfully. This may not turn into such a bad week after all. He'd have all kinds of reasons to keep Amber near and there'd be news to tell Joe on Sunday.

"We can't stay long today," said Amber, "but there's one more thing we found out." She made quick work of telling him about Stanley Petty, his physical description plus his last known address.

After they took their leave Ryan said, "Here's what I think we should do, if you're game." He put on his bravest face. "You need to get back to the Wrights', so why don't I go talk to the Buchanans and get what information they have for us."

Amber looked hesitant. "But the race is in nine days. You need to get ready."

"It'll be okay. I can make up for lost time tomorrow. This way Trey won't be upset."

"You'd do that for me?" He nodded and Amber reached into her clutch. "Then at least take this for the train."

He closed his hand over hers as she handed him some change and he stood looking into her eyes. Love without counting the cost. Yes, it felt good. He should try it more often. His sacrifice would save Amber from Trey's wrath even if it meant giving up an afternoon with this special girl. "Let's meet again on Monday at the bank. Same time." *I'll be counting every minute until then, my love.*

SIXTEEN

Ryan sat in the Buchanan's front room and wished Amber was next to him. She'd be holding her necklace and glancing nervously at him, and he'd smile reassuringly at her and nod, telling her without words that everything was going to be all right. Somehow. Somehow, he would get her away from Trey or come to a place in his heart when he could release her to the care of the Wrights. Somehow, he'd earn the money to stay in school. Somehow, this conversation with the reverend would bring about the answers they sought. Somehow, God would allow him to remain friends with Amber, even if she and Trey got married.

He took a deep breath. "Reverend and Mrs. Buchanan, Amber received your letter this morning. The Pinkerton agent who originally held this case has allowed me to consult on it. I hope you don't mind."

"Not at all, not at all," answered the older woman shakily. "Welcome to Oakwood Hills, my boy. Have you been here before?"

"Yes, with Amber," Ryan answered quietly. He didn't want to admit he'd also followed her there.

"My husband is hard of hearing, mind you, so speak loudly, if you will."

"Reverend, you said you remember a Tabitha from about twenty years ago?" Ryan said with more volume than normal. "A Tabitha Murray? Or perhaps Tabitha Grantham?" He wasn't sure which name a woman who was hiding from a Pinkerton husband would go by. Perhaps she had used another alias altogether. Amber's excitement from

217

this morning was rubbing off on him. This was it. He could feel in his bones something out of the distant past was about to be brought out for everyone to see.

The reverend nodded his head enthusiastically. "Not Murray. Graham. Tabitha Graham. When my missus here told me the timeframe of the woman's death, I knew it had to be the same person."

"That's right," put in Mrs. Buchanan. "As soon as my dear husband said her last name, I remembered her. Red haired little thing," she said, waving her hand in Ryan's direction. "Like your sweet gal Amber."

"Did you say, Graham, sir?" Ryan said. "We're looking for someone with the last name Grantham."

"Anthem? No, never did know anyone by that name. But I can tell you Tabitha Graham's funeral was one I didn't well enjoy performing." Reverend Buchanan shook his gray head. "Sad day, that was. Only one person besides me at the gravesite. I sent the letter because I figured if your Amber was related to the woman, I wanted her to know she was buried in peace."

Graham. How unusual. Maybe they had the wrong Tabitha after all and the MacDonald piece was purely coincidental. "We didn't see a headstone in the church yard."

Reverend Buchanan leaned in and on hearing Ryan's statement a second time, said, "That's because she was buried on her own property. By an old shack, just north of town."

♦♦♦

Everything was going to be all right. Somehow. Somehow, Trey would understand her heart and let her into his. Somehow, Ryan's conversation with the reverend would be productive. Somehow, God would allow her to remain friends with Ryan, even after she and Trey got married.

"Why have you been gone so long? I thought you were only going to stay an hour or two at the orphanage."

Amber cringed at the sound of Trey's voice behind her on the sidewalk. He grabbed her by the arm and halted her progress before she had a chance to turn around.

"I asked you a question. I expect an answer." Trey was toe to toe with her, fiery eyes glaring down into hers.

"Let go, Trey." Amber wrenched her arm from his grip and continued walking toward home. And that's what it was. Home. No matter Trey's unpredictable moods, it was where she belonged. She would show Trey Wright he didn't need to check up on her. She was not being rebellious toward him in any sense of the word.

Trey caught up with her quick steps and put his arm around her, steering her across the street to where the family's driver sat waiting. "I won't ask again." He squeezed her shoulders. Hard.

Might as well answer the man. He wasn't about to let it drop. "I had something I wanted to talk to Christian about." There. That ought to appease him. She was wrong.

"I saw someone walking away from you as I was getting out of the carriage," he said as she settled onto the leather seat. "Who were you talking to?"

From the time she was born, she hadn't been anyone's property. Had watched out for herself and answered to no one. Even Mrs. MacDonald had taken a lackadaisical approach to her care. She'd spent countless hours in the woods behind their little house, and when she'd come in for dinner, her caretaker never once asked where she'd been all day. Then it was in and out of various places, sleeping behind buildings and finally on to the King's Castle, where, from the first day, she took the role of big sister to so many. Christian and Summer's close watchfulness had been the one exception in her life, and that she welcomed. This made her recoil.

"I don't need to tell you everything, Trey. It's not like we're engaged or promised to one another." Amber felt ashamed the moment the words were out of her mouth. The Wright family was prepared to give her the one thing she wanted and she was pushing it away. Again.

Before she could amend her statement, Trey spoke, in a softer tone this time. "No. You're right. I haven't made anything official." He removed his arm from her shoulders and looked out the window. "Sorry I overreacted. Forgive me?" Who could resist that sheepish face?

Amber reached over and took his hand in hers. She needed to let him know how sorry she was for hiding the fact she'd been meeting with Ryan. No, she couldn't apologize for that. Not just yet. She and Ryan were so close to finding out the truth. But she could show Trey her affection.

Leaning over to give his cheek a kiss she said, "You're forgiven. Truce?" She smiled to seal the deal.

"That's my girl. Give me some more of those kisses and we'll be well on our way." Trey turned to grin at her impishly. "But I am going to ask you to stay home this week. Just through next Sunday." The air suddenly felt like it was a fifty-pound weight on her chest. Trey went on as though his request was the most natural thing in the world. "This is a big week for me and I don't want anything to ruin it. I plan to win that race next Sunday. I need to bring Benz and Daimler into the equation to make my plan work."

Ah, yes. His plan of cleaning Waterford Cove of its street trash. "The factory. I remember. I'm sure getting the interview with them would help your cause."

"I knew I could count on you to stand by me." The horses drew up to the Wright's front steps and Amber and Trey alighted. Trey took both of Amber's hands in his. "Promise me you'll idle around here for a few days, just until the race is over. Spend time in the kitchen. Read a book. Put your feet up and start to see what your life could be like. Let the servants run to the bank for you or whatever else you would normally deem as your responsibility." Trey leaned down and brushed his lips across hers. "Practice being the lady of the house. It just might be your position to take one day." He twinkled his eyes down at hers. "And the sooner the better, as far as I'm concerned."

Amber smiled up at him, imagining what he would look like after they'd been married twenty years. He would be dashing with grey at his temples and smile lines around his eyes. Her smile widened when she realized it would be their children's antics that would help put both of those attractive features there over time.

And she would be the perfect helpmate, cheering him on in whatever endeavor he undertook. Starting with this one. "Of course, Trey. I'll stay right here." It was only for a little over a week. She'd learn sooner or later what Ryan had found out in Oakwood Hills. Plus, she was certain that between now and next Sunday, she could convince Trey to let her attend the race. She couldn't miss the chance to see how the runabout would perform with its modifications.

The sooner the better. The words rang like wedding bells in her head as she and Trey climbed the steps and entered this home she had grown to love so much. Winnie and Yvette were busy getting the puppies ready to take out back for a romp in the yard. Grandmother and Sheila had the Easter brunch menu laid out before them on the game table, heads bent over their work. Millie came into the foyer and gave Amber a quick hug, telling her she had something to show her later that afternoon. All of the friendly hubbub gave Amber a well-rounded contented feeling, as if nothing could ever go wrong again.

◆◆◆

Ryan was going to have to fudge the truth. Again. Share as little information with Joe as possible. Tell him he was close but not give any specific details. Even tell a lie or two to indulge Joe's hunger for the win.

Ryan raised his hand to knock on the Schneider's back door. He'd be repeating the motion only a few more times. The assignment was almost over. He was grateful Friday had overwhelmed Amber to the point that she forgot to ask about Joe. Grateful, yet a knot of dread was forming in his stomach. He didn't want to lie to Amber or even withhold information. He wanted them to share everything. But not yet.

He rocked back on his heels, hands in his pockets while he waited. A full minute passed before he tried again. Maybe the man was asleep. He went to the window near the back door and banged with enough force to wake the neighbors. Nothing.

Ryan walked around to the front of the house and cupped his hands to the only window. Even though Joe and his wife lived in squalor, it was easy to see that the mess before his eyes wasn't normal. The place had been ransacked.

The front door stood slightly ajar and Ryan pushed it open with a squeak. He gingerly picked his way past overturned tables and chairs at the front of the house. "Joe? You here?" Ryan said loudly. "Joe?"

A short hallway to his left revealed two closed doors. Ryan recalled his father's threat on Joe's life and a wiggle of fear ran up his spine and prickled over his scalp. He carefully turned the knob to the farthest room. "Joe?" Nothing. Nothing except more overturned furniture and an empty bureau.

One more. Ryan cringed to think what might be lying behind the final door. He pushed it open with his foot to reveal a small office. Newspaper clippings had been torn into pieces and lay haphazardly on the floor. But no Joe. Ryan breathed a sigh of relief. One of the article's headlines caught his eye. *York Mansion.* That's where he and his father lived. The clipping had been torn in two and Ryan took a moment to find its mate. *Pierce Purchases York Mansion on Fifth Street.* Joe had been keeping up with his old partner. In a few minutes, Ryan had some of the other scraps pieced back together.

Jewelry Missing from Mayor's Home. Fraudulent Scammer on the Loose. Lone Thief Takes All.

He didn't need to see anymore. Ryan shut the front door behind him and was grateful the neighborhoods he passed through were quiet on this Sunday morning. William. This was his father's doing even if he had no way of proving it. Ryan should go to the police. But how would he explain his presence at the Schneider's this morning? Jelly Joe wasn't exactly a seemly sort of character. According to William, his old partner hadn't kept his nose perfectly clean throughout the years. If he went to the authorities, the ransacking may very well be pinned on him. Perhaps that's what his father intended all along.

Up ahead, the church's belfry stood quiet, a pinnacle pointing straight to heaven, a place that was looking more and more appealing than this earth. Ryan breathed deep of the fresh air. It cleared his head enough to know one thing: he needed to be inside that church.

Quiet as his heavy feet would let him, he slipped inside and took the back pew. The neat little line he had drawn in his heart had just been blurred irreversibly. No longer could he pretend his duties for his father didn't affect his heart. Joe and his wife were dead. Somehow, Ryan knew. Father had made good on his threat. Even if he was wrong, this was the final push off the edge of the cliff he had been walking for so long. He was falling headlong into a bottomless pit. Drowning, smothering. He needed to breathe. *I have set before you life and death, blessing and cursing: therefore choose life.* His heart told him this was the place to do it.

Life and death. Ryan remembered what he'd read in the book of John. Men loved darkness rather than light, because their deeds were evil. *That's my father. He's loved evil, not good, all his days. I'm glad I'm not like that.*

"If you'll open to James chapter 1," intoned the pastor. "It's not exactly a traditional Palm Sunday passage, but bear with me." He stood at a high desk of sorts, looking joyous and solemn at the same time. James. That sounded familiar. *Must be the other part of the Bible Christian asked me to read.*

"Verses thirteen, fourteen, and fifteen have been on my heart all week as we lead up to Easter Sunday, a day when we celebrate Christ's sacrifice on the cross and His resurrection that ensures our eternal life," said the pastor. "We all deal with sin, even me. It's inescapable, but that's not an excuse to revel in it. In fact, God sets out a pattern for us in this chapter, a sequence if you will, of how sin progresses if we do not turn away from it and choose God's ways. Listen as I read.

"'Let no man say when he is tempted, I am tempted of God: for God cannot be tempted with evil, neither tempteth he any man: But every man is tempted, when he is drawn away of his own lust, and enticed. Then when lust hath conceived, it bringeth forth sin: and sin, when it is finished, bringeth forth death.'"

It certainly does.

But there was something else to be unearthed in these words. The pastor continued, but Ryan's mind was reviewing what the passage had said. Ryan had lust. The lust, the desire to do just a little bit of wrong. How many times had he justified the means to redeem the result?

The truth was, he had lied. Those lies had led to thievery. Ryan Pierce was a liar and a thief. And it wasn't William's fault. Ryan had done it to himself. He needed to take responsibility for his actions. He could have said no to his father. He could have stood up for what was right. Just like Amber had said, everyone was a sinner. Ryan was a sinner. He wondered why he'd never seen himself for what he really was before now.

The scariest part of this realization wasn't that God could see his sins; somehow, Ryan was all right with that. He needed God to know everything. The most troubling thought was the slippery slope he was on. A slope that ended in the same miry pit of evil William was in. It wasn't his father's sin that had pushed Ryan off the ledge, it was his own and it would lead to more death. And not just physical death. Ryan could see he had been walking around dead his entire life. Dead in his heart and he knew it. More words from John came back to him as the other congregants turned in their Bibles to another passage.

I am the light of the world: he that follows Me shall not walk in darkness but have the light of life. *Yes, Lord, save me. Save me from this path I'm on. I want to follow You.* A hot tear slipped down his check as the pastor began to wrap up his sermon, speaking about the life-giving blood of Jesus that cleanses from all sin. *Give me life, Lord. Let me walk in Your light.*

A sweet and unfamiliar feeling settled his heart into a rhythm of perfect peace. His head still down, he pictured the cross hanging behind the pastor. He now knew why so many gravestones held that special symbol. It was the only way to eternal life, the only hope for this life and the life to come. And now it was his. Nothing and no one could take it away, not a lack of money or the absence of an education, not even his father. *It doesn't matter that my mother and father rejected me. I'm God's boy now. You are my Lord.*

Ryan brushed his cheek and looked up, his eyes coming into focus for the first time in several minutes. Ahead and to the right, he caught sight of slim shoulders and fire red hair. Amber. His heart was too jumbled to fake a smile if she caught him after the service. In fact, the thought of faking anything ever again turned his stomach sour. He didn't know what he was going to do about his father, but he knew things would look different from here on forward.

I can be a con man or a man of God, but I can't be both. Lord, help me.

◆ ◆ ◆

"Father? Are you in here?" If Ryan thought he felt trepidation when he entered the church, this was hundred-fold. He knew nothing about following God. Had no inkling of what it looked like to serve Christ as King, but he knew it had to start now, in this room with William.

"Come on in, Ryan." William motioned for him to sit down. "How did it go with Joe this morning?"

Wow. No wonder Ryan had been so successful over the years. He'd learned from the best. If his father had committed a heinous crime, he wasn't giving anything away in either his tone or demeanor. He looked perfectly relaxed.

How did it go with Joe? What a question to answer. Well, one thing he knew to do: speak the truth. "I wasn't able to talk with him."

"Oh? That's too bad. Well, just as well. He's getting to be just a middle man in this whole thing anyway." William cocked an ankle on a knee. "You can just tell me what you were going to tell him. Come on, don't be shy." William grinned.

"Well, I've confirmed that Tabitha lived in Oakwood Hills but that's about all. Died in 1879. Kind of a dead end."

"Is that a fact?" William's disposition was way too casual. By now he'd normally have thrown something, at very least a temper tantrum.

"Yes, sir."

"Nothing else to go on, then? No other leads?"

This couldn't be happening. He expected it would be several days before he'd be tested in his brand-new faith. *Lord, help.*

It hit Ryan in that moment that God had set before William life and death as well. He had the same freedom to choose that Ryan did. William wasn't worse than Ryan; they were both born into sin, just like Amber had said. Jesus had told Nicodemus that whoever believed in Him would have eternal life. Whoever. That included him. That included William. It wasn't too late for him. It wasn't too late for anyone.

"Father, something happened to me today that I'd like to talk to you about."

"If it doesn't have to do with the missing money, I don't want to hear about it." William's feet hit the floor with a thud and he stood abruptly. "If you've got nothing else to report, I'd just as soon go make myself some lunch, how about you?"

"No, thank you. I think I'll make some notes and head on out to the carriage house for the afternoon."

Ryan walked to the next room over and sat down at his desk. Thankfulness over not having to tell William about Amber or the Buchanans or suspicions over a former bank employee was soon taken over by questions of what could have happened to Joe. If Joe was out of the way, William had a straight shot to getting the money, if it still existed.

The thoughts stayed with him as he wrote a detailed account of everything he knew up to this point. The last thing he recounted was his visit with the Buchanans and the name Tabitha went by in Oakwood Hills. Graham. As in Amber Graham. It was a common enough last name. When he was finished, Ryan looked up and stared at nothing in particular for a long moment.

♦♦♦

In the short span of one week, William would have almost everything in hand. By next Sunday, Trey Wright would bring the Chariot to victory, transporting William's business to the top of the automotive game. Everyone would be clamoring to buy his piece of fabricated genius. The win would ensure the future mayor of Waterford Cove would be in his pocket, which William knew was likely to come in handy on more than one occasion. The prize money would make the next two mortgage payments and after he found his missing money, he'd be set for life.

The money. It belonged to him now that Joe was out. William didn't kid himself for a second that the grudge his old partner held down for twenty years wasn't about to pop up its ugly head. The hefty debt William now owed to his contacts in the underworld to carry out the deed was a small price to pay. He only wished he could have seen for himself the look on Joe's face when he realized his game was over.

William chuckled as he pulled back the curtains and looked out the window. He could see the edge of Ryan's shirt as he bent over that heap of a project. The runabout, or whatever Ryan had called the fool thing, didn't stand half a chance of beating the Chariot. To be on the safe side though, it might be wise to tweak something to ensure the win. No matter. That was easily accomplished.

The boy was becoming more trouble than he was worth. Hanging around Red, letting her take up time that should be spent finding William's cash. Ryan had nothing to show for all the weeks he'd squandered his time. Unless—

William dropped the curtain and raced down the hall to Ryan's study. Lately, Ryan had been leaving the top of the desk cleared of any personal effects. History told William that Ryan didn't tell him everything. It was entirely possible Ryan was hiding facts about the money to keep it for himself. A quick pick of a lock would remedy Ryan's error and put William at the tiller once again.

Sure enough, at the very bottom of the stack of papers in Ryan's top drawer was a detailed list of everything he needed to know. The buffoon. What a sorry day it was when a father realized his only offspring could be so easily buffaloed. William had spent a decade training the boy to dupe others for a living and Ryan didn't even have the wherewithal to cover his own tracks.

The chair he thought was directly behind him didn't catch his weight when he sat down hard. William swore as he picked himself up off the floor but he didn't take his eyes from Ryan's notes. What was written there was astonishing. Implausible. Yet everything fit together. He seated himself correctly this time and scooted his chair closer to the desk, settling in to review Ryan's notes one more time. Everything seemed so obvious when he saw it written out, though he thought he maybe should have seen it sooner.

The papers back in place, William walked to his own desk, his back a little straighter, his head held erect. Ryan's withholding of these monumental facts ensured a last-minute act of retribution was needed. It was time for William to not just take Ryan out of the race, but out of commission. Permanently. After he had time to formulate his plan, he'd be at Trey Wright's back door.

SEVENTEEN

I need you to do a favor for me."

Amber looked down from her open bedroom window at two figures standing on the side lawn. The top of one head she recognized immediately. Trey. Her Trey. Who was the other? From this vantage point, he looked vaguely familiar. Something in the cut of his shoulders and his stance as he stood there with arms crossed over a massive chest.

"I'm already doing you more than one and I've done everything you've asked. To the letter." Trey's voice.

"Good, but you're gonna like this one the best. Trust me." The other man lowered his voice and bent his head close to Trey's, cutting off his words to Amber's ears.

She quickly took off her shoes and padded down the servants' staircase and to the room nearest where the two men were talking. If she couldn't know what they were saying, she could catch a glimpse of this stranger Trey was consulting with.

Keeping her back against the wall between two windows of an unused music room, Amber took a gamble and peered around the window frame as inconspicuously as possible. In the half second she had a glimpse, what she saw surprised her more than anything that had happened recently. A man in his late forties stood talking with Trey, a man who looked exactly like Ryan.

Tiptoeing back to her room, Amber stood by the window to see if she could hear another snippet of their conversation. She wasn't even aware Trey and William knew each other.

"I can't do it, sir."

"You will or you won't be driving the Chariot. You have until tomorrow night. See that it's done." William's brown duster jacket flared out as he spun around and disappeared through a stand of eastern redbuds that were starting to put out their purple flowers.

Amber watched as Trey stood there for a full minute, his hand rubbing the back of his neck. Then he strode purposefully toward the carriage house. His father's new Packard was on the road before Amber could try to comprehend everything that had transpired.

What did Trey have till tomorrow night to accomplish for a man who had a serious criminal background? And if it wasn't something that needed to be kept quiet, they would have met in the front parlor or perhaps Mr. Wright's office.

But just as she had trusted Ryan even though he was related to William, she needed to be fair and give Trey the benefit of the doubt. For all she knew, he could be planning something that would be a blessing to his family and friends.

Amber left her shoes by the window and wandered back down to the music room. The entire family but Trey had gone to a Good Friday service but Amber had politely declined their repeated invitations.

Running her hand along the grand piano, Amber renewed her commitment to keep her word to Trey and not cause him any grief this week. And if that meant missing out on family events and being a no-show to her meeting with Ryan a few days ago, then so be it. Maybe if she was successful in convincing Trey to let her come to the race, she could talk with Ryan there. Explain why she hadn't come on Monday. Plus, it would be fun to catch up with him.

As she pressed a few ivory keys, a series of chords resonated in the room, ones she had heard during a special day when the King's Castle first opened. "Mendelssohn's Wedding March" from *A Midsummer Night's Dream* had been played while Christian and Summer walked down the makeshift aisle created for them in the large living room.

Amber had turned twelve by the time they got married and was thrilled to throw flower petals as the couple ran down the aisle after they had made their vows.

I wonder how long it will be until I wear white and meet my man at the altar, Amber mused as she played a few more measures from memory. A picture of Ryan wearing his best suit and smiling that broad smile popped into her mind, unbidden. Oh, Ryan. He had so much potential. So much life before him. How she cared for him. *Lord, draw Ryan to Yourself and bring him a wife of Your choosing. Give him wisdom, God, as he makes final preparations for the race. And, Lord?* Amber sighed. *Please surround him with Your love and protection. Amen.*

The last of the stanza was played *ff*, the way a bride should boldly enter life with her new husband. She couldn't wait until she and Trey were that couple.

True, she didn't know everything about the man, including the story of how he came to know Christ, but she would in time. In fact, she could start today. What better time to ask him what he believed than Good Friday. The final notes died away to reveal a motor idling out front. Amber ran to greet Trey.

"You weren't gone long," she said breathlessly.

"I didn't know you knew I'd left," he replied, jumping to the ground. A package wrapped in brown paper was under his arm.

"What do you have there?" Amber asked, pointing.

She'd never seen Trey blush before, but red trailed up his neck and he shifted the parcel to his other side. "Nothing much. By the way, how have you been enjoying your week as resident princess?" He chucked her under the chin. "I hope you're getting used to a life of luxury. Must be quite the change for you."

I'll choose to ignore that. "Very much, thank you. But I was wondering something." She hesitated. She'd bided her time all week. The race was less than forty-eight hours away. It was now or never. "I would love to be at the race on Sunday to cheer everyone on. Would you mind if I came?"

A range of emotions crisscrossed Trey's face, so many it was hard to decipher each one. Certainly there had been a bit of alarm followed by resignation. Then she could almost visibly see Trey place a final veil over all his other feelings. A look of confidence with a hint of charm settled into place. "I can't promise that just yet, but I do have a surprise up my sleeve for tomorrow night. Just you wait. You'll be so ecstatic, you won't care about seeing a handful of dusty men try to beat each other to the finish line."

"Is that a fact?" she teased back. What a fascinating man. What a lifetime of wonderment awaited her with each passing year they would have together. She imagined this was how it would always be. Forever something to look forward to. Stories to tell their grandchildren one day that they would pass on to their grandchildren.

"Tomorrow night, my darling." He sealed his promise with a soft kiss on her cheek and walked away, smiling back at her over his shoulder. Not until that evening as she and the Wright sisters lay whispering about the likelihood of an upcoming wedding did Amber realize she forgot to ask the question that had been weighing on her mind about this man who was the key to her future.

♦♦♦

"Something you said when I was here last week got me thinking," said Ryan loudly to the Buchanans. Spring break had given him plenty of time to ponder their last conversation and there was something that wouldn't leave him alone. "You told me Tabitha was buried on her own property?"

"That's right." Reverend Buchanan shook his head. "The woman was a recluse. What a shame that only one person showed up to her funeral."

"That's just it," said Ryan, perplexed. "Don't you mean to say, *their* funeral? The woman died in childbirth and as we understand it, the child perished as well."

"Oh, no," answered the reverend. "It was just the woman."

The tiny hairs on the back of Ryan's neck prickled. Even though he still had a few final tweaks to make to the runabout, it had definitely been worth his time to make the trip to Oakwood Hills this clear Saturday morning. "Can you tell me where the grave is?" Ryan asked, trying to not let his voice shake like Mrs. Buchanan's. Bridget MacDonald had lied. The baby hadn't died. Christian had a child living somewhere in this big, scary world. A child he thought he had lost.

"Don't think that would do you any good. The house, if you can call it that, is all rotten boards by now, what with the roof half blown off and woods growing up all around it. A woman and the child lived in it for a time but when I drove my buggy back there a few years ago, there wasn't much left but brambles and birds' nests, if you get my meaning. The grave marker itself was only a little wooden cross. Probably gone by now too." The reverend's face turned sympathetic. "I wish I could tell you more."

"Where is this place? Even if there's not much left, I'd like to come back with Amber if possible."

"North of town, down at the very end of Pine Lane. Coming in from Waterford Cove, turn right at the town square, and you'll run into Pine in a couple of miles. It'll be on your right. Take that all the way to the back and you'll see the house at the dead end."

If he would have had this information a week ago, he may very well have made quick tracks over there, found the money and been done with this whole thing. Everything was different now. He didn't want to go to Tabitha's grave without Christian and Amber. "You've been very helpful," Ryan said politely as he made ready to leave. "We may stop by again if we have other questions."

"Anytime," said Mrs. Buchanan. "Anytime." She stopped him at the door and laid her hand on his arm. "You take care of that girl of yours. She's a precious gift from the Lord."

♦♦♦

It was done. Lining up the runabout parallel to the other four contenders on WCU's campus green, Ryan turned the valve to cut the fuel, bringing the runabout's engine to a rest. As he hopped down and went to look over his competition, Ryan thought about the forthcoming conversation he'd be having with Christian. He'd see him at the race tomorrow but what would the man's reaction be to finding out his child was alive? *Lord, give me the right words to say.*

Sizing up the competition didn't take long. The Chariot was there, of course, but Ryan ignored Trey's entry to the race and examined the others. One car had wooden, wagon-type wheels with a flat deck and a short seat. Nothing looked particularly innovative about it, but looks could be deceiving. There was a closed-cabin, heavy-looking vehicle, as tall as it was long next to another entry that had clearly started life as a farm wagon.

"You don't stand a chance, Pierce."

Ryan looked up from examining the linkage connecting six levers to one of the engines only to find Isaac Jennings's jeering smile raining down on him. "Hello, Jennings. Thought everyone else had gone home to get a good night's sleep before the big day tomorrow."

"Nah. We're all going over to Trey's place for the big pre-party. You're not going, eh?"

Isaac's voice was just about as grating as Trey's. The two hung out together too often, it seemed. "No, I didn't know about it until now."

"Ah. Too bad. Well anyway, come take a look at my beauty. It cranks better than anything you've ever seen. Benz and Daimler are gonna go nuts over my invention."

"I doubt that," Ryan said skeptically. In fact, his win was banking on the fact that every vehicle but his needed to be hand-cranked and couldn't match the power of his two engines working in tandem. While the other boys were busy trying to start their engines, he'd be half a mile down the road, and that counted for a lot in a fifteen-mile race.

"Come see for yourself." Isaac sat behind the tiller of his project car and pulled the choke, then moved the lever to retard the timing. "You should be ready to give it a good turn."

"You want me to crank it now?"

"Yeah. Go ahead. I want to show you something. Trust me. This thing's gonna start right up."

Ryan shrugged and got into place. Getting a cold engine to turn over was always challenging and required a perfect balance of ignition timing and proper fuel mixture, not to mention a strong arm that could spin the engine fast enough to make it all come to life. Hence, his senior project and the invention that would hopefully get noticed in the industry. "All right. I'm ready."

Isaac quickly pulled the lever to fully advance the timing as Ryan used all the muscle in his right arm to rotate the crank. He knew it normally took at least a full rotation but before he had made it two-thirds of the way, the advanced spark ignited. Suddenly, the handle whirled in the opposite direction quicker than he could remove his hand. A sickening crunch was closely followed by a loud yowl from Ryan as he hit the grass.

Jennings came to his side. "You okay?"

"No," Ryan ground out. "My hand's broken."

Isaac whistled sharply through his teeth at a buggy that was passing by on the street. "Hey! Stop! Can you help us?" Ryan heard him ask the driver. "This man's hurt."

Fool, Ryan thought as an hour later, he looked at his bandaged hand. He was well aware of the dangers of a hand crank. There were numerous ways the starting process could go wrong and countless men had broken thumbs and hands and arms doing exactly what he did. And rather than learning from the stories he'd heard, he walked right into trouble.

"Take a dose of this when the pain gets too unbearable." The doctor who had set the bone was giving him last minute instructions before sending him home. "What I gave you should hold you over for a few hours." He wagged his finger at Ryan. "But you put your feet up for the next week or so. You had a bad break and I don't want you doing too much activity."

A nurse called him a cab and Ryan climbed inside a little unsteadily.

"Where can I take you to, sir?" the driver asked.

My own bed. "The old York Mansion on Fifth Street." Ryan cradled his right arm with his left and laid his head back on the seat. All he needed was some rest. In the morning he'd be fit for the Endurance Race. He had to be.

Lord, he prayed silently, let me be in that race tomorrow if it's Your will. It felt so good to be able to say that word, Lord. Jesus Christ was the Lord of his life. He had spent half of the week doing the final modifications to the runabout and the other half reading the Bible, soaking up books like Colossians and Ephesians. *Lord, thank you for making me a new creation. Thank you for putting people in my life like Mack and Christian and Amber.* He paused. *Lord, be with Amber tonight. Give her whatever she needs. Protect her.*

A strange feeling overcame him as soon as he made the request. He picked up his head and sat up straight. Rest would have to wait. "Driver, change of plans. Take me to the Wright's on Crescent Lane."

"Yes, sir."

The horses made a sharp left turn, and Ryan winced at the pain of having to steady himself on the seat. It was worth it. He had to see Amber. When she hadn't shown up at their meeting on Monday, Ryan had written it off, figuring something must have come up, and he'd spent the rest of the day with Christian, learning what it meant to live as a believer.

Wednesday, Ryan had planned to drop a note off to one of the Wright girls to give to Amber but as he approached the house, he could see Trey with Amber on the front porch swing. Yesterday, he thought of directly knocking on her front door but decided to pay the Tituses a visit instead to inquire after her. No one at the King's Castle had seen her all week.

Something wasn't right. And it was time to get to the bottom of it. Trey was throwing a party for the competitors; Ryan figured he could walk in like he owned the place, quell the rumors that he was out of the race and maybe get the chance to talk with Amber about what he'd learned from the Buchanans.

And, he thought as he ascended the wide front steps of the Wright mansion, see with my own eyes that Amber is all right.

The double doors stood wide open and the string quartet playing in the front parlor muffled his approach. With the number of guests in attendance, he would have remained inconspicuous if only he was dressed for the occasion.

A few students and professors nodded his direction as he cautiously wove his way through the crowd. His arm was bumped more than once but he ignored the pain as his eyes scanned each room for Amber. There. Standing with one hand on Trey's arm, the other on her necklace. She was nervous. Trey said something Ryan couldn't hear and the group that was crowded around them laughed. Amber only smiled.

"Ryan." It was Mack Wright. "I thought you couldn't come. You look
—" He cut himself off. "Isaac Jennings told us what happened. How
bad off are you?"

"I know what you're asking, sir, and I can't answer that just yet. I will
let you know in the morning."

"Fine by me. If I know you, you'll be there if you can. I trust you."

*Yes, you do. That's one of the things that helped me get to where I
am today.* "Thank you, Mack. That means everything to me. If you'll
excuse me?"

Ryan faltered as he walked away, but it wasn't the medicine that
made him off-kilter. This was where his plan stopped. Should he just
walk up to Amber in front of Trey and ask if there was anything wrong?
He didn't have time to finish his thought. William was approaching
Amber's group and slapping Trey on the back.

"Gonna win that race for me tomorrow, aren't you?" The confidence
with which his father carried himself tonight made him look like he
belonged there.

Trey grinned back at William. "No, sir. Gonna win that race for me.
I want that interview."

"I see how it is," William answered good-naturedly. He must have
caught sight of Ryan from the corner of his eye for he turned to him
but not before he shot Trey a murderous look. "Ryan. My boy. And
what happened to you?"

If Mack Wright had already heard about the accident, Ryan figured
William had as well. Probably everyone in attendance knew. "Evening,
all. Father. Trey." He nodded at each person in turn and let his eyes
linger on Amber's last. *Are you okay?* he tried to silently communicate.
I've missed you. He hoped she got the message.

"We heard about what happened. How are you feeling?" she asked.
She gazed at him with concern but also with a sense of detachment.

Ryan knew then he was about to lose her for good. Trey would win
both the race and the girl. *Your will be done, Lord.*

Trey piped up before Ryan could answer her question. "Must have been
quite the blow, Pierce. If you can't use your right hand, guess you're out of

the race. Too bad. But you can pull up a seat at the finish line and watch me win. And you're here just in time for another victory. Everyone!" Trey clapped his hands and led Amber to stand in the foyer in front of the open double doors. "Everyone, may I have your attention, please?"

What seemed like the entire senior class of WCU and most of the professors gathered around the couple, and Ryan had to stand on tiptoe to see Amber's face.

"Tonight is a very special night, and not simply because of my sponsor, William Pierce, and the win we plan on grabbing tomorrow." These statements were followed by soft clapping and the other drivers shaking their heads and elbowing each other. "Tonight, I secure my future in more ways than one." Ryan's stomach did a flip flop when Trey got down on one knee and pulled out a velvet-covered jewelry box. "Amber Graham, will you marry me?"

Loud cheering wasn't enough to drown out the beating of Ryan's heart that thundered in his ears as he watched Trey bend close to Amber's ear and remove her necklace. Trey put the priceless heirloom in the box and proceeded to put the ring on her finger. Amber, no! Ryan wanted to shout. Don't give up your past or your future to that man. *I love you.*

◆◆◆

It was a good trade. The old for the new. Her barren life for a family tree. Her beloved necklace for a ring that symbolized what was to come. If she could wear the necklace just one more time on her wedding day, she'd have something old, something new, and something borrowed, leaving her only to find something blue.

She glanced across the room, searching for Ryan. His blue eyes stood out from the crowd. Her heart sank when she saw a mixture of sadness and dread in them. He mouthed something that looked like the words *I love you* and held her gaze for a full five seconds before she watched him turn and walk out of the room.

Well-wishers teemed around the newly engaged couple. Amber tore her eyes from where Ryan had disappeared. She reached to finger her necklace and remembered it was no longer there. Amber sighed and put a big smile on her face. She was officially part of the Wright family. All the lonely nights had been worth it. Trey had certainly delivered on his promise.

Millie and Winnie and Yvette pushed their way through the throng and gave Amber a group hug.

"Do you think you and Trey will live at the big house with us?" Millie wanted to know.

"Oh, please say you will," put in Yvette. "Now that you'll be our real sister, I can't stand the thought of you leaving."

"Girls, girls," Sheila Wright joined the happy group. "Let her and Trey decide that. And give them half a minute to breathe."

"Congratulations, son," said William Pierce. Amber had met him earlier in the night and learned he was Trey's sponsor. No wonder the two men had met yesterday at the house. They were probably going over last-minute details about the race. "You've got quite a looker there."

Amber squirmed under William's penetrating gaze and wanted to shrug Trey's arm off of her shoulder when he made a comment about her hair in front of this stranger.

"As good as you did in the wife department, you and I need to talk," said William. His face had grown dark and Amber saw in his eyes the same look he'd given her fiancé when Ryan had walked up to the group.

"If you'll excuse me, gentlemen." Amber tried to exit their presence graciously but Trey's comment about her looks made her feel like running from the room. She wanted her husband-to-be to love her for who she was. She wanted Trey to praise her love for children or her volunteer work or the way she made him feel.

If only she could find Ryan. He would know what to say to bring her back to the merry feeling she had when Trey asked for her hand. Everything felt so right in that moment; now she only wanted to escape.

Despite accepting the dozens of felicitations of faces both familiar and new, Amber made good time as she beelined for the kitchen's back door. The moonless canopy of stars overhead became an instant sanctuary, her own personal chapel where she could gaze at the heavens. It was astonishing how her future had gone from ambiguous to certain with four life-changing little words. She needed to line it all up in neat little columns in her mind, making sense of what had at one time seemed like a frivolous daydream. A dream that had suddenly become reality.

Ryan's handsome face came to mind at the thought of dreams as she leaned up against the cool stone of the house. Amber didn't have any doubt he could achieve his larger-than-life aspirations to be part of what he saw as the next wave of transportation innovations. She whole-heartedly believed he was different from his father, capable of becoming someone who lived life with peace and purpose.

Trey's dream of becoming mayor was just as grand. Now that she'd be his constant companion, he could accomplish anything he desired. Especially if he won the race tomorrow. Having two of the biggest names in the industry bend their ears his direction couldn't hurt his endeavor of building that factory.

God had made for her rivers in the desert, just like Grandmother Wright had spoken of the second time they met. *Yes, God, I see it. This is Your provision.* Trey cared for her. Amber knew that.

"I love you," Ryan had mouthed across the room. Had he really said what she thought he did? Trey had never expressed his affections for her in words, only kisses. Ryan had held her in his arms on the dance floor that first night they officially met and since then had held her hand on numerous occasions. Trey's embraces had helped her believe she could one day be part of this family. Ryan's gentle touches helped her believe she was accepted just as she was.

Love. What a strange and wonderful word. Love is of God and God is love. That's what First John chapter four told her. And she believed it. That meant everything God did and said displayed His love. He was gentle and patient. He didn't keep a record of her wrongs and instead forgave her continuously. He gave up everything He had for her, His very own Son. He was merciful, not only withholding punishment when she deserved it but taking that punishment on Himself in her stead.

When she thought about it, she realized Trey had not shown her anything remotely resembling God's kind of love. He was harsh and impatient, making her pay for ways he felt she didn't measure up. She had dismissed the numerous times he'd covered his cruelty with a mask of humor or arrogance.

Amber was glad the night was pitch black with the exception of the distant twinkling stars. She didn't like the direction her thoughts were taking her, didn't want anyone to see the struggle turning violent inside her heart. "Oh, God," Amber started to whisper.

Then she shook her head fiercely. She didn't want to hear the answer to her unspoken question. Trey was her ticket to first-class passage for the journey of the rest of her life. She couldn't let it flutter to the ground to be picked up by someone else. This was hers to claim.

"Is Jesus your servant or your King?" Mrs. Buchanan's words were not welcome as they flashed in her mind like a bold newspaper headline.

"Of course You're my king," she growled low. A servant does what they're told, no questions asked, no matter what. She'd demand from a servant but worship a king.

She tilted her chin toward the sky, trying to take in the sheer number of stars, knowing God had fashioned each one, just as He'd formed her in her mother's womb. With great care, He had spoken the heavens into existence and with His very own hands He had made Amber. He was the King of the universe. He was her King.

She remembered a story from Genesis with a similar theme. God had shown Abraham the stars and promised him that one day his descendants would be as numerous as the stars in the sky, that his wife who was past her child-bearing years would have a baby. From all accounts, it didn't seem possible. When it looked like God wasn't going to deliver, Abraham went forward with his own plans. He went from faith in God to faith in himself. And the results were disastrous.

The nation of Israel was to begin with Abraham and Sarah—a family tree designed by God to bless all nations on Earth. Amber sighed into the night. How Abraham must have hoped and dreamed for the day, just like Amber had. Then when an alternate solution presented itself, he jumped at the chance.

Her head as far back as she could get it, she tried to remember the moment life pivoted, the moment she began insisting Trey must be God's plan for her life. It was that first night visiting the Wrights, the night her heart felt the sum of all the losses she had experienced over the years not being adopted as a Wright girl.

Then when Trey had shown her interest, everything came together. She could conceive a relationship with him and reclaim what had been stolen from her. It had made perfect sense, yet Amber couldn't deny she'd never prayed about Trey, instead expecting God to get her to the finish line she had drawn. She had assumed being folded into the Wright family was God's way of paying her back.

I can answer you now, Mrs. Buchanan. I've made Jesus my servant and I've become king in His place. She had not bowed her knee to God's will; instead she had asked God to bow to hers. A good king made decisions based on love for his people. Amber had been making decisions based on what was best for her.

Her own desires had dug this pit, but she knew what to grab onto to start climbing out. And it was at the same time the easiest and the hardest thing to do. "Lord, You are my inheritance. I see that now. No matter what You have for my future, You are enough. I'm here for You, not the other way around. Show me Your plan and help me to follow You. And Lord, please forgive my willfulness. Forgive me."

As soon as she'd spoken the words, instead of the shame she thought she'd feel, the peace of God seemed to guard her heart and her mind. She would trust the Lord of her life to be the Lord of her future. He was worthy of that. *For My thoughts are not your thoughts, neither are your ways My ways.*

"Yes, Lord. I see that now. Help me to know what to do next." She didn't know where to start, but in this new season of trust, she would wait on the Lord. His ways were higher than hers. Amber was just starting to take a deep, cleansing breath when the kitchen door banged open, flashing a momentary rectangle of light onto the dark grass.

"You botched the whole thing." William's voice. Amber would bet her life on it. She slid down the stone wall until she was out of sight behind a lilac bush. Who was he talking to?

"I'm sorry, sir." Trey. "I knew I could injure him to the point that he wouldn't be able to race tomorrow but I couldn't kill him. I've never done anything like that before." His voice sounded wheedling and puny.

Trey had been sent to take Ryan out of play? For good? Amber felt like she was going to be sick. William, wanting his own son to be murdered. Her fiancé, willing to harm an innocent man to garner a small victory for himself. It was too much to take in.

Head in her hands, Amber sat there for so long that when she finally looked up, the stars had moved in the sky. William and Trey had gone inside not long after she learned the awful truth, but she didn't seem to have the gumption to move her body. She felt frozen in place. Is this what the world felt like on this very night almost two thousand years ago? The darkest night in history as the Savior of the world lay motionless in a grave. The King of the world crucified, His followers' hopes nailed to the cross.

Thankfully, the story didn't end there. And neither did hers.

Amber stood and signed a cross over her chest, a symbol of her belief in not only Jesus' death for her but the hope of what Sunday morning would bring. Her twentieth birthday. The sun would rise over Waterford Cove in less than six hours, and as she pictured the empty tomb the soldiers found on Easter morning, Amber knew exactly what she needed to do.

EIGHTEEN

The pain in Ryan's right hand woke him before the chirping of the birds early Sunday morning. He shifted on the seat of the runabout and moaned at the movement. Slowly sitting up, he placed his feet on the floorboards and rolled his stiff neck as he looked across the campus green. Cramped hours in the crisp evening air was a price he was willing to pay to protect his design and his spot in the race.

The more Ryan had thought about the events of last evening, the more he suspected Isaac Jennings had purposefully set out to cause him injury. And a job well done, Ryan thought ruefully. If Jennings or anyone else couldn't deter him from entering, the next best thing was to sabotage his vehicle. Ryan admitted he may have jumped to conclusions, but like a pioneer sleeping outside to protect his horses, he had done his due diligence and sat wakeful through the midnight hours.

The sun broke the horizon, turned the morning a rosy pink, and Ryan reached for the Bible he had hurriedly packed in his overnight bag. Easter had never held any meaning to him before now. Growing up, it had just been another inconsequential holiday. This week, Christian had helped him to see the Christian faith would be dead if the gospel story stopped with Jesus on the cross.

He turned to the book of Mark and read the account of Jesus's sacrifice for him. His new faith had been confirmed by truth after truth from God's Word all throughout the week, but seeing the sunrise and reading the words *He is risen* on this resurrection morning seemed to set a seal over his heart.

Jesus had appeared to His disciples afterward, telling them they had a new job to do: go and preach the gospel. Short, sweet, and to the point. A clear directive: tell the truth about Me to all creation.

Ryan took the words to heart. Suddenly it didn't matter if he won the race, if his design was recognized in the industry, or even if he had lost Amber. He wanted those things, but the words of the Lord's Prayer he had memorized a few days ago made more sense in light of Jesus's commission. Thy kingdom come. Thy will be done in earth, as it is in heaven. Ryan had been redeemed for a purpose.

Waterford Cove University's campus remained quiet until the noon hour when spectators and participants alike began to trickle in. Ryan felt refreshed from the cold water of the campus pump, but his pain was becoming more noticeable. Medication wasn't an option; he wanted to be sharp for the task ahead.

As the time grew closer to the green flag going down, his doubts began to rise. Maybe he didn't need to drive today. Maybe he should stay behind and sit with Christian or start trying to tell anyone who would listen about the new life that could be found in Jesus Christ.

Mack was the first to walk up to him when he saw the Wright family approach the grounds. Ryan didn't see Amber among the group.

"So you made it after all. That's my boy. Trey was fit to be tied when you showed up last night. I'm glad you're here; the competition will give him the gas he needs to push to the finish line."

The deep throbbing in his hand that had started a few hours ago was working its way up his arm. Ryan needed to be honest with his sponsor. "Sir, I appreciate your faith in me, but I'm not sure how I'm going to manage the tiller with my left hand."

"You're supporting your right arm with your left." Mack rubbed his chin. "I do see your point. Well, if I've learned anything in my fifty years on this earth, it's that God has a way of providing just what we need at the moment we need it." Mack looked over his shoulder and nodded at someone then turned back to Ryan, smiling broadly. "Even if it's something we never would have expected."

It was then that Ryan saw who Mack had seen. Amber Graham, wearing a pair of trousers with a set of aviator glasses perched atop her fire red hair. "Happy Easter, Ryan." Her precious necklace was back in place, resting against a cream-colored chambray shirt.

"Ha—happy Easter." The way Amber glowed from the inside made Ryan feel like he was thirteen again and reacting to his first puppy love. "Why are you, I mean, what are you, I mean, how are you this morning?"

A deliciously free laugh escaped her lips. Ryan knew Amber well enough to see she wasn't having fun at his expense. "Why, I'm here to be your driver, of course."

Ryan's eyes darted to Mack's and back to Amber's. "I—I don't know if that's allowed."

Mack slapped Ryan on his good shoulder. "This was my race from the beginning. If anyone has a problem with it, they can take it up with me."

"Shall we?" Amber asked, leading the way to the driver's door of the runabout. She had her bag over her shoulder and set it on the grass. Ryan followed, still trying to understand what was happening. Amber belonged to Trey now.

"Are you hungry?" she asked, bending down and producing a wrapped parcel. "I didn't know if you'd eaten yet, and we had so much left over from our Easter brunch. Here. Eat up. We've got a long drive ahead of us."

Bewildered beyond words, Ryan carefully held his arm and took a seat in the shade of the runabout.

"I made you a sling so you don't have to hold your arm. I noticed last night you didn't have one." She pulled a dark blue piece of fabric from the bag and slipped it over his head. Her movements were slow and tender. Leave it to Amber to know exactly what he needed. The woman was a wonder. He should tell her so.

"You're a wonder, Amber." Finally, he could speak. "Thank you. But what are you doing here? Trey's going to be pretty bent out of shape."

She waved her hand in the air as if swatting away a pesky fly. "He already knows. I told him after I talked with his father this morning."

"And?" Ryan let his question hang.

Amber's laugh tinkled again. "He wasn't too happy about it, but he was pretty distracted about something else, so I don't know if it's sunk in yet."

I can imagine. Ryan figured he knew pretty well how Trey was feeling. Newly engaged to this glorious creature. If the roles were reversed, Ryan supposed he wouldn't care about some crummy race either.

"We'll have to start taking our places here in a few minutes. If you're finished with that, I can start cleaning up."

So, she really was set on this. "Have you ever driven before?" Ryan was beginning to have some major hesitations.

"As a matter of fact, twice. James Cole's 1895 Duyrea." She looked triumphant, and Ryan had the realization again that this woman could do anything. "Granted, that was a year ago, but I think I got the hang of it. I can't imagine this one being much different. That is, except for your fantastic modifications." She looked so confident and courageous. "I'll take to it like a duck to water, just you see." Amber sealed her pep talk with a wink.

Oh, to have and to hold this woman for always. But that wasn't meant to be. *But my sweet Amber,* Ryan thought with a smile as he reached into his pocket for a dose of medicine, *I've got you all to myself for at least the next hour. And if that's how God chooses to bless me today, I'll gladly take it.*

◆◆◆

"I missed you this week."

Amber looked over at Ryan as they hit a divot in the dirt road. The quick start from the battery combined with the joint power of the electric motor and the gas engine had given them at least a three-minute head start. No other entrants could be seen behind them and to Amber it felt like the day she and Ryan had driven to Oakwood Hills. Yet, there was something different in the set of Ryan's jaw, a change in the way he looked at her, a softness in his voice. Amber began to wonder if she really had read his lips correctly.

"I missed you, too," Amber answered honestly. "I'm sorry I couldn't meet you on Monday. I hope you didn't wait long." She looked at him nervously, but his gaze only echoed back friendship with a hint of something new. Grace, perhaps?

With his good arm, he reached over and patted her hand. "I figured out pretty quick you were probably laying low this week for Trey's sake."

"How did you know? But you're right. He asked me to stay home all week. In fact, he didn't even want me at the race." *But boy, am I glad I came.*

With the sun overhead, the wind in her face, she thrilled at their speed. It was exhilarating. And if she could capture the win for Ryan, she would be happiness personified.

"Then why are you here?" Ryan asked.

Should she tell him? No, not yet. This was too fun, and she didn't want any more talk of Trey Wright to ruin it.

Amber looked at Ryan saucily. "Shouldn't the birthday girl get her pre-rogative?"

"I didn't know it was your birthday." He seemed surprised. "And here I thought I knew so much about you."

"A grand ol' twenty years old today. And your birthday is July 4."

Now it was Ryan's turn to look amazed. "How did you know that?"

"Christian told me. Said your father had an alibi for the night of the Waterford Cove Holdings Robbery." She jerked a thumb in his direction. "You."

Ryan whistled low through his teeth. "Boy, do I wish Christian was here right now. I've got solid evidence that speaks the exact opposite." Amber looked at him questioningly. "My mother's journals. I recently found a couple, and that was one of the first entries I turned to. William was missing from the day before my birthday till the day after. She never knew where he went."

"So he did do it. Oh, Ryan, I am sorry." How awful.

"Don't be. I didn't know that's what Christian thought all these years."

"I guess I'm realizing I didn't put his alibi in my notes. But really, I am sorry."

Ryan was quiet for a moment, studying the map. "The first checkpoint is coming up." He pointed to a table set up by the roadside. "We don't have to stop. They'll read the number on the side of the runabout."

A whole host of people, including Christian, Summer, and their girls cheered and waved as the runabout drove by and Ryan gave them a thumbs up with his left hand.

"How are you doing? Hanging in there?" Amber knew all the jostling wasn't helping Ryan's cause.

"Are you kidding? This is a dream come true for me. I don't even care if I win. Just being here with you, using our design, that's good enough for me."

The smile Ryan gave her made her want to pull over and soak up as much of this man as she could. "The next checkpoint isn't too far from here, right?" *Time to get my mind back on the race.*

"Yes, at Oakwood Hills' town square. About a mile ahead. By the way, I went and saw the Buchanans like we talked about. Twice. Learned something pretty outstanding. Been waiting for a chance to talk with you about it. But after what happened last night, I didn't figure I'd ever get you alone again."

"Last night," Amber began, then stopped. "What did the Buchanans say?" That was paramount.

"I'm glad you're sitting down because the reverend told me he didn't remember a Tabitha Murray but he did remember a Tabitha Graham."

"You mean, Grantham?"

"That's what I said. I knew he was hard of hearing and figured there was a breakdown in communication. But no, that's what he said. Graham. But that's not the crazy part. Get this," Ryan paused, and Amber felt like she would fly to pieces if he didn't spit it out.

"When I asked where she and the baby were buried, he told me only Tabitha died. The baby lived on the property where Tabitha was buried with another woman for a while. Christian's child is still alive, as far as we know. Can you beat that?"

Amber whipped the goggles from her eyes and blinked rapidly. She tried to clear her vision while her pulse pounded in her ears. *It can't be. It just can't.* She reached up and grabbed her necklace, grateful she had given Trey back his ring this morning.

"Amber?" Ryan's caring voice sounded far away, his hand on her shoulder felt like it wasn't really touching her. "Amber, what's wrong?"

"I'm Amber Graham," she said chokingly.

"Right," Ryan said slowly with a hint of a question to his voice.

She could see the town square just ahead and quickly glanced over at her friend. "I never told you I had a caretaker for the first few years of my life after my mother died." The words felt like they would strangle her if she didn't get them past her swollen throat. "Her name," Amber coughed, "her name was Mrs. MacDonald."

Ryan pointed at the central square the town was built around. "Turn right. Right here."

"What? Ryan, what are you talking about? The checkpoint is the other direction. This is where we turn to go south for a few miles before heading to the coast and then back to the university."

"Trust me. This is more important than winning the race."

Amber followed the directions Ryan gave, but once they were on an unused road called Pine Lane, she couldn't remember the steps it had taken to get there. Her mind was racing to fill in a timeline she didn't dare hope belonged to her.

A little girl toddling around a rundown house while Mrs. MacDonald did the chores. A church with a stained-glass window where a Man hung on a cross. A missing woman who had red hair, just like hers. A grave marker of a Bridget MacDonald who died the same year Amber had begun her five-year journey to the King's Castle. A man named Christian Titus who had always treated her like family. Two little girls she'd helped raise.

"I think this is the place." Ryan pointed to a dilapidated house almost completely overtaken by forest overgrowth.

Amber stopped the car and jumped down without a word. Memories began in earnest as she walked the old path to the front door. Mrs. MacDonald making soup and crusty bread. Countless hours spent outside playing with her rag doll under the tree canopy. A birthday cake and her first time at church the day she turned six.

"Graham," she said, pushing open the door that hung by only one hinge. Amber turned to see if Ryan had followed her. "This is where Mrs. MacDonald told me my last name. The same day she gave me this." She held the necklace away from her body, showing it to Ryan like she had done one night by the fire, long ago. "The day I left home."

The house's boards had shrunk over the years, letting in not only moisture but forest animals as well. Sunlight striped the dirt floor while Amber spun in a circle, in and out of its rays. She came to a stop, her mind full of images of those early years. Things she didn't know she remembered until now. Amber felt as though she were tipping sideways through the memories, and she reached out for something to grab on to. Behind her, she felt something solid. A strong arm enveloped her, and Amber closed her eyes, leaning against Ryan. He set his chin on her head and suddenly, she was at peace.

This may all be a surprise to her, but God already knew. He had orchestrated each moment of her life, and though this was a pinnacle, she knew it wasn't the end. Like Abraham, God had tested her faith and was preparing her for the next big adventure ahead.

"Tell me about your mother." Ryan's breath against her hair felt warm and real in this place that had only existed in her mind up until a few minutes ago.

"My mother." *Tabitha Graham.* "I didn't know her. I guess she died the day I was born, according to the letter Mrs. MacDonald sent. Bridget lied to my—my father." *My father is Christian Titus. I'm a Titus.* "My caretaker never told me any stories about her. I've never seen a picture. It was as if she didn't exist until Bridget gave me the necklace. Told me to go out back to the woods and find the bee tree. Said there was something there my mother wanted me to have, though I wasn't old enough yet. Mrs. MacDonald told me to hide it and take it with me. That it would help me."

Ryan slowly turned her around and kept his hand on her shoulder. "And what did you find?"

Amber shook her head. "Nothing. I looked and looked, but it began to grow dark, and I had to go to the church Mrs. MacDonald had taken me to the week before." She looked into Ryan's face, so glad for his presence. "That was the last time I was here."

Ryan's eyes took on a strange look, "Can I see your necklace again?"

When she held it toward him, he said, "I mean, can you take it off for me? I want to have a better look at it."

Going out the back door for more light, Amber sat on the sagging stoop and removed the keepsake. "Except for last night, this hasn't been off of my neck for fourteen years. Fourteen years ago today, as a matter of fact." Trey had been the one to undo the clasp last night before putting it directly into the box that had held the ring, so it felt strange to hold the whole thing in her hand, chain and all.

"Turn it over for me," said Ryan. "Is anything engraved on the back?"

"Not that I know of." But still, Amber obliged. She looked closely and at first didn't see anything written there. But a brush of her finger over the back caused her to look again. "Here. Feel those bumps?"

Ryan's thumb caressed the gold. "Might be writing." He held it up to the afternoon sun and peered closer. "Yes. There is something here. Some of it's been rubbed away." He winked at Amber.

"Guess I can take the fall for that." It felt good to smile.

After another look, Ryan said, "But I can make out a few letters. *Bi* and maybe a *j*, then a space, then a lowercase letter *d*, then something that starts with *Art*." Ryan snapped his fingers. "Bijoux d'Artisan. Do you know it? That's where my pocket watch came from. The one my mother gave me that I had to sell. Mr. Dandurand is a master craftsman. He can do anything with any kind of metal."

"Justine Cole has a couple of pieces from him. A silver necklace in the shape of a fawn with Psalm 42:1 engraved on the back. And that's where Garrett had Justine's wedding ring made."

Splaying the fingers of her left hand for a brief moment, Amber looked at Ryan. Had he seen that Trey's ring didn't occupy her fourth finger?

"I noticed you weren't wearing your ring today." Guess that answered that question.

"Not today or any other day." She couldn't hold it in any longer. She wanted Ryan to know she was free. "I broke it off with Trey this morning."

◆◆◆

Only one other moment in Ryan's life rivaled the elation he was feeling. Christ had given him freedom and eternal life; Amber was offering him the promise of tomorrow. A loud *whoop* escaped his lips and he threw his left arm around her shoulders. "Praise the Lord." Then he sobered. "Sorry about that," he said sheepishly. "I'm just so doggone happy for you. Although I'm sure that was a difficult decision to make." After a moment he ducked his head to look her in the eye. "May I ask why?"

He left his arm still embracing her. Amber surprised him by laying her head on his shoulder. "Last night, I found out something he did. Something very wrong. He's not living a life pleasing to the Lord. So this morning, I asked him straight-out about his faith in Christ. He told me he doesn't have time for such foolishness." Amber lifted her head and stood abruptly. He saw her put the necklace in her pant's pocket but she kept her back to him. "I'm ashamed I worked so hard to join my life to someone who's my opposite in every way."

Last year's leaves crunched under his feet as he came to stand beside this woman he was growing to love. They stood looking at the expanse of tangled woods lining the back of the property. "What did Trey do?" he asked, low. Although it might be for the better if Amber didn't tell him, something inside Ryan said he already knew.

"He was asked to take you out." She paused and looked at him. "By your father."

"To injure me?" Ryan laughed humorlessly. "Well, he certainly accomplished that."

"No. That was Trey's idea." Amber faced him and ran her fingers down his left arm, her caress ending at his hand. Her small thumb ran a smooth line from his thumb to his wrist. "Listen to me, Ryan. Your father—" He could see Amber visibly swallow. "Your father wanted you dead."

Ryan let the words sink in. He had been right to stay with the runabout last night. If he had been home—that was a thought he'd rather not finish.

"It doesn't make sense," Amber said. "Kill you just to win the race?"

This was it. The moment he'd been dreading. But Lord help him, he'd do the right thing. "Maybe that was part of it, but Amber," it was Ryan's turn to swallow, "do you remember the day you saw me at WCU sitting on the bench? The day you left your job? That was my low point, the day I found out my father emptied my bank account. The same day I got a payment notice in the mail from the university. The money from the watch, all the odd jobs I'd taken for over a year," he paused, "gone. My education. My career. Everything. He stole it all."

"Oh, Ryan."

"No, just wait. There's more." This was harder than he thought. But the Lord asked him to put away lying and speak truth to his neighbor. He'd read that this week. "Before all of this, I had decided I'd no longer be my father's lackey. I was done lying for him, stealing money from honest men." He looked up at the hundreds of budding branches reaching toward the blue sky. "Everything came to a head when I realized the crime you were trying to solve as a sort of pastime was the same money my father was suddenly desperate to find. I knew he stole the money, Amber. I'm sorry I couldn't tell you sooner."

Amber let go of his hand and walked farther toward the edge of the tree line. "Did you follow me to Oakwood Hills the first time I went?" She turned around. "The bowler hat? The brown duster?"

"Yes." He wouldn't hide anything now. "I wanted to see why you had my father's file. It wasn't until later I learned William was being pigeonholed by an old associate to find the money."

"Joe Schneider," Amber whispered.

"Yes," Ryan said again. He had no idea if Amber would give him another chance now that she knew, but it felt good to speak the truth. "He was threatening my father's life if he didn't have the money in hand in a matter of weeks. Once a week I had to report to Joe and tell him my progress. But something good came out of that weekly visit."

Amber looked wary at best. "What's that?"

"I became a Christian." Ryan couldn't keep a huge smile from splitting his face. "I would walk by Waterford Cove Chapel every Sunday morning on my way home from his house and hear the singing, even sit on the steps to hear part of the sermon. Last Sunday, Palm Sunday, I went inside and God met me there. I was the man on the slippery slope, headed toward spiritual death. I was already walking dead. Do you know what I mean?"

Her face had gone a little soft, and she kicked at an old log that looked like it had been there for ages. Its rotten wood splintered a bit when her foot hit it. She nodded slowly.

She understands. Thank you, Lord. "I always thought if I could just get away from William, I'd be a good man. The Lord showed me that day I was no different than my father. Sure, I'd never killed anyone or physically stolen any cash, but my deeds were just as wicked. It was that passage from James, remember? I was that man, tempted and drawn away by my own lust. My lust for success, for freedom at any cost. My desires led me down the path of sin. I needed a Savior."

When she finally spoke, it was with a different voice than Ryan expected. He thought she'd hurl insults his way or at the very least snub him with her piety. She was so good, so right. He remembered the many times he thought he could somehow take her goodness and make it his own. How wrong he had been. Only Jesus could do that.

"First of all, I'm so thrilled for you," she said. "You're a Christian, Ryan! This makes my heart so happy." He believed her as he looked into her radiant face. It was the same expression Christian wore when Ryan had told him. Amber pulled him into a hug then quickly let go. Turning serious she said, "I know how hard that must have been to tell me. Thank you for being honest."

"You should know I didn't share very many of the details of our searching with my father. I only told him bits and pieces, enough to keep him assuaged."

"None of that matters now." Amber held his gaze and smiled her lovely smile. "Life's going to look a lot different for both of us going forward, don't you think?"

"You can say that again. Everything's about to get turned inside out and flipped upside down. You have a new family waiting for you back in Waterford Cove with half-sisters and everything, and I'm about to lose the only family I've got. You ready for this?"

"Definitely," Amber said confidently. "If God is for us, who can be against us?"

"Well said. Now let me see that necklace again. I don't know if this will lead anywhere, but hear me out. You know how Christian said that Tabitha made a trip to Waterford Cove and was gone a couple of days, and her trip put her there at the time of the robbery? Well, what if she took the money William had just stolen and stuck around long enough to have Mr. Dandurand fashion some way to hide a key to a security deposit box or a safe?"

Amber's eyes were bright. "Like in a handcrafted necklace?"

Three hands were suddenly turning the necklace this way and that, trying to see if there was anything to Ryan's theory. Amber put her thumb and forefinger on the bee. "This has always had a bit of a wiggle to it."

"Give it a good twist," Ryan prompted her.

"It moved," she said excitedly, looking up.

"Keep going. See how far it goes."

The bee turned ninety degrees and came loose from its setting.

Their eyes locked for an instant and then Amber pulled the bee all the way out. "It's a key!" they said in unison.

"A tiny key," Amber put in. She'd never seen anything like it. "What do you suppose it goes to?"

"What did you say Mrs. MacDonald told you when she gave it to you?"

"To go out back to the woods and find the bee tree. There was something inside that would help me." She swiveled her eyes to his. "Do you think —?"

"You bet your bottom dollar I do. It would be a perfect place to hide a strong box. Put it right in among an active hive. Smart."

As if on cue, Ryan and Amber began to slowly walk through the woods, their necks craned high, searching for any sign of such a tree.

"We could be here for days trying to figure out which one it is," said Amber. "Plus, it's been fourteen years. The bees have probably found a new home by now."

"Yeah, but if they've moved on, they've left evidence behind, and it'll be easier to search without the risk of getting stung."

After a few minutes of climbing over fallen logs and through brambles, Amber said, "Why don't we bring back reinforcements? We need a search party out here."

They walked back to the edge of the woods and stood looking one last time. Amber put one foot on the rotten log she had kicked. Her shoe went right through. An "Ouch!" came out of her mouth but not before they both heard a metallic *thunk*.

"Here, let me help you." Ryan stood solid and let Amber lean on him to get her foot loose.

Once she rolled her ankle and found it undamaged and rubbed her bruised shin, they peered inside the hollow log that had broken into two pieces when it had fallen long ago. "I see something." Amber bent and reached into the end of the log, pulling out an old honeycomb. She handed it to Ryan then reached back inside. She was on her stomach now, both arms in up to her shoulders. After a minute of removing more debris, she pulled out something dark covered in dirt and bits of splintered wood. A square box, about a foot in length and height.

She set it next to the log and brushed her hand over its top. "Here's the keyhole," Amber said, her hand and her voice a little shaky.

"Do the honors, my Little Bumble Bee."

Amber inserted the odd little key and gave it a turn. Ryan heard the lid click open. Inside lay restitution for those who had been robbed so many years before.

"I'll take that, Red."

◆◆◆

A voice from behind caused Amber to jump. She put the key in her pocket and shut the lid before she stood up and turned around. William.

"Give it to him, Amber." Ryan stood rigid at her side, his voice subdued and sounding much calmer than she felt. Amber didn't think for one moment he wanted his dad to sweep in for the win. Ryan's testimony rang with sincerity, and she knew with all of her heart he was a changed man. He was just trying to protect her.

"Oh, yes, Amber, is it?" William said in a mocking tone of voice. "Nice to finally make your acquaintance. You look like your mother, you know. Let's just hope you don't try to double-cross me like she did." Before she could blink, he had pulled a pistol from his pocket.

"Ryan?" she asked timidly. He'd said he hadn't told his father much. How did William know they would come across the money today?

"I didn't tell him, Amber. I promise."

"That's all together true," he said. "You should have. But it was easy enough to learn your secrets." William looked smug. "The top drawer of your desk has been quite convenient lately." He *tsked*. "I've taught you better than that, although your oversight gave me exactly what I needed." His face turned threatening as he pointed the gun at Amber. "My plan became very simple when I figured out you were Tabitha's daughter. Now hand it over."

He won't be able to open it without the key. Amber's thoughts raced wildly, and she looked to Ryan for direction. He nodded, almost imperceptibly.

"It's okay, Little Bumble Bee. If God is for us, who can be against us?"

Amber took a step forward and handed William the box. "Here." Ryan was right. William might look like he was winning, but she would put her trust in God and not repeat the mistake of taking matters into her own hands.

As soon as he had his treasure under one arm, William sprinted around the house, looking back once to fire a stray bullet.

"We'll take the runabout and go back to Christian at the first checkpoint. It's time to turn this over to the authorities."

Amber picked an unopened red trillium from the wood's edge and laid it on the log. "I'll be back to find your grave, Mother," she said softly. And she would. One day soon. "But first, I want to give my daddy a big hug."

EPILOGUE

Waterford Cove, Virginia
February 14, 1900

J ust a minute!" Amber hurriedly finished buttoning her boot when she heard a knock at the front of the house.

"I'll get it," Christian said from outside her bedroom door. "Take your time."

As Summer secured a pin in Amber's hair, Mirabel and Fiona took turns fluffing out her skirt.

"You look boo-tiful, Sissy."

Amber picked up little Fiona and held her close, disregarding the wrinkles in her dress. "Thank you, my sweet girl." She set her back on the floor and knelt to look both girls in the eye. "You two know what to do tonight, right?"

Mirabel nodded with a twinkle in her eye while Fiona whispered loud in Amber's ear, "Give Mommy and Daddy our Val-um-time's present."

Mirabel rolled her eyes. "It's Valentine's, silly," she said, emphasizing the pronunciation. Mirabel obviously didn't remember that only last year she had said it the same way. Amber chuckled.

"Yes, but keep it a secret till it's ready, okay?" Both girls nodded enthusiastically. "I'll be back in a few hours." Amber pulled them both into her arms.

"Let's get you out there," said Summer, ushering Amber toward the bedroom door. "Can't keep your man waiting forever."

Ryan stood by the front window of the Titus home, his black hair gleaming in the candlelight. He was wearing a new suit coat and Amber thought he'd never looked so dashing. She told him so.

"I've got to keep up with the most beautiful girl in Waterford Cove, don't I?" Ryan said with a wink. He had become so winsome over the last year, love for God and His people seemed to ooze out of him at every turn. He pulled a bouquet of tulips from behind his back. "I got them from the Ag Department at the university. Once they knew who they were for, I had no trouble getting them to part with some."

"My favorite." She kissed him on the cheek. "Thank you, Ryan."

"What about me?" her father teased.

"You get one too," Amber said happily. "And a hug." She felt she could never spend too much time with this wonderful man who had always loved her like his own. "Thank you, Daddy. For everything."

"Why are you thanking me?" said Christian with mock disbelief. "I should be thanking you. You're the one who's made this family complete. Now, go and have a great time at that party. We won't wait up for you."

"You ready for this?" Amber smiled at Ryan after they bid her family farewell and climbed into his new car. It was *Number 001* in production from the factory where Ryan had been hired to oversee research and development. Benz and Daimler hadn't cared that Ryan didn't finish the Endurance Race. Once they saw the runabout's performance for themselves, they began to pass word around to industry leaders. Before the end of the year, a young man who was trying to make a name for himself had swept into town and started the Waterford Cove Automobile Company. The production line was now open, and Ryan's little beauty had been completed a week ago. This was only Amber's second time taking a ride on its luxurious leather seats.

Rather than sighing at the question, Ryan set his shoulders back and smiled. He threw the knife switch and the electric motor caused the car to lurch into motion. "Yes," he said confidently. "It may not be a traditional way to celebrate the most romantic holiday of the year, but it's the right thing to do."

Amber squeezed his hand for encouragement as Ryan parked in front of the prison. William came into the visitation room, his hands cuffed in front of him. He spat on the floor when he saw who had come to call. "Get out of here, boy. I've no desire to lay eyes on you again."

It may not be the same words they'd heard once a week for the last eleven months, but William always delivered the same message. *Go away.*

"Hello, Father." Ryan sat at the table, and Amber came to stand behind him, hands on his shoulders. "It's good to see you."

William remained silent.

"This is a special night for Amber and me, you know," Ryan went on as though this was a normal conversation. "A year ago tonight we officially met at the Wright's party. I drew her name and got to dance with her for the first time." Ryan turned to wink at Amber and her heart took a dip in her stomach. "But it definitely wasn't the last."

After five minutes of chatter from only one side of the table, they took their leave. At the door, Ryan added, "God loves you, Father. And so do I."

Hard words to say, Amber knew, but even harder to live out consistently. Yet Ryan did. Not once since William was caught had she heard Ryan slander his father or complain about having to move out of the big house. He repeatedly told Amber he loved living in the little cottage that used to be hers. He seemed just as content with his situation as she was living as a Titus. She smiled to herself as they climbed back into the car. It also didn't hurt that Ryan was only a stone's throw away from her front door.

"Are you ready?" Ryan returned Amber's question as they pulled into the Wright's curving driveway.

"Yes," Amber said, smiling. "This *is* the most romantic way to spend the holiday, in my opinion. Returning to the scene of the crime."

"Oh, a crime, was it?" teased Ryan, cutting the motor. "I like to think of it as the first chapter to a beautiful story."

Just like last year, the welcoming committee stood on the front porch, only this time there was no blizzard. "Sheila! Girls!" Amber took turns hugging her friends while Emma and one of her yearling pups tried to get in the mix. "Sorry we're a little bit late." The words brought to mind all she thought she'd lost by missing her chance to become an adopted Wright sister. It was clear now she hadn't been late—God hadn't been late. He was always right on time.

"Thank you for inviting us," Amber continued.

"Are you kidding? Wouldn't be the same without you," said Millie, taking Amber's wrap.

"Come on into the front parlor," said Winnie as she led the way. "Everyone's here and we've got games going by the fire until we're ready to begin."

Amber's heart took a little dip when she saw Trey playing checkers with a young lady she didn't recognize. Even though he'd been back at school since the turn of the New Year, this would be the first time she'd spoken to him since he'd returned from visiting relatives in Georgia. "Hello, Trey. You're looking well."

He put his elbows on the table and regarded Amber, but there was a different look in his eyes. A new modesty rested over his features, replacing some of the cunning that had been there before. "As are you. May I introduce you to Miss Annabelle?"

Amber politely finished the conversation and went to stand by the fireplace, taking a deep breath. Ryan's hand on her back along with his encouraging words were enough to remind her all things could be made new. And that included William and Trey. Her God could do anything. She believed that now. The Maker of the stars could take her little seed of trust and grow it into something that would produce abundantly as she continued to follow Him. He was a God of plenty who didn't disappoint.

Ryan leaned to whisper in her ear, "Just so you know, I've rigged it so I'm guaranteed to draw your name tonight."

"Full of surprises, are you?" Amber teased. "Well, you're not the only one."

"Oh, really? What are you up to?"

Amber looked around at the little groups clustered here and there in the parlor and decided this was the perfect time. "I have something for you," she said as she reached into her purse, suddenly a little shaky.

Amber's plan had been in the works since the day she'd been rehired at the university, so she didn't know what there was to be nervous about.

"What's this?" Ryan looked at her inquisitively when she handed him a square jewelry box.

"You'll see," she said, her stomach feeling like the day they were going all-out in the race, heading to the first checkpoint with both engines at full power. "Go ahead. Open it."

"Amber, you didn't." Ryan's voice was one of awe as he lifted out his Carmouche pocket watch. By now, the others in the room must have noticed something happening because they came crowding in. Everyone but Trey. "How in the world—"

Even though she felt everyone watching, Amber's focus was on Ryan's face. He bore a look she'd been anticipating since Mr. Dandurand had agreed to let her make monthly installments. "Every time you open it, you can be reminded of your mother's love for you. And," Amber went on boldly, "of mine."

Ryan pulled her into an embrace, and she heard half a dozen hands slap Ryan on the back.

"Good show," Mack said, coming into the room. "And a great way to kick off the night."

"Yes," Sheila agreed, sending Amber a gracious smile. "Everyone," here she looked at the room at large, "dinner will be served in five minutes in the dining room." She turned back to the foyer at a knock on the door.

Before Amber could grasp what was happening, Fiona and Mirabel came tumbling into the room while Sheila greeted Christian and Summer who were followed shortly behind by Grandmother and Grandfather Wright.

"Surprise, Sissy," said Mirabel.

"Yes, it is," said Amber, helping the little girls out of their coats. "But what are you doing here? You're supposed to be helping Mother and Daddy have their special evening."

"They are," said Ryan, who had appeared unnoticed at Amber's side. "Aren't you, girls?" He wiggled his eyebrows at them.

With that unusual statement, Ryan proceeded to take Amber's hand

and ask her the same question Trey had in this very house not so long ago. This time, Amber could see the present melding seamlessly with her her future, with no qualms anywhere in sight.

"I will, Ryan Pierce," she said as he slipped his mother's ring on her finger. Then they were being hugged on every side with well wishes all around.

Grandmother Wright broke up the revelry and told Amber and Ryan to go outside and have a moment to themselves. Ryan took Amber's hand and led her to the edge of the front porch where they had a clear view of the winter sky.

Amber looked up at the innumerable stars, remembering God's promise to Abraham. He who promised had been more than faithful.

"You've been planning this for a while, haven't you?" Ryan wanted to know.

"Me? What about you?" she said with a laugh and threw her arms around him.

"I couldn't wait any longer to make you my wife or to go get our little Biddy and bring her home."

Amber grinned. "Let's go get a houseful."

DISCUSSION QUESTiONS

1. Amber is convinced she has missed out on what should have been hers—belonging to the Wright family like the other girls.

- How do you think her life would have been different had she been adopted by them? Do you think she would have turned out to be the same person?
- Does God have a Plan B for our lives or are the circumstances we find ourselves in His ultimate will? Back up your answer with Scripture.

2. Ryan wishes he had come from an honorable family. We all know that no family is perfect. There may even be times you wished you had come from a different heritage.

- Read Acts 17:24–28. What does this passage tell us about God? About our lives?

3. When Amber loses her job and her home, she feels she's in too deep with Trey. There's a sense she has to move forward with the relationship, even though she may have some doubts.

- Do you agree she couldn't have backed out?
- What do you think would have happened if Amber would have prayed about the situation before acting?
- What did Amber need to believe about God during that time in her life?
- Are you in a situation where you've given up or you think it's too

267

late to turn things around? What do you need to believe about God and His promises in your circumstance?

4. When William belittles Ryan again and again, Ryan passes it off as a chance to toughen up. Do you think William's words helped him or hurt him?

- What does God's Word say about encouragement in Ephesians 4:29–32 and Hebrews 10:23–25?
- Who in your life do you need to build up with encouragement?
- Who has God put in your life to encourage you when it's hard to see the truth?

5. Amber says she knows from experience that sometimes the days are long but the years are short. Where have you experienced this to be true in your life?

- How does looking back on that season give you different perspective on what God may have for you in your current season?

6. How does it change your perspective on how your days should be spent when you read what Mrs. Buchannan said to Amber (from parts of 2 Corinthians 4:16–18)?

- "But you know, these bodies, and our heads, mind you, weren't meant to last. We have a forever home just a waitin' for us on the other side of that sky." Mrs. Buchanan reclined again in her chair and pointed to the ceiling. "Though our outward man perish, yet the inward man is renewed day by day. We look not at the things which are seen, but at the things which are not seen: for the things which are seen are temporal; but the things which are not seen are eternal."
- Amber said she had used those verses to help her through especially hard days. What Scripture do you think of when you need new perspective?

7. Ryan learns that sacrifice can bring joy. It's a new concept to him, one he'd been avoiding all of his life. Sacrifice often sounds uncomfortable. Painful, even.

- In John 15:13, Jesus says "Greater love hath no man than this, that a man lay down his life for his friends."

- That's exactly what Jesus did for us, and we will be reaping the benefits of His sacrifice into eternity.
- God asks us to lay down our life, our preferences, our agenda to love our spouse, our family, our friends, our co-workers, even strangers. When we love like Jesus loved, we see how beautiful sacrifice can be.

8. Ryan feels he has carefully divided his heart into two sections. He's convinced himself he can go ahead with certain sins and still maintain hope.

- Psalm 86:11 says "Teach me thy way, O Lord, I will walk in Thy truth: unite my heart to fear thy name."
- This is one of my favorite verses because it describes my heart struggle so well. I want God to teach me. I promise to walk in the truth of His Word. Yet, most days, I find my heart still divided.
- Lord, show me the sins in my heart that allow me to remain divided. Forgive me of my sins, O God, and make me wholly devoted to You.

9. Love without counting the cost. That's how Amber describes how the Coles and Tituses live. Why do you think she says this about them?

- Who in your life has loved you like this?
- Who is God specifically laying on your heart, right now, that needs God's love shown to them in this way?
- How can you practically carry that out this week?

10. The Scripture Ryan hears while sitting on the church steps is from Deuteronomy 30:19–20. "I call heaven and earth to record this day against you, that I have set before you life and death, blessing and cursing: therefore choose life, that both thou and thy seed may live: That thou mayest love the Lord thy God, and that thou mayest obey his voice, and that thou mayest cleave unto him: for he is thy life, and the length of thy days: that thou mayest dwell in the land which the Lord sware unto thy fathers, to Abraham, to Isaac, and to Jacob, to give them."

- Ryan felt he was stumbling around in the dark. He tried to find the light and life by getting away from his father, but he realized that believing in and surrendering to God was the only way to truly choose between life and death. Have you chosen new life in Christ?

11. If it's been awhile, read through the story of Abraham in the Old Testament. God had shown Abraham the stars and promised him that one day, his descendants would be as numerous as the stars in the sky, and that his wife, who was past her child-bearing years, would have a baby. From all accounts, it didn't seem possible. When it looked like God wasn't going to deliver, Abraham went forward with his own plans. He went from faith in God to faith in himself. And the results were disastrous.

- Amber realizes she's done the same thing in her life. She made Jesus her servant and not her King.
- She had not bowed her knee to God's will; instead she had asked God to bow to hers. A good king made decisions based on love for his people. Amber had been making decisions based on what was best for her.
- Amber realizes her own desires have dug her into this pit.
- What does she do to get out?
- If you are finding yourself in this position, what prayer do you need to pray, right now? God is waiting with arms open wide as you make Him Lord of your life!

12. Ryan's faith is only a week old when he reads the account of Jesus's death and resurrection on Easter morning as the sun rises.

- Have you experienced the feeling he had of a seal being placed over your heart on an Easter morning at sunrise?
- That can be quite an experience, but even if you've never had it, God tells us in Ephesians 1 that when we believe in Jesus, He seals us with the promised Holy Spirit, who is the guarantee of our inheritance.
- Praise God today that nothing and no one can take away the inheritance God has kept in heaven for you (1 Peter 1:4).

13. After Jesus was resurrected, He appeared to His disciples, telling them they had a new job to do: go and preach the gospel. Ryan sees it as a clear directive: tell the truth about Me to all creation.

- Ryan takes the words to heart and suddenly all the things he's been working for don't have the same significance. He understands he's been redeemed for a purpose.

- No matter how rotten your roots, God can redeem you as well. Let today be the day you say *yes* to God and walk in the new purpose He has for your life.

.

DEAR READER

could read and write love stories all day long. How about you? Sometimes I wonder why we never get tired of them, then I realize maybe
it's because we picture ourselves in the story. We want to be the one
who is loved and treasured, secure in the safe arms of someone who
will love us unconditionally.

There's a repeated theme from Genesis to Revelation—God wants
you and will go to any length to draw you close to Him. Relationship
existed in the Trinity before time began, and because of Jesus, we will
have eternal relationship with our God. There's no doubt about it—God
is the author of relationship and it's His gift to us—with each other and
with Himself. What a generous God we serve.

But if you are married, it probably didn't take long for you to realize you married a sinner—and so did they. Most of us live within our
marriage relationship with a contract mentality rather than a covenant
commitment. *You do your part, I'll do mine. You broke your end of the
agreement, which gives me license to break mine.* Our God is the original
Covenant Maker and the only **Covenant Keeper**, and He asks us and
inspires us to treat our marriage like the covenant it is.

When our husband-wife relationships don't go the way we originally thought they would, we tend to want to hide. But what if, in full
view of the sin that exists between us, we stepped forward and shouted
loud about a covenant God? What if others saw God's covenant love

for us lived out in this one challenging yet freeing act of commitment: *I will love my spouse the most when they deserve it the least.* Try it and see what God will do.

No matter where you and your spouse have been, you can come out from the shadows of shame that have been cast by a contract marriage and step into the light of the gospel of Jesus Christ being lived out in your home with this theme resonating daily within your heart: *Marriage is a covenant TO GOD that says, "Lord, I will give YOUR best to this person, I will serve them, I will love them, I will be YOUR hands and feet in their world, even when they break their promise."*

The Vows Written in Permanent Ink Contest is an opportunity to share how God's covenant love to YOU has affected your covenant to your spouse. The two couples who won the contest for *Roots Redeemed* not only got the opportunity to have their first names as the characters in the story, they wanted to share a bit of their marriage testimony with you as well.

It is my pleasure to introduce to you the real-life Amber and Ryan, Sheila and Mack. It is their hope that their stories would give you hope for your own marriage and reveal glimpses of our covenant God's faithfulness.

Ryan and Amber's Testimony

Things haven't always been great for me. My previous marriage was difficult and my husband at the time mentally and physically abused me. God was with me through it all, and I stayed faithful to Him during this time, knowing He would see me through it. God had better plans for me, and He gave me the strength to get out of the situation.

Over the next few years, I worked on my relationship with God and through my church, met Ryan. Ryan and I worked in the youth group together (this was secretly set up by some in the church who thought we should be dating). Ryan had recently been through a situation with his then-fiancée that ended similarly. We starting dating and praying about our future and what God had in store for us. A year later we were engaged and the rest is history.

Today, we have a four-year-old son and continue to walk the path God set forth for us. We don't always understand why we go through the things we have to in life, but God's plan is perfect, and if you trust and lean on him, He will see you through. Ryan and I love each other, we love our son, but we understand we must first love Christ if we are to have a solid marriage.

Sheila and Jeff's (Mack's) Testimony

Jeff and I met as friends in the early 1990s, during my freshman year and his junior year of college. I was engaged to another guy when I met him, but the relationship with the young man I was with was not the Lord's will for my life. Not long after getting to know each other, it became evident God's hand was clearly at work, and He began to set in motion a series of events that brought Jeff and I together. The Lord was gracious in allowing me to see in Jeff an honesty and transparency that never existed in any other guy I had known before him. His down-to-earth straightforwardness was a breath of fresh air, and we began a deep friendship that was easy and natural—and the time I spent with him felt like…home. After developing a strong bond as friends, we knew God was moving in our lives to bring us into a deeper relationship and to a forever commitment in marriage.

Jeff and I had each been raised by hard-working and loving single moms, but we knew firsthand the emotional hardship and difficulty of being a child of parents who went through a painful marriage breakup. We both had a personal knowledge of the profound struggles that accompany divorce. We had shared with each other our stories and were steadfast in our strong convictions that if we were going into a marriage, that the commitment would be something we were going to approach with serious consideration. The very vows we would make were promises before God to love, honor, and make a lifetime together as one flesh. We both individually realized these vows were forever and would be said not only before all of our friends and family, but most importantly, the Lord Himself. This would mean it was a lifetime commitment, and we were going to do everything we could, by God's grace and only through His power, to stay together. We both were dedicated in our resolve to never put ourselves or our future children through the trauma of what we, our parents, and our siblings had experienced from the pain of divorce.

Neither of us were perfect, and we saw that the difficulties of being two independent young people learning how to each live sacrificially and humbly with each other in the first years of our marriage were real. It was not easy, and we had a lot to learn and much to put into practice as we grew in our knowledge of each other. The quality of being self-sacrificing was not natural, and became a daily battle that needed our constant attention. To be intentional in our love for each other required effort that we realized was not a "50-50" compromise, but would take Jeff and I each giving 100 percent of ourselves. We knew it was not in our own flesh that this would take place, and the "until death do us part" commitment would only be obtained by giving our wills over to the maker of marriage Himself—Jesus Christ.

With every hardship, we dug our heels in more and found our hope to stay committed to one another would only be realized from leaning harder on the Lord for *His* strength and in *His* way, not our own. Through God's wisdom we found that by becoming closer to Him, we fortified our vows, and our marriage covenant would be all the more secure and strong. It would not be because of a personal resolve to avoid divorce that we made as young newlyweds, but from the power of the Holy Spirit in submitting ourselves to His authority in our lives. By keeping God first, we saw that our love for each other would then be the way the Lord had intended it to be!

By God's grace alone, 2022 marks the twenty-ninth anniversary of our wedding vows. The time has flown by, and through all of the changes we have experienced, we remain firm in our commitment to one another. We have been blessed beyond measure to be parents as well, and marvel at the path God placed us on to be in each other's lives. It has not been an easy road, but our faith being put into action has helped to fortify the foundation the Lord has us standing on. From a young age we saw how deceptive it is to think that to "throw in the towel" and give up on our marriage commitment would somehow be an answer to persistent struggles. We know for certain—God is faithful through our weaknesses and failures. He must remain the center and love of our lives for us to succeed in our marriage and to ultimately know the full joy He intended us to experience as husband and wife. There isn't any obstacle He cannot help us overcome. We both understand and continue to live in the truth that our marriage is a covenant relationship. To this day, Jeff and I are still best friends and are still 100 percent committed to our "forever together."

A last note from the author

When I read these testimonies, I hear the theme song of hope being played. No matter where your marriage is today, our God provides hope. Who or what are you putting your hope in today? Place it in our covenant God who can teach you to love the most when your spouse deserves it the least. Lean in when you feel like pulling away. Pour out even when the only one pouring into *you* is God. You will see the fruit of your obedience to God's Word and you will be blessed.

"The steadfast love of the LORD never ceases; his mercies never come to an end; they are new every morning; great is *your* faithfulness. 'The LORD is my portion,' says my soul, 'therefore I will hope in *him*'" (Lamentations 3:22–24, my emphasis).

For more encouragement and truth for your marriage, visit VowsToKeep.com where you will grow closer to your spouse and closer to the heart of God's design for your marriage.

Going shoulder-to-shoulder with you for biblically healthy marriages,

Tracy Michelle Sellars

ABOUT THE AUTHOR

Tracy Sellars was born to speak the truth of God's Word to your heart. She and her husband of twenty years live in the rolling hills of Ohio with their three teenagers. Tracy can usually be found on her front porch with her computer or in the recording studio with a microphone, teaching the body of Christ how to passionately pursue both their spouse and their Savior.

She is from the beautiful Black Hills of South Dakota but has moved twenty-eight times (and she's enjoyed every one). The shortest stay was three months. The house she lives in now is the longest—eight years!

Tracy and David have owned and restored almost 100 wrecked and classic vehicles. Currently, as a family they are working on a 1941 Buick Sedanette, a 1983 Mercury Capri, a 1983 Mustang, and a 1960 VW Bug.

If Tracy could write a novel in the bathtub, she'd be one happy camper. Pick up Tracy's new historical romantic suspense novels and learn how to grow closer to your spouse and closer to the heart of God's design for your marriage at VowsToKeep.com.

Penniless.
Scared.
Alone.

*Caught in a web of
deception and mystery,
will they trust God
to show them the way out?*

Roots Run Deep.

Available in bookstores and from online retailers.

 CrossRiver Media
crossrivermedia.com

Discover more great fiction at CrossRiverMedia.com

WALTZ WITH DESTINY

The splendors of Detroit's ballrooms spin Esther (McConnell) Meir around like a princess in a fairy tale Here she meets junior engineer Eric Erhardt. But will Eric abandon his playboy ways for Esther? Award-winning historical fiction author Catherine Ulrich Brakefield weaves fiction with real-life events to create this inspirational fourth book of the Destiny series.

OBEDIENT UNTO DEATH

Sinister forces are at work to destroy the fledgling Christian faith in Ephesus, and Sabina is in their way. A young scribe is murdered during a covert Christian worship service. Sabina, a member of this outlawed religion, can't believe a member could be the killer. But when her Roman magistrate father arrests the church bishop for murder, she realizes all is not brotherly love among the faithful. Racing to stop the bishop's execution, Sabina scrambles for proof of his innocence. Will she discover the truth in time, or will she be thrown in prison herself for her faith in Christ?

LOVE FINAL SUNRISE

Ruth Jessup, a New Yorker, and Joshua Stutzman, an Amish man, couldn't be more different—yet their lives collide as they face a psychopath and the chaos of the New World Order. Struggling with amnesia, Ruth awakens in a world of buggies and lanterns, far removed from modern life. As the biblical seven-year tribulation unfolds, an unexpected bond grows between them. Can Joshua's Amish ways help them endure the next three-and-a-half years without taking the mark of the beast?

Bold faith starts here.

DIVINE DETOUR   WOOD

UNBEATEN   LINDSEY BELL

ABBA'S HEART   CLYMER

ABBA'S ANSWERS   BUTTERFIELD

ABBA'S LESSONS   LAKE

SURVIVING CARMELITA   MIURA

OBEDIENT UNTO DEATH   EYERLY

FORTUNES OF DEATH   EYERLY

ROOTS REDEEMED   SELLARS

Available in bookstores and from online retailers.

CROSSRIVERMEDIA.COM

If you enjoyed this book, will you consider sharing it with others?

- Please mention the book on Facebook, Twitter, Pinterest, or your blog.

- Recommend this book to your small group, book club, and workplace.

- Head over to Facebook.com/CrossRiverMedia, 'Like' the page and post a comment as to what you enjoyed the most.

- Pick up a copy for someone you know who would be challenged or encouraged by this message.

- Write a review on the platform of your choice or Goodreads.com.

- To learn about our latest releases subscribe to our newsletter at www.CrossRiverMedia.com.

www.ingramcontent.com/pod-product-compliance
Lightning Source LLC
Chambersburg PA
CBHW070638260626
47161CB00007B/2757